THE YELLOW DOG &
NIGHT AT THE CROSSROADS

In the windswept seaside town of Concarneau, a local wine dealer is shot. Someone is out to kill all the influential men, and the town is soon sent into a panic. For Inspector Maigret, the answers lie with the downtrodden waitress Emma, and a strange yellow dog lurking in the shadows . . . And in *Night at the Crossroads*, Maigret has been interrogating Carl Andersen for hours without a confession. Why was the body of a diamond merchant found at his mansion? Why is his sister always shut in her room? And why does everyone at Three Widows Crossroads have something to hide?

Books by Georges Simenon
Published in Ulverscroft Collections:

PIETR THE LATVIAN
& THE LATE MONSIEUR GALLET
THE HANGED MAN OF SAINT-PHOLIEN
& THE CARTER OF *LA PROVIDENCE*
A CRIME IN HOLLAND
& THE GRAND BANKS CAFÉ

GEORGES SIMENON

THE YELLOW DOG
&
NIGHT AT THE
CROSSROADS

Complete and Unabridged

ULVERSCROFT
Leicester

The Yellow Dog first published in French as
Le Chien Jaune by Fayard in 1931

This translation first published in the USA as
Maigret and the Yellow Dog
by Harcourt Brace Jovanovich 1987

First published in Great Britain as *The Yellow Dog*,
with minor revisions, by Penguin Books in 2003

This edition, with further minor revisions,
published by Penguin Books in 2013

Night at the Crossroads first published in French as
La nuit du carrefour by Fayard 1931

This translation first published in Great Britain by
Penguin Books in 2014

This Ulverscroft Edition published 2019
by arrangement with
Penguin Random House UK
London

The moral rights of the author and translators
have been asserted

A catalogue record for this book is available
from the British Library.

ISBN 978–1–4448–4333–0

Published by
F. A. Thorpe (Publishing)
Anstey, Leicestershire

Set by Words & Graphics Ltd.
Anstey, Leicestershire
Printed and bound in Great Britain by
T. J. International Ltd., Padstow, Cornwall

This book is printed on acid-free paper

Contents

The Yellow Dog

Translated by LINDA ASHER

1

Nobody's Dog

Friday, 7 November. Concarneau is empty. The lighted clock in the Old Town glows above the ramparts; it is five minutes to eleven.

The tide is in, and a south-westerly gale is slamming the boats together in the harbour. The wind surges through the streets. Here and there a scrap of paper scuttles swiftly along the ground.

There is not a single light on Quai de l'Aiguillon. Everything is closed. Everyone is asleep. Only the three windows of the Admiral Hotel, on the square where it meets the quay, are still lighted.

They have no shutters, but through their murky greenish panes the figures inside are just barely visible. Huddled in his booth less than a hundred metres away, the customs guard stares enviously at the people lingering in the café.

Across from him in the harbour is a coaster that had come in for shelter that afternoon. There is no one on deck. Its blocks creak, and a loose jib snaps in the wind. And there is the relentless din of the gale and the rattle of the tower clock as it prepares to toll eleven.

The hotel door opens. A man appears, still talking to the people inside. The gale snatches at him, flaps his coat-tails, lifts off his bowler hat.

3

He catches it in time and jams it on his head as he walks away.

Even from a distance, it is clear that he is a bit tipsy; he is unsteady on his legs and is humming a tune. The customs guard watches him and grins when the man decides to light a cigar. A comic struggle then develops between the drunk and the wind, which tears at his coat and his hat as it pushes him along the pavement. Ten matches are blown out.

The man spots a doorway up two steps, takes cover there and leans forwards. A match flickers, very briefly. The smoker staggers, grabs for the doorknob.

Was that noise part of the storm, the customs guard wonders. He can't be sure. He laughs as he sees the fellow lose his balance and reel backwards at an impossible angle.

The man lands on the ground at the kerb, his head in the filth of the gutter. The customs guard beats his hands against his sides to warm them and scowls at the jib, irritated by its racket.

A minute, two minutes pass. He takes another glance at the drunk, who has not moved. A dog has turned up from somewhere and is sniffing at him.

'That was when I first got the feeling there was something wrong,' the customs guard said later, at the hearing.

★   ★   ★

The comings and goings that followed are harder to establish in strict chronological order. The customs guard approaches the fallen man, not

4

reassured by the presence of the dog, a big snarling yellow animal. There is a street lamp eight or ten metres away. At first he sees nothing unusual. Then he notices a hole in the drunk's overcoat and a thick fluid flowing from the hole.

He runs to the Admiral Hotel. The café is nearly empty. Leaning on the till is a waitress. At a marble table, two men, their chairs tilted back, their legs stretched out, are finishing their cigars.

'Quick! A crime . . . I don't know . . . '

The customs guard looks down. The yellow dog has followed him in and is lying at the waitress's feet.

There is hesitation, a vague feeling of fright in the air.

'Your friend, the man who just left here . . . '

Some seconds later, the three of them are leaning over the body, still sprawled at the kerb. A few steps away is the town hall, with the police station. The customs guard, needing to do something, dashes over and then, breathless, runs to a doctor's doorbell.

Unable to shake off the sight, he keeps repeating, 'He staggered backwards like a drunk, and he went three or four steps, like this . . . '

Five men, then six, seven. Windows opening everywhere. Whispering . . .

On his knees in the mud, the doctor declares: 'A bullet fired point-blank into the belly. He must be operated on right away. Someone phone the hospital!'

Everyone recognizes the wounded man. It is Monsieur Mostaguen, Concarneau's biggest wine dealer, a good fellow, without an enemy in the world.

The two uniformed policemen — one of them has come out without his cap — don't know where to begin the investigation.

Someone is talking: Monsieur Le Pommeret, whose manner and voice show him to be someone important. 'He and I were playing cards at the Admiral café, with Servières and Dr Michoux. The doctor left first, half an hour ago. And then Mostaguen . . . He's afraid of his wife; he left on the stroke of eleven . . . '

A tragicomedy: everyone is listening to Monsieur Le Pommeret; they have forgotten about the wounded man. Suddenly he opens his eyes, tries to get up, and, in a voice so surprised, so gentle, so feeble that the waitress bursts into nervous laughter, he whispers, 'What happened?'

But a spasm of pain racks him. His lips twist. The muscles of his face tighten as the doctor prepares his syringe for a shot.

The yellow dog circles among the many legs. Puzzled, someone asks, 'You know this animal?'

'I've never seen him before.'

'Probably off some boat.'

In the charged atmosphere, the dog is troubling. Perhaps it is his colour, a dirty yellow. He's tall and lanky, very thin, and his huge head calls to mind both a mastiff and a bulldog.

Five or six metres away, the policemen are questioning the customs guard, who is the only witness.

They look at the doorstep. It is the entrance to a large private house, whose shutters are closed.

To the right of the door, a solicitor's sign announces the sale of the building at auction on 18 November: *Reserve price: 80,000 francs.*

A policeman fiddles for a long while without managing to force the lock. Finally, the owner of the garage next door cracks it with a screwdriver.

The ambulance arrives. Monsieur Mostaguen is lifted on to a stretcher. The onlookers are left with nothing to do but contemplate the empty house.

It has stood empty for a year now. A heavy smell of gunpowder and tobacco hangs in the hallway. A torch beam picks out cigarette ashes and muddy tracks on the flagstone floor, indicating that someone had been waiting and watching for a good while behind the door.

A man wearing only a coat over his pyjamas says to his wife, 'Come on! There's nothing more to see. We'll find out the rest from the paper tomorrow. Monsieur Servières is here . . . '

Servières, a plump little man in a raincoat, had been with Monsieur Le Pommeret at the Admiral. He is an editor at the *Brest Beacon*, and, in addition, writes a humorous piece every Sunday.

He is taking notes, giving suggestions — not to say orders — to the two policemen.

The doors along the hallway are locked. The one at the rear, which opens on to the garden, is swinging open. The garden is surrounded by a wall no higher than a metre and a half. Beyond the wall is an alley that runs into Quai de l'Aiguillon.

'The murderer went out that way!' proclaims Jean Servières.

7

It was on the following day that Maigret established this rough account of the event. For the past month he had been assigned to Rennes to reorganize its mobile unit. There he had received an agitated phone call from the mayor of Concarneau.

And he had come to the town with Leroy, an inspector with whom he had not worked before.

The storm never let up. Heavy clouds dropped icy rain over the town. No boats left port, and there was talk of a steamer in distress out past the Glénan Islands.

Of course, Maigret installed himself at the Admiral Hotel, the best in town. It was five in the afternoon and just dark when he stepped into the café, a long, gloomy room with marble tables and sawdust scattered on the dingy floor. The room was made drearier still by the green windowpanes.

Several tables were occupied. But a quick survey was enough to tell him which was the one with the regulars, the established customers, whose conversation everyone else tried to overhear.

Someone rose from that table — a baby-faced man with round eyes and a smile on his lips.

'Inspector Maigret? My good friend the mayor told me you were coming . . . I've heard a lot about you. Let me introduce myself: Jean Servières . . . Well, now — you're from Paris, I believe? So am I! I was manager of the Red Cow in Montmartre for some time; I've worked for the *Petit Parisien*, for *Excelsior*, for the *Dispatch* . . . I was a close friend of one of your chiefs — Bertrand, a fine fellow. He retired to the country last year, down in Nièvre. And I've done the same thing: I've retired, so to speak, from public life . . . I help out at the *Brest Beacon* now, to keep busy . . . ' He jumped around, waving his arms.

'Come, now, let me present our group — the finest band of merry men in Concarneau. This is Le Pommeret: unrepentant skirt-chaser, a man of independent means and vice-consul for Denmark.'

The man who rose and offered his hand was turned out like a country gentleman: checked riding-breeches, custom-made gaiters without a trace of mud, white piqué stock at his throat. He had a fine silver moustache, smoothly slicked hair, a fair complexion and florid cheeks.

'Delighted, inspector.'

Jean Servières went on: 'Dr Michoux, the son of the former deputy. A doctor on paper only, incidentally, since he's never practised. You'll see, he'll eventually sell you some land; he owns the best building plots in Concarneau, and maybe in all of Brittany.'

A cold hand. A narrow, knifelike face, with a nose bent sideways. Reddish hair already thinning, though the doctor was no more than thirty-five.

'What will you drink?'

Meanwhile, Leroy had gone off to learn what he could at the town hall and the police station.

The atmosphere in the café had about it

9

something grey, or grim — impossible to say exactly what. Visible through an open door was a dining room, where waitresses in Breton dress were laying the tables for dinner.

Maigret's gaze fell on a yellow dog lying beneath the till. Raising his eyes, he saw a black skirt, a white apron, a face with no particular grace, yet so appealing that throughout the conversation that followed he hardly stopped watching it.

Whenever he turned away, moreover, the waitress, in turn, fixed her agitated gaze on him.

★　★　★

'If it weren't for the fact that it nearly killed our poor Mostaguen — the best fellow in the world, except that he's scared silly of his wife — I'd swear this was just some tasteless joke,' Servières said.

Le Pommeret called in an easy tone: 'Emma!'

And the waitress came forwards. 'Well? What will you have?' There were empty beer mugs on the table.

'Time for an aperitif,' said the journalist. 'Otherwise known as Pernod hour. Pernods all round, Emma. That all right, inspector?'

Dr Michoux was deeply absorbed in studying his cufflink.

'Who could have known that Mostaguen would step into that doorway to light his cigar?' continued Servières' resonant voice. 'No one, right? Le Pommeret and I live on the other side of town; we don't go past that vacant house. At that time of night, there'd be no one but the three of us out in the streets . . . Mostaguen isn't the type to have enemies. He's what you call a good-natured fellow — his sole ambition is to get the Légion d'Honneur some day . . . '

'Did the operation go well?'

'He'll pull through . . . A funny thing is that his wife made a scene at the hospital. She's convinced it has to do with some woman! Can you imagine? The poor man would never dare even lay a hand on his secretary!'

'Give me a double,' Le Pommeret told the waitress as she poured the mock absinthe. 'And bring some ice, Emma.'

Some customers left, since it was now dinnertime. A gust of wind blew in through the open door and set the tablecloths in the dining room flapping.

'You'll read the article I've written on this business — I think I've covered all the hypotheses. Only one makes sense: that we're dealing with a madman. We know everyone in town, and we can't for the life of us work out who might have lost his mind . . . We're here every night. Sometimes the mayor comes by to play a game with us. Or else Mostaguen. Or sometimes, for bridge, we go and fetch the clockmaker who lives a few doors away.'

'And the dog?'

The journalist shrugged. 'No one knows where it came from. At first we thought it belonged to the coaster that arrived yesterday — the *Sainte-Marie*. But apparently not. They do have a dog on board, but it's a Newfoundland, and I

11

defy anyone to say what breed this hideous hound is.'

As he spoke, he picked up a pitcher of water and poured some into Maigret's glass.

'Has the waitress been here long?' the inspector asked quietly.

'Oh, for years.'

'She didn't go out last night?'

'She didn't budge . . . She waited for us to leave before she went up to bed. Le Pommeret and I, we were going over old times, memories of the good old days when we were handsome enough to get ourselves women without paying for them. Isn't that right, Le Pommeret? . . . He's not saying a thing! Once you get to know him better, you'll see that when it comes to women he can go on all night . . . You know what we call the house he lives in, across from the fish market? The House of Depravity!'

'To your health, inspector,' said the man in question, not without embarrassment.

Maigret noticed just then that Dr Michoux, who had barely opened his mouth, was leaning forwards to examine his glass against the light. His brow was furrowed. His face, by nature colourless, wore a look of enormous anxiety.

'Just a minute!' he exclaimed suddenly.

He put the glass to his nostrils, then dipped a finger in and touched it to the tip of his tongue.

Servières burst into loud laughter. 'He's letting the Mostaguen business get to him!'

'What's the matter?' asked Maigret.

'I think we'd better not drink this . . . Emma, go and ask the pharmacist to come over right away. Even if he's at dinner . . . '

That created a chill. The room looked emptier, more dismal. Le Pommeret tugged nervously at his moustache. Even the journalist squirmed in his seat. 'What's bothering you?'

The doctor was still staring gloomily at his glass. He rose and went to get the Pernod bottle from the shelf. He twisted it in the light, and Maigret made out two or three small white granules floating in the liquid.

The waitress returned, followed by the pharmacist, whose mouth was full.

'Here, Kervidon, analyse the contents of this bottle and the glasses right away.'

'Today?'

'This minute!'

'What shall I test for? What do you have in mind?'

Maigret had never seen the pale shadow of fear spread so swiftly. In seconds, all the warmth had drained from the customers' expressions, and the rosy blotches on Le Pommeret's cheeks looked artificial.

The waitress leaned an elbow on the till and licked a pencil before setting down some figures in a black oilcloth-covered account book.

'You're crazy!' Servières exclaimed with some effort.

It rang false. The pharmacist held the bottle in one hand, a glass in the other.

'Strychnine,' whispered the doctor.

He shoved the pharmacist out of the door and came back to the table, his head low, a yellow pallor to his complexion.

13

'What makes you think — ' Maigret began.

'I don't know — just a hunch . . . I saw a grain of white powder in my glass, and the smell seemed odd to me.'

'The power of suggestion!' declared the journalist. 'If I described this in my article tomorrow, it would close every bistro in Finistère.'

'You always drink Pernod?'

'Every evening before dinner. Emma's so used to it that she brings the bottle as soon as she sees our beer mugs are empty. We have our little habits. Evenings, it's calvados.'

Maigret went over to the liqueur shelf, reached for a bottle of calvados.

'Not that one. The flask with the broad bottom.'

He picked it up, turned it in the light, saw a few specks of white powder. But he said nothing. It was unnecessary. The others had understood.

Leroy entered and announced offhandedly, 'Well, the police haven't seen anything suspicious — no drifters reported in the vicinity. They don't understand it.'

The silence in the room suddenly registered, the dense throat-grabbing anguish. Tobacco smoke coiled around the electric lights. The green felt of the billiard table spread like a trimmed lawn. There were a few cigar butts on the floor in the sawdust, along with gobs of spittle.

'Seven, carry one . . . ' Emma counted, wetting the tip of her pencil. Then, raising her head, she called into the wings, 'Coming, madame!'

Maigret tamped his pipe. Dr Michoux stared stubbornly at the floor, and his nose looked more crooked than ever. Le Pommeret's shoes

14

gleamed as if they had never been used for walking. Servières shrugged his shoulders from time to time as he mumbled to himself.

All eyes turned towards the pharmacist when he came back with the bottle and the empty glass.

He had run and was breathless. At the door, he gave a kick, trying to drive something away, muttering, 'Filthy mutt!'

He was no sooner inside the café than he asked: 'It's a joke, isn't it? Nobody drank any?'

'Well?'

'It's strychnine, yes! Someone must have put it into the bottle less than half an hour ago.' He looked with horror at the full glasses, at the five silent men.

'What's all this about? It's outrageous! I have every right to know! Last night, a man was shot right near my house, and today . . . '

Maigret took the bottle from his hand. Emma came back from the dining room, looking impassive, and from over the till turned towards them her long face with its sunken eyes and thin lips. Her Breton lace cap was slipping as usual to the left on her unkempt hair, which it did no matter how often she pushed it back in place.

Le Pommeret strode back and forth, his eyes on the gleam of his shoes. Servières, unmoving, stared at the glasses, then suddenly, his voice choked by a sob of terror, cried, 'Good God!'

The doctor hunched his shoulders.

2

The Doctor in Slippers

Inspector Leroy, who was twenty-five years old, looked more like what's called a well-bred young man than a police inspector.

He had just got out of college. This was his first case, and for the past few minutes he had been watching Maigret unhappily, trying to catch his attention. Finally, blushing, he whispered, 'Excuse me, inspector . . . but . . . the fingerprints.'

He must have thought that his chief belonged to the old school and was unaware of the value of scientific procedures, because Maigret merely puffed on his pipe and said, 'If you want . . . '

So off went Leroy, carefully carrying the bottle and glasses to his room, where he spent the evening constructing a packing kit — he carried the instructions in his pocket — specifically developed for transporting objects without losing the fingerprints on them.

Maigret took a seat in the corner of the café. The proprietor, in white smock and chef's toque, looked round his establishment as if it had been devastated by a cyclone.

The pharmacist had talked. People could be heard whispering outside.

Jean Servières was the first to put his hat on.

'Well, enough of this. I'm a married man, and Madame Servières is expecting me. I'll see you later, inspector.'

Le Pommeret stopped his pacing. 'Wait for me. I'm going home to dinner too . . . You staying, Michoux?'

The doctor only shrugged.

The pharmacist was determined to play an important part. Maigret heard him tell the proprietor: ' . . . and, of course, it's imperative to analyse the contents of all the bottles! . . . There's someone here from the police; all he has to do is give me the order.'

There were over sixty bottles of various aperitifs and liqueurs on the shelves.

'What do you think, inspector?'

'It's an idea . . . Well, yes, that might be wise.'

The pharmacist was short, thin and nervous. He fussed three times as much as necessary. Someone had to get him a bottle crate. Then he phoned a café in the Old Town to tell his assistant he needed him.

Bareheaded, he shuttled between the Admiral and his shop five or six times, but found the time to speak to the spectators gathered on the pavement.

'What's to become of me if they carry off all my liquor?' whimpered the proprietor. 'And no one's even thinking about eating! You're not having dinner, inspector? . . . And you, doctor? Are you going home?'

'No. My mother's gone to Paris, and the maid's off.'

'You're sleeping here, then?'

17

It was raining. The streets were running with black mud. The wind was rattling the blinds on the second floor. Maigret had eaten in the dining room, not far from the table where the doctor sat, looking despondent.

Beyond the little green windowpanes, inquisitive faces moved, sometimes pressing up to the glass. The waitress was gone for half an hour, long enough to have her own dinner. Then she took up her customary place, to the right of the till, one elbow resting on it, a towel in her hand.

'Give me a bottle of beer,' Maigret said.

He was well aware that the doctor was watching him as he drank, and then afterwards, as if waiting for signs of poisoning.

Jean Servières did not return, as he had said he would. Nor did Le Pommeret. Apparently no one cared to enter the café, still less to have a drink. Word had spread that all the bottles were poisoned. 'Enough to kill off the whole town!'

From his house out near White Sands beach, the mayor telephoned to find out what was happening. After that, all was gloomy silence. In a corner, Michoux leafed through newspapers without reading them. The waitress did not move. Maigret smoked placidly, and from time to time the proprietor looked in, as though to make sure there had been no new calamity.

The clock in the Old Town sounded the hours and the half-hours. On the pavement, the shuffling footsteps and talking died away. Then there was nothing but the monotonous moan of

18

the wind and the sound of the rain beating on the windows.

'You're spending the night here?' Maigret asked the doctor.

In the silence, the mere act of speaking aloud was disquieting.

'Yes . . . I do that sometimes . . . I live with my mother, about a mile outside town — in a huge house . . . My mother's gone to Paris for a few days, as I said, and the maid asked for time off to go to her brother's wedding.'

He rose, hesitated, then said abruptly, 'Good night.' And he disappeared up the stairs. He could soon be heard taking off his shoes, just over Maigret's head. No one was left in the café but the waitress and the inspector.

'Come here!' he said to her, leaning back in his chair. And as she stood stiffly before him, he added, 'Sit down . . . How old are you?'

'Twenty-four.'

There was an exaggerated humility about her. Her cowed eyes, her way of gliding noiselessly about without bumping into things, of quivering nervously at the slightest word, were the very image of a scullery maid accustomed to hardship. And yet he sensed, beneath that image, glints of pride held firmly in check.

She was anaemic. Her flat chest was not formed to rouse desire. Nevertheless, she was strangely appealing, perhaps because she seemed troubled, despondent, sickly.

'What did you do before you came to work here?'

'I'm an orphan. My father and brother were

lost at sea, on the ketch *Three Kings*. My mother'd died long before . . . I used to be a salesgirl at the stationery shop near the post office . . . '

What was she watching for, with her restless glance?

'Do you have a lover?'

She turned away without answering. Maigret watched her face steadily, puffed on his pipe slowly and took a swallow of beer. 'There must be customers who make a play for you! . . . Those men who were here earlier — they're regulars, they come every evening, and they like good-looking girls . . . Come! Which one?'

Her pale face twisted wearily as she said, 'The doctor, mainly . . . '

'You're his mistress?'

She looked at him with half a mind to trust him.

'He has others too . . . Sometimes me, when he feels like it. He'll stay here for the night and tell me to come to his room.'

Maigret had rarely heard a confession so flat in tone.

'Does he give you anything?'

'Yes . . . not always. Two or three times, on my day off, he's had me go to his house. Like the day before yesterday . . . while his mother's away . . . But he has other girls.'

'And Monsieur Le Pommeret?'

'The same thing — except I only went to his house once, a long time ago. A woman from the sardine-packing plant was there, and . . . I didn't want that! They get new girls every week.'

'Monsieur Servières too?'

'Not the same. He's married. They say he goes into Brest to play around. Here, he doesn't do more than flirt a little, or he'll give me a pinch.'

It was still raining. From the distance came the sound of a foghorn, probably from a ship trying to find its way into port.

'And that's the way it goes all year round?'

'Not all year . . . In the winter, they're all alone here. They'll drink once in a while with some travelling salesman . . . But in the summer there are people around. The hotel is full. At night, ten or fifteen of them get together to drink champagne or throw a party at somebody's house. There are lots of cars, pretty women . . . And we're really busy here . . . In summer, I don't do the serving — there are waiters. I'm downstairs then, washing dishes.'

What could she be looking around for? She was fidgeting on the edge of her chair and seemed ready to snap to attention.

A shrill bell sounded. She looked at Maigret, then at the electric panel behind the till. 'Will you excuse me?'

She went upstairs. The inspector heard footsteps, an indistinct murmur of voices in the doctor's room.

The pharmacist came in, a little drunk.

'All done, inspector! Forty-eight bottles analysed, and carefully. I promise you that! Not a trace of poison except in the Pernod and the calvados. The proprietor can take back all his stock . . . So, now, what do you think, just between you and me? Anarchists — right?'

21

Emma returned, stepped outside to close the shutters and then waited by the door to lock up.

'Well?' said Maigret, when they were alone again.

She turned her head away without answering, unexpectedly embarrassed, and the inspector felt that if he pressed her, even a little, she would burst into tears.

'Good night, child!' he said.

★   ★   ★

When Maigret went downstairs the next morning, the sky was so dark with clouds he thought he must be the first one up. From his window he had seen a solitary crane at work, unloading a sand barge in the deserted port, and, in the streets, a few umbrellas and raincoats hurrying along close to the buildings.

Halfway down the stairs, he had passed a travelling salesman, who had just arrived; a porter was carrying his bags up.

Emma was sweeping the café. On a marble table stood a cup with some coffee stagnating in the bottom.

'Was that my officer's?' Maigret asked.

'A while ago he asked the way to the station. He was carrying a big package.'

'And the doctor?'

'I took him his breakfast upstairs. He's sick. He doesn't want to go out.'

And the broom went on stirring the mixture of debris and sawdust. 'What will you have?'

'Black coffee.'

She had to pass close to him to reach the kitchen. When she did, he gripped her shoulders with his heavy paws and looked her in the eyes. His manner both gruff and kindly, he said: 'Tell me, Emma . . . '

She made only a timid effort to get free, then stood motionless, trembling and making herself as small as possible.

'Just between us, now, what do you know about all this? . . . Quiet! You're about to lie! You're a sad little girl, and I don't mean to make trouble for you . . . Look at me! The bottle, eh? Tell me, now . . . '

'I swear — '

'Don't bother swearing.'

'It wasn't me!'

'For heaven's sake, I know it wasn't you! But who was it?'

Her eyelids puffed up suddenly. Tears poured out. Her lower lip trembled. The waitress looked so touching that Maigret loosened his grip. 'The doctor . . . last night?'

'No! . . . It wasn't for what you think.'

'What did he want?'

'He asked me the same thing you did. He threatened me. He wanted me to tell him who'd been handling the bottles. He nearly hit me . . . And I don't know! On my mother's head, I swear — '

'Bring me my coffee.'

It was eight o'clock. Maigret went out to buy some tobacco and took a walk around the town. When he came back, about ten, the doctor was downstairs in the café, in his slippers and with a

23

foulard around his neck in place of a collar. His features were drawn, his red hair tousled.

'You're not looking in very good shape.'

'I'm sick . . . I should have expected it. Kidney trouble. The slightest upset or excitement, and it shows up. I didn't get a wink of sleep last night.' He kept watching the door.

'You're not going back to your house?'

'There's no one there. I'm in better hands here.'

He had sent out for all the morning papers, and they lay on his table. 'You haven't seen my friends? Servières? Le Pommeret? . . . It's odd they haven't turned up to see if anything's happened.'

'Oh, they're probably still asleep,' Maigret mumbled. 'Incidentally, I haven't seen that awful yellow dog . . . Emma, have you seen any more of that dog? . . . No? Here comes Leroy. He may have run across him in the street . . . What's new, Leroy?'

'The bottles and the glasses are on their way to the laboratory. I stopped by the police station and the town hall . . . You were asking about the dog, I think? Apparently some peasant saw him this morning in Dr Michoux's garden.'

'In *my* garden?' The doctor jumped. His pale hands shook. 'What was he doing in *my* garden?'

'From what I was told, he was lying on the doorstep. When the peasant approached, he growled so viciously that the man decided to give him a wide berth.'

Maigret was watching their faces from the corner of his eye. 'Now, doctor, why don't we take a walk over to your house together?'

A strained smile. 'In this rain? In my condition? That would put me in bed for a week . . . What does that dog matter? Just an ordinary stray, probably.'

Maigret put on his hat and coat.

'Where are you going?'

'I don't know. Get a breath of air. You coming with me, Leroy?'

When they were outside, they could still see the doctor's long head, distorted by the windowpanes, which made it even longer and gave it a greenish tinge.

'Where are we going?' asked the young man.

Maigret shrugged his shoulders. He wandered for a quarter of an hour around the harbour, as if he were interested in boats. At the jetty, he turned right, on to a road whose signpost indicated it was the way to White Sands.

Leroy cleared his throat. 'I wish we'd had a chance to analyse the cigarette ashes they found in the hallway of the empty house — '

'What do you think of Emma?' Maigret interrupted.

'I . . . I think . . . The problem, as I see it — especially in a place like this, where everyone knows everyone else — the problem must have been getting hold of such an amount of strychnine.'

'That's not what I'm asking you . . . Would you, for instance, be interested in making love to her?'

The poor officer could find nothing to say.

Maigret made him stop and open his coat so that he could light his pipe away from the wind.

★　★　★

The beach at White Sands, rimmed by a few houses — one, grand enough to rate the term 'chateau', belonged to the mayor — stretches between two rocky headlands, about a mile from the centre of town.

Maigret and his companion scuffed through seaweed-strewn sand, scarcely looking at the empty, shuttered houses.

Beyond the beach, the land rises. Steep rocks crowned with firs plunge into the sea.

A large sign read: *White Sands Property Company*. A map indicated with one colour the plots already sold, and with another those still available. A wooden booth was labelled *Sales Office*. Beneath were the words: *Address inquiries to Monsieur Ernest Michoux, Director*.

In the summertime, the whole place was probably bright and cheerful, freshly painted. But in the rain and the mud, with the din of the surf, it was sinister.

In the centre of the cleared area stood a big new house of grey stone, with a terrace, an ornamental pool and flower beds laid out but not yet planted.

Further along were the foundations of other houses, and stretches of wall that already indicated the layout.

Some windowpanes were missing in the booth. Piles of sand stood waiting to be spread on the new road, which was half blocked now by a steamroller. At the top of the cliff was a hotel — a future hotel, rather — with unfinished stucco walls and windows sealed by planks and cardboard.

Maigret calmly pushed open the gate of the grey-stone house, Dr Michoux's. When he was on the doorstep and reaching for the knob, Leroy murmured: 'We have no warrant! Don't you think . . . ?'

Once again, Maigret shrugged. On the path, they could see the deep tracks left by the yellow dog's paws. There were also other prints: those of enormous feet, in hobnail boots — size twelve at least!

The knob turned. The door opened as if by magic, and on the carpet inside were the same muddy tracks, of the dog and of those amazing boots.

The house, elaborate in its architecture, was just as pretentious inside. Nothing but nooks and crannies everywhere, filled with couches, low bookcases, Breton closet-beds transformed into vitrines, little Turkish or Chinese tables, dozens of rugs and hangings. The place strained for a kind of folk-modern effect.

There were a few Breton landscapes, and some signed nude drawings with dedications on them: 'To my good friend Michoux,' 'To the artists' friend.'

The inspector gazed sullenly at all the bric-a-brac, but the young Leroy was rather impressed by the false elegance.

Maigret opened doors, glanced into the rooms. Some were unfurnished. The plaster was barely dry on the walls.

Finally he pushed one door open with his foot

and gave a grunt of satisfaction on seeing the kitchen. On the pine table stood two empty Bordeaux bottles.

A dozen cans had been roughly opened with a knife. The table was smeared with dirt and grease. Someone had eaten straight from the cans — herring in white wine, cold cassoulet, mushrooms and apricots.

The floor was filthy. Scraps of meat lay around. There was a broken bottle of brandy, and the stench of alcohol mingled with that of the food.

Maigret looked at his companion with an odd smile. 'Well, Leroy, do you suppose the doctor is the pig who eats like this?'

When the dumbfounded Leroy did not answer, he went on: 'Not his mum, either, I hope! Or the maid. Look! You like prints. These are more like crusts of mud. That'll give you a perfect outline of the soles — size eleven or twelve, I'd say. And the dog's tracks too!'

He filled a new pipe, picked up some matches from a shelf. 'Take whatever evidence there is to take in here. You've got a big job ahead of you. See you later!'

His hands in his pockets, the collar of his coat turned up, he went off along the White Sands beach.

When he stepped into the Admiral café, the first person he saw was Dr Michoux, in his usual corner, still in his slippers, unshaven, his scarf around his neck.

Next to him sat Le Pommeret, turned out as meticulously as the night before. The two men watched silently as the inspector approached.

It was the doctor who finally said, in a hoarse voice, 'You know what I just heard? Servières has disappeared . . . His wife is going out of her mind . . . He left here last night, and nobody's seen him since.'

Maigret gave a start, not because of this news, but because he had just caught sight of the yellow dog, stretched out at Emma's feet.

3

Fear Reigns in Concarneau

Le Pommeret had to confirm Michoux's story, for the pleasure of hearing himself talk.

'She came to my house a while ago, begging me to look for him. Servières — his real name is Goyard — is an old friend . . . '

Maigret's gaze moved from the yellow dog to the door as it flew open for a newsboy, who entered like a gust of wind, and then to a headline in type big enough to read from across the room:

FEAR REIGNS IN CONCARNEAU

The subheadings read:

New mystery daily
Disappearance of our colleague Jean Servières
Bloodstains in his car
Whose turn next?

Maigret caught the newsboy by the sleeve. 'Have you sold a lot of those?'

'Ten times as many as on a regular day. There are three of us running them from the station.'

Set free, the boy raced off along the quay calling, '*Brest Beacon*! Sensational news!'

The inspector had hardly had time to start reading the article when Emma announced, 'You're wanted on the phone.'

It was the mayor's voice. He was furious. 'Hello, chief inspector! Are you behind this idiotic article? . . . And I didn't know a thing! I insist — do you hear me? — I insist on being the first person informed about what happens in this town. I'm the mayor! What is this story about the car? And this man with big feet? In the past half-hour I've had over twenty phone calls from panicky people asking me if the news is true! . . . I repeat, from now on I want — '

Without turning a hair, Maigret hung up and returned to the café, where he sat and began to read. Michoux and Le Pommeret scanned a copy of the paper on the marble table.

Our esteemed colleague Jean Servières reported in these very pages the recent dramatic events in Concarneau. That was Friday. A respected businessman of that town, Monsieur Mostaguen, left the Admiral Hotel, stopped in the doorway of a vacant house to light a cigar and was shot in the stomach by a bullet fired through the letter-box in the door.

On Saturday, Chief Inspector Maigret, recently seconded from Paris to head the Rennes Flying Squad, arrived on the scene. This did not prevent a new drama from occurring.

Indeed, that very evening, a telephone call informed us that, as they were about to

31

drink an aperitif, three prominent local figures — Messieurs Le Pommeret, Jean Servières and Dr Michoux — noticed that the Pernod served them contained a strong dose of strychnine.

Then this morning, Sunday, Jean Servières' empty car was found near the Saint-Jacques River. Its owner has not been seen since Saturday evening.

The front seat is stained with blood. One window is shattered, and all the evidence suggests that a struggle took place.

Three days: three incidents! Little wonder that Concarneau is in the grip of terror, as anxious citizens wonder who the next victim will be.

The public is particularly disturbed by the mysterious presence of a yellow dog, which no one knows, which seems to have no master and which reappears with each new misfortune.

This dog appears to have given the police a significant lead. They are looking for a person, still unidentified, who has left curious footprints — larger-than-average footprints — in several places

A madman? A drifter? Is he the perpetrator of all these crimes? Whom will he attack tonight?

He will certainly meet opposition from now on, because the frightened citizenry will be armed and ready to shoot at the slightest alarm.

Meanwhile, today, Sunday, the town is

deathly still, an atmosphere reminiscent of towns in northern France during the War when the air-raid sirens sounded.

Maigret stared out through the windowpanes. The rain had let up, but the streets were still thick with black mud, and the wind still blew violently. The sky was a livid grey.

People were coming out of Mass. Almost all of them carried a copy of the *Brest Beacon*. Faces were turned towards the Admiral Hotel, and several people quickened their step as they passed.

There was indeed a dead feeling about the town. But wasn't that how it was on any Sunday morning? The telephone rang again. Emma could be heard answering. 'I don't know, monsieur. I haven't heard. Do you want me to get the inspector? . . . Hello! Hello! . . . They hung up!'

'Who was that?' growled Maigret.

'A Paris newspaper, I think. They asked if there were any new victims . . . They reserved a room.'

'Call the *Brest Beacon* for me.'

While he waited, he paced up and down, without a glance at the doctor, who was huddling in his chair, or at Le Pommeret, who was contemplating the many rings on his fingers.

'Hello! The *Brest Beacon*? Inspector Maigret here. The editor, please . . . Hello — is that the editor? Good! Would you tell me what time your paper was printed this morning? . . . Nine thirty, eh? Who did the piece on the business at

33

Concarneau? . . . Ah, no, seriously! . . . Really? The article just turned up in a sealed envelope? . . . Unsigned? . . . So, then, you publish whatever material you get, name or no name, just like that? . . . Well, I take my hat off to you!'

He tried to go out to the quay but found the door locked. 'What does this mean?' he asked Emma, looking straight into her eyes.

'The doctor insisted . . . '

Maigret stared at Michoux, whose expression was more evasive than ever, shrugged his shoulders and went out through the hotel door. Most of the shops had their shutters closed. People in Sunday clothes hurried by.

Beyond the harbour, where boats were tugging at their moorings, Maigret found the mouth of the Saint-Jacques River. It was at the very edge of town, where houses thinned out and shipyards took over. Several half-finished vessels stood on the ways. Old boats lay rotting in the mud.

A stone bridge crossed the river where it emptied into the harbour, and there a group of inquisitive people stood around a small car.

The nearby wharves were blocked by building sites, so Maigret had to make a detour to get there. From the looks he received on the way, he realized that everyone already knew who he was. He saw anxious people talking quietly in the doorways of the closed shops.

Finally, he reached the car abandoned at the side of the road. He pulled the door open brusquely, scattering shards of glass, and easily made out the brown streaks on the seat cover.

The onlookers crowded around him, mainly

34

kids and young people in their Sunday best.

'Monsieur Servières' house?'

A dozen people led him to it. It was a quarter of a mile away, rather secluded — a middle-class house with a garden. His escort stopped at the gate. Maigret rang the bell and was let in by a little maid who looked upset.

'Is Madame Servières here?'

She was already opening the door to the dining room.

'Oh, inspector! . . . Do you think he's been killed? I'm going out of my mind! I . . . '

She was a handsome woman, about forty, with the look of a scrupulous housewife, an impression confirmed by the tidiness of her home.

'You haven't seen your husband since — '

'He was home for dinner last night. I could see that he was worried, but he didn't want to say anything to me . . . He'd left the car at the gate, which meant that he was going out again that night . . . to play his regular card game at the Admiral. I asked him if he'd be late coming home . . . At ten o'clock, I went to bed. I was awake a long time. I heard the clock strike eleven, then half past. But he often came home very late . . . I must have fallen asleep finally. I woke up in the middle of the night and was upset not to find him beside me . . . Then I decided that he must have gone on to Brest with some people. There's not much going on here, so sometimes he . . . I couldn't get back to sleep. From five o'clock on, I was up and watching out of the window. He doesn't like me to wait up for

him, and even less for me to check on him . . . At
nine, I ran over to Monsieur Le Pommeret's
. . . I was coming back another way when I saw
people gathered round his car . . . Tell me! Why
would anyone want to kill him? He's the kindest
man on earth . . . I'm sure he has no enemies.'

A small group still clustered at the gate.

'They say there are bloodstains! I saw people
reading a newspaper, but no one showed it to
me.'

'Did your husband have much money on
him?'

'I don't think so . . . The same as usual
— three or four hundred francs.'

Maigret promised to keep her informed and
even took the trouble to give her a few bland
words of comfort. A scent of roast lamb came
from the kitchen. The maid, in her white apron,
led him back to the door.

The inspector had gone no more than a
hundred yards when a man approached him
eagerly. 'Excuse me, inspector. Let me introduce
myself: Monsieur Dujardin, teacher. For the past
hour, people — mostly the parents of my
students — have been coming to ask me whether
there's any truth to what the newspaper says.
Some of them want to know whether they have
the right to shoot if they see that man with the
big feet — '

Maigret was no angel of patience. Shoving his
hands into his pockets, he snarled, 'Leave me
alone!'

And he headed back to the centre of town.

It was idiotic! He'd never known anything like

it. It made him think of a storm in a film: you're seeing a cheerful street scene, a clear sky. Then an image of a cloud slides over the scene, it blocks the sun. A violent wind sweeps through; dim light, banging shutters, whirling dust, some fat drops splash, and suddenly the street is lashed by rain, under a dramatic sky.

Concarneau was changing before his eyes. The piece in the *Brest Beacon* was only the beginning: for some time now, word of mouth had far outstripped the written version.

And besides, it was Sunday. The townspeople had time on their hands. You could see them deciding, for their walk, to go and take a look at Jean Servières' car, where two policemen had been posted. The idlers hung around for an hour or so, as the better-informed among them explained the situation.

When Maigret got back to the Admiral Hotel, the proprietor, in his chef's toque, clutched nervously at his sleeve. 'I've got to talk to you, inspector . . . This is becoming impossible.'

'Just give me some lunch.'

'But — '

Maigret, in a temper, sat down in a corner and ordered. 'Bring me a beer! . . . Have you seen my officer?'

'He went out. I think he was called over to the mayor's house . . . Someone just telephoned again from Paris. A newspaper has reserved two rooms, for a reporter and a photographer.'

'Where's the doctor?'

'He's upstairs. He told us not to let anyone up.'

'And Monsieur Le Pommeret?'

'He's just left.'

The yellow dog was gone. Several young fellows, flowers in their buttonholes, hair slicked down with pomade, were seated around the tables, but they were not drinking the lemonades they had ordered. They had come to watch and they were visibly proud of themselves for their boldness.

'Come here, Emma.'

There was an instinctive rapport between the waitress and the inspector. She approached readily and let him draw her into the corner.

'You're sure the doctor never went out last night?'

'I swear I didn't sleep in his room.'

'So he might have gone out?'

'I don't think so. He's afraid . . . I told you he made me lock the door to the quay this morning.'

'How come that yellow dog knows you?'

'I don't know. I've never seen him before . . . He comes, he goes . . . I wonder who feeds him.'

'Has he been gone long?'

'I wasn't paying attention.'

Leroy came back in a nervous state. 'You know, sir, the mayor is furious . . . And he's a very influential man! He told me he's a cousin of the minister of justice. He claims all we're doing is churning things up and throwing the town into a panic . . . He wants us to arrest someone, anyone, to calm people down. I promised him I'd talk to you about it. He kept telling me our careers — yours and mine, that is — are on the line.'

Maigret scraped serenely at the bowl of his pipe.

'What are you going to do?' asked Leroy.

'Nothing at all.'

'But — '

'You're young, Leroy! . . . Did you pick up any worthwhile evidence at the doctor's house?'

'I've sent everything to the laboratory — the glasses, the cans, the knife. I even made a plaster cast of the footprints, the man's and the dog's. That was hard, because the plaster they've got here is very poor quality . . . Do you have any ideas?'

By way of answer, Maigret pulled a notebook from his pocket. The officer, more baffled than ever, read:

Ernest Michoux (known as Doctor): Son of small manufacturer in Seine-et-Oise who served as deputy for that department for one term and then went bankrupt. Father dead. Mother a schemer. Tried, with son, to establish property development at Juan-les-Pins. Complete failure. Started again at Concarneau. Set up a company, trading on dead husband's name. Invested no capital herself. Now trying to get town and department to underwrite development costs.

Ernest Michoux was married, then divorced. His former wife married a notary in Lille.

Degenerate type. Has difficulty paying bills.

Leroy looked at his chief as if to say, 'Meaning?'
Maigret showed him the next entry:

Yves Le Pommeret: Prominent family.
Brother Arthur runs biggest canning plant
in Concarneau. Minor gentry. Yves the playboy of the family. Never worked. Long ago
ran through most of his money in Paris.
Came back to live in Concarneau when he
was down to 20,000 francs a year. Manages
to come across as gentry even if he does
polish his own shoes. Many affairs with working girls. A few scandals hushed up. Hunts at
all the big estates in the neighbourhood. Big
shot. Through connections got himself named
vice-consul for Denmark. Pulling strings now
for Légion d'Honneur. Sometimes borrows
from brother to pay his debts.

Jean Servières (pseudonym for Jean Goyard):
Born in Morbihan. Long-time journalist in
Paris, manager of small theatres, etc. Came
into small inheritance and settled in Concarneau. Married former usherette who'd been
his mistress for fifteen years. Middle-class
household. Occasional flings in Brest and
Nantes. Lives off small investments more
than off newspaper work, but very proud of
latter. Decorated by Academy.

'I don't understand,' stammered Leroy.
'Of course not. Give me your notes.'
'But . . . who told you I . . . '
'Let's see them.'

The inspector's notebook was a cheap little graph-paper pad with an oilcloth cover. Leroy's was a loose-leaf day-book in a steel binder.

His manner paternal, Maigret read:

1.*Matter of Mostaguen*: The bullet that hit the wine dealer was certainly intended for someone else. As there was no way to foresee that anyone would stop randomly at that doorway, the real target must have been expected there, but never came, or came too late.

Unless the purpose was to terrorize the population. The perpetrator knows Concarneau intimately. (Neglected to analyse cigarette ashes found in hallway.)

2.*Matter of poisoned Pernod*: In wintertime, the Admiral café is empty almost all day. Anyone who knew this could enter and put poison in the bottles. In two bottles. Thus it was aimed specifically at the drinkers of Pernod and calvados. (Note, however, that the doctor spotted, in time and easily, the grains of white powder floating in the liquid.)

3.*Matter of yellow dog*: He knows the Admiral café. He has a master. But who? Seems to be at least five years old.

4.*Matter of Servières*: Determine by handwriting analysis who sent article to *Brest Beacon*.

Maigret smiled, handed the book back to his companion and remarked: 'Very good, my boy.'

41

Then, with an irritable glance at the gawkers' silhouettes beyond the green windows, he added, 'Let's go and eat!'

A little later, when they were in the dining room, along with the travelling salesman who had arrived that morning, Emma informed them that Dr Michoux was feeling worse and had asked for a light meal to be sent to his room.

★   ★   ★

That afternoon the Admiral café was like a cage in the zoo, what with sightseers filing past its small dim windows in their Sunday best. They then headed towards the far end of the harbour to the next attraction — Servières' car, still guarded by two policemen.

The mayor phoned three times from his sumptuous house at White Sands. 'Have you made an arrest?'

Maigret barely bothered to answer.

The young crowd, those from eighteen to twenty-five, invaded the café. Noisy groups took over tables and ordered drinks, which they never touched. They weren't in the café more than five minutes before their jokes petered out, their laughter died down, and awkwardness gave way to bluffing. And one by one they left.

The difference in the town was more apparent when it came time to light the street lamps. It was four o'clock. Ordinarily at that hour the streets would still be busy. That evening, they were deserted, and deathly silent. It was as if the strollers had passed the word. In less than a quarter of an hour the streets had emptied, and when footsteps sounded, they were the hurried ones of someone anxious to get to the shelter of home.

Emma leaned on her elbows at the till. The proprietor went back and forth between the kitchen and the café, where Maigret stubbornly refused to listen to his lamentations.

Ernest Michoux came downstairs at about 4.30, still in slippers. Stubble covered his cheeks. His cream silk scarf was stained with sweat.

'Ah, you're here, inspector!' The fact seemed to comfort him. 'And your officer?'

'I sent him off to look around town.'

'The dog?'

'Hasn't been seen since this morning.'

The floor was grey, the marble of the tables a harsh white veined with blue. Through the windows, the glowing Old Town clock was dimly visible, now showing ten minutes to five.

'We still don't know who wrote that article?'

The newspaper lay on the table. By this point only one headline stood out:

WHOSE TURN NEXT?

The telephone jangled. Emma answered. 'No . . . Nothing . . . I don't know anything.'

'Who was it?' Maigret asked.

'Another Paris paper. They said their reporters are arriving by car.'

She had hardly finished the sentence when the phone rang again.

'It's for you, inspector.'

The doctor, pale as a ghost, kept his eyes on Maigret.

'Hello! Who's there?'

'It's Leroy . . . I'm over in the Old Town, near the channel inlet. There's been a shooting here . . . A shoemaker saw the yellow dog from his window and — '

'Dead?'

'Wounded! Badly. In the hindquarters. The animal can barely drag himself along. People don't dare go near him . . . I'm calling from a café. The dog is in the middle of the street — I can see him through the window. He's howling . . . What should I do?' And despite his effort to keep calm, the officer's voice was tense, as if the wounded yellow dog were some supernatural creature. 'There are people at every window . . . What should I do, inspector? Finish him off?'

His colour leaden, the doctor stood behind Maigret, asking fearfully, 'What is it? . . . What's he saying?'

And the inspector saw Emma leaning on the counter, her expression blank.

4

Field Headquarters

Maigret crossed the drawbridge, passed through the Old Town ramparts and turned down a crooked, poorly lit street. What the people of Concarneau call 'the closed town' — the old section still surrounded by its walls — is one of the most densely populated parts.

As the inspector advanced, however, he entered a zone of ever more ambiguous silence, the silence of a crowd hypnotized by a spectacle and trembling with fear or impatience. Here and there, a few isolated voices, those of adolescents determined to sound bold, could be heard.

One last bend in the street and he reached the scene: a narrow lane, with someone at every window, the rooms behind them lit with oil lamps; a glimpse of beds; in the street a mob blocking the way, and, beyond, a large open space, from which came the sound of hoarse breathing.

Maigret pushed through the spectators, mostly youngsters, who were startled by his arrival. Two of them were pelting the dog with stones. Their companions tried to stop them. They heard — or rather, sensed — the warning.

One of the boys flushed to the ears when Maigret shoved him to the left and strode towards the wounded animal. The silence then took on a different character. It was clear that a few moments earlier an unwholesome frenzy had been driving the crowd, except for one old woman, who cried from her window:

'It's shameful! You should haul them all in, inspector. The whole bunch of them were torturing that poor creature . . . And I know perfectly well why. They're afraid of him!'

The shoemaker-gunman withdrew sheepishly into his shop. Maigret leaned down to stroke the dog's head; the animal gave him a look that was more puzzled than grateful. Leroy came out of the café from which he had telephoned. The crowd began reluctantly to move away.

'Someone get a wheelbarrow.'

Windows were closing one after another, but inquisitive shadows hovered behind the curtains. The dog was filthy, his dense coat matted with blood. His belly was muddy, his nose dry and burning. Now that someone was showing kindness, he took heart and stopped trying to creep along the ground through the dozens of large stones that lay around him.

'Where should we take him, inspector?'

'To the hotel . . . Easy there . . . Put some straw under him.'

The procession could have looked ridiculous. Instead, by some eerie effect of the anguish that had grown steadily stronger since morning, it was stirring. With an old man pushing it, the wheelbarrow bounced over the cobblestones of the twisting street and on to the drawbridge. No one dared follow it. The yellow dog panted hard, an occasional spasm stiffening his four legs.

Maigret noticed an unfamiliar car parked opposite the Admiral Hotel. He pushed open the café door and found the atmosphere transformed.

A man squeezed past him, saw the dog being lifted out of the wheelbarrow, aimed a camera at the animal and set off a magnesium flash. Another, dressed in plus fours and a red sweater, with notebook in hand, touched the visor of his cap.

'Inspector Maigret? Vasco, from the *Journal*. I've just got here and already I've been lucky enough to meet Monsieur . . . ' He indicated Michoux, who was in his corner, slouching against the moleskin banquette. 'The *Petit Parisien* is right behind. They broke down about ten kilometres back.'

'Where do you want the dog?' Emma asked the inspector.

'Isn't there a spot for him in the hotel?'

'Yes, near the courtyard . . . a porch where we store empty bottles.'

'Leroy! Phone a vet.'

An hour earlier, the place had been deserted, seething with silence. Now, the photographer, in an off-white trenchcoat, was shoving tables and chairs around and yelling, 'Wait a minute! Hold it, please! Turn the dog's head this way . . . ' And the magnesium flared.

'Le Pommeret?' Maigret asked Dr Michoux.

'He left not long after you did . . . The mayor phoned again. I think he may be on his way over . . . '

47

★   ★   ★

By nine that evening, the place had become a sort of military headquarters. Two more reporters had arrived. One was working on his story at a table towards the back. From time to time the photographer came down from his room. 'You wouldn't have any rubbing alcohol? I've absolutely got to have it to dry my film . . . The dog looks terrific! . . . Did you say there's a pharmacy nearby? . . . Closed? Doesn't matter.'

At the hall phone, a reporter was dictating his story, in an offhand voice: 'Maigret, yes — M as in Maurice, A as in Arthur . . . Yes. I as in Isidore . . . Take down all the names first . . . Michoux — M, I, choux, that's chou as in choucroute . . . No, no, not like pou. Now wait — I'm going to give you the headlines . . . Will this go on page one? . . . Absolutely! Tell the boss it's got to go on the front page . . . '

Feeling lost, Leroy kept looking at Maigret as if to get his bearings. In a corner, the lone travelling salesman was preparing his next day's route with the help of the regional directory. Now and then he would call over to Emma.

'Chauffier's . . . is that a big hardware outlet? . . . Thanks.'

The vet had removed the bullet and set the dog's hindquarters in a cast. 'These animals, it takes a lot to kill them!'

Emma had spread an old blanket over straw on the blue granite floor of the porch that gave on to both the courtyard and the cellar stairway.

48

The dog lay there, all alone, inches from a scrap of meat he never touched.

The mayor arrived by car. He was a very well-groomed elderly man with a small white goatee; his gestures were curt. His eyebrows rose as he entered and noticed the atmosphere of a guardroom — or, more precisely, a field headquarters.

'Who are these gentlemen?'

'Reporters from Paris.'

The mayor was very touchy. 'Wonderful! So tomorrow the whole country will be talking about this idiotic business! . . . You still haven't found out anything?'

'The investigation is still going on!' growled Maigret, as if to say, 'None of your business!'

For the atmosphere was really tense. Everyone's nerves were on edge.

'And you, Michoux, you're not going home?' The mayor's look of contempt made clear that he thought the doctor a coward.

'At this rate,' he said, turning back to Maigret, 'there'll be full-scale panic within the next twenty-four hours . . . What we need — as I told you before — is an arrest, no matter who.' He emphasized his last words with a glance at Emma. 'I know I have no authority to give you orders . . . As for the local police, you're ignoring them completely . . . But I'll tell you this: one more crime, just one, and we'll have a catastrophe on our hands. People are expecting trouble. Shops that on any other Sunday stay open till nine at night have already closed their shutters . . . That idiotic piece in the *Brest*

Beacon terrified the public . . . '

The mayor, who had not taken his bowler off his head, now pulled it down farther as he left, saying, 'I'll thank you to keep me informed, inspector . . . And I remind you that whatever happens now is your responsibility.'

'A beer, Emma!' Maigret snapped.

There was no way to keep the reporters from descending on the Admiral Hotel, or from installing themselves in the café, telephoning and filling the place with their noisy commotion. They demanded ink, paper. They interrogated Emma, whose poor face looked constantly alarmed.

Outside, the night was dark, with a beam of moonlight that heightened the melodrama of the cloudy sky instead of brightening it. And there was the mud, which clung to every shoe, since paved streets were still unknown in Concarneau.

'Did Le Pommeret tell you he was coming back?' Maigret suddenly asked Michoux.

'Yes. He went home for dinner.'

'His address?' asked a reporter who had nothing else to do.

The doctor gave it to him, as the inspector shrugged and pulled Leroy off into a corner.

'Did you get the original manuscript of this morning's article?'

'I just got it. It's in my room . . . The handwriting is disguised. It must have come from someone who thought they'd know his writing.'

'No postmark?'

'No. The envelope was dropped in the newspaper's box. It says 'Extremely Urgent' on it . . . '

'Which means that at eight this morning, at the latest, someone knew about Jean Servières' disappearance, knew that the car was, or would be, abandoned near the Saint-Jacques River, and that there would be bloodstains on the seat . . . And that same someone also knew that we'd discover the tracks of an unknown man with big feet . . . '

'It's amazing!' sighed Leroy. 'But about those fingerprints — I wired them off to Quai des Orfèvres. They've already checked the files and called me back. The prints don't match those of any known offender.'

There was no doubt about it: the tension was getting to Leroy. But the person most thoroughly infected, so to speak, by that virus was Ernest Michoux, who looked even more colourless in contrast to the newspapermen's sporty clothes, easygoing manner and self-assurance.

He had no idea what to do with himself. Maigret asked him: 'Aren't you going to bed?'

'Not yet . . . I never fall asleep before one in the morning . . . ' He forced a feeble smile, which showed two gold teeth. 'Frankly, what do you think?'

The illuminated clock in the Old Town tolled ten. The inspector was called to the telephone. It was the mayor.

'Still nothing?' It sounded as if he, too, was expecting trouble.

But, actually, wasn't Maigret expecting trouble himself? Frowning, he went out to visit the yellow dog. The animal had dozed off; now, without alarm, he opened one eye to watch

Maigret approach. The inspector stroked his head, pushed a handful of straw beneath his front legs.

He felt the proprietor come up behind him.

'Do you suppose those newspaper people will be staying long? . . . Because if they are, I ought to think about supplies. The market opens at six tomorrow morning . . . '

For anyone not used to Maigret, it could be unsettling to see his large eyes stare blankly at you, as now, then to hear him mutter something incomprehensible and move on as if you were not worth noticing.

The reporter from the *Petit Parisien* returned, shaking his dripping raincoat.

'Is it raining?' someone asked. 'What's new, Groslin?'

The young man's eyes sparkled as he spoke quietly to his photographer then picked up the telephone.

'*Petit Parisien*, operator . . . Press service — urgent! What? You have a direct line to Paris? . . . Well then, hurry . . . Hello! *Petit Parisien?* Mademoiselle Germaine? Give me the copy desk. This is Groslin!'

His tone was impatient. And he darted a challenging look at the colleagues listening to him. Passing by, Maigret stopped to listen.

'Hello, is that you, Mademoiselle Jeanne? . . . Rush this through! There's still time to get the story into a few of the out-of-town runs. The other papers will only be able to get it into their Paris editions. Tell the copy desk to rewrite what I give you; I don't have time. Here we go.

'The Concarneau Case. Our predictions were correct: another crime . . . Hello? Yes, *crime*! A man's been killed. Is that better?'

Everyone was silent. Spellbound, the doctor drew close to the reporter as he went on, excited, triumphant.

'First Monsieur Mostaguen, then the news-paperman Jean Servières and now Monsieur Le Pommeret! . . . Yes, I spelled the name earlier. He's just been found dead in his room . . . at home. No wound. His muscles are rigid. All evidence points to poisoning. Wait — end with: 'Terror reigns' . . . Yes! Rush this to the managing editor . . . I'll call back in a while to dictate a piece for the Paris edition, but the information has to get to the out-of-town desks now.'

He hung up, mopped his face, and threw a jubilant look around the room.

The telephone was ringing again. 'Hello. Inspector? We've been trying to get through to you for a quarter of an hour. I'm calling from Monsieur Le Pommeret's house . . . Hurry! He's dead!' And the voice repeated, in a wail, 'Dead!'

Maigret looked around. Empty glasses stood on almost every table. Emma, her face drained, followed his eyes.

'Nobody touch a single glass or bottle!' he ordered. 'You hear me, Leroy? Don't leave here.'

Sweat dripping from his brow, the doctor snatched off his scarf; at his skinny neck, his shirt was fastened by a toggle stud.

★　★　★

53

By the time Maigret reached Le Pommeret's apartment, a doctor from next door had already made the initial examination.

A woman of about fifty was there. She was the owner of the building, the person who had telephoned.

It was a pretty house of grey stone, facing the sea. Every twenty seconds, the glowing brush of the lighthouse beacon set the windows on fire. There was a balcony with a flagstaff and a shield bearing the Danish coat of arms.

Outside, five people watched wordlessly as the inspector went in.

The body lay on the reddish carpet of a studio crowded with worthless knick-knacks. On the walls were publicity shots of actresses, framed pictures clipped from sexy magazines and a few signed photos of women.

Le Pommeret's shirt was pulled out of his trousers, his shoes were still crusted with mud.

'Strychnine,' said the doctor. 'At least so far I'd swear to that. Look at his eyes. And notice especially how rigid the body is. The death throes took over half an hour. Maybe more . . . '

'Where were you?' Maigret asked the landlady.

'Downstairs. I sub-let the whole second floor to Monsieur Le Pommeret, and he took his meals at my place . . . He came home for dinner around eight o'clock. He ate almost nothing. I remember he said there was something wrong with the electricity, but the lights seemed perfectly normal to me. He said he'd be going out again, but that first he'd go up and take an aspirin, because his head felt heavy . . . '

The inspector looked questioningly at the doctor.

'That's it! The early symptoms.'

'Which appear how long after absorbing the poison?'

'That depends on the dose and on the person's constitution. Sometimes half an hour, sometimes two hours.'

'And death?'

'Doesn't come until after general paralysis sets in. But there is local paralysis first. So he probably tried to call for help . . . He would have been lying on this couch . . . '

The couch that had earned Le Pommeret's place the name House of Depravity! Pornographic prints crowded the walls around the couch. A night light gave off a rosy glow.

'He'd have gone into convulsions. Like an attack of delirium tremens . . . He died on the floor.'

Maigret walked to the door as a photographer started to come in and slammed it in the man's face.

'Le Pommeret left the Admiral a little after seven o'clock,' Maigret calculated. 'He'd had a brandy-and-water . . . A quarter of an hour later, he drank and ate something here . . . From what you say about the way strychnine works, it's just as possible he was poisoned back there as here . . . '

Abruptly, he went downstairs, where the landlady was crying, with three of her neighbours around her.

'The dishes, the glasses from dinner?'

It took her a moment to understand what Maigret wanted. By the time she replied, he had

55

already looked into the kitchen and seen a basin of warm water, clean plates and glasses laid out to the right, dirty to the left.

'I was just washing up when . . . '

A local policeman arrived.

'Watch the house,' Maigret told him. 'Put everyone out except the landlady . . . and no reporters, no photographers! Nobody is to touch a glass or a plate.'

It was 500 metres, through the downpour, to the hotel. The town was dark except for two or three distant lighted windows. Then on the square, at the corner by the quay, the Admiral Hotel's three square windows shone out, though their green panes made the place look like a huge aquarium.

As Maigret drew near, he heard voices, the telephone ringing, and then the roar of a car starting up.

'Where are you heading?' he asked the reporter in it.

'The phone is tied up. I'm going to look for another one. In ten minutes it'll be too late to make my Paris edition.'

Standing in the café, Leroy looked like a teacher monitoring prep. Men were writing without pause. The travelling salesman watched, bewildered but excited by a scene that was entirely new to him.

Glasses still stood on the tables — stemware for aperitifs, beer mugs slick with foam, small liqueur glasses.

'When did you last clear the tables?'

Emma thought back. 'I can't say exactly. I

picked up some glasses as I went by. Others are left from this afternoon.'

'What about Monsieur Le Pommeret's?'

'What did he drink, Dr Michoux?' she asked.

It was Maigret who answered: 'A brandy-and-water.'

She looked at the saucers, one after another, checking the prices on them. 'This one says six francs . . . But I served one of those men a whisky, and that's the same price . . . Maybe that glass over there? . . . Maybe not . . . '

The photographer, sticking to business, was taking pictures of the glassware spread on the marble tabletops.

'Go and get the pharmacist,' the inspector ordered Leroy.

And from then on it was a long night of glasses and plates. Some were brought from the vice-consul of Denmark's house. The reporters made themselves at home in the pharmacist's laboratory, and one of them, a former medical student, even helped out with the analyses.

The mayor, by telephone, merely remarked sharply: 'Entirely your responsibility.'

The proprietor suddenly appeared and asked, 'What's become of the dog?'

The place where he had been lying on straw was empty. The yellow dog was incapable of walking, or even crawling, because of the cast immobilizing his hindquarters, but he had vanished.

The glasses revealed nothing.

'Monsieur Le Pommeret's may have been washed already . . . I can't tell in all this commotion!' said Emma.

At his landlady's, too, half the dishes had already been washed in warm water.

Ernest Michoux, his face ashen, was more disturbed over the dog's disappearance. 'Someone came through the courtyard and took him! There's a way through to the quay, a kind of alleyway . . . That gate has to be sealed, inspector! Or else . . . To think that someone got in without anybody knowing! And then left with that animal in his arms!'

It looked as if the doctor didn't dare move from his corner, as if he was keeping as far as possible from the doors.

5

The Man at Cabélou

It was eight in the morning. Maigret, who hadn't gone to bed, had taken a bath and was now shaving at a mirror dangling from the window latch.

It had turned colder, and the rain was mixed with sleet. A reporter was waiting downstairs for the Paris newspapers. The 7.30 train had sounded its whistle, and soon the newsboys would arrive with the latest sensational issues.

Below the inspector's window, the square overflowed with the weekly market. Yet the usual liveliness of a market was missing: people talked in low voices; farmers looked uneasy.

In the open square stood some fifty stalls, piled with butter, eggs, vegetables, pairs of braces, silk stockings. To the right, carts of all kinds were lined up. And the whole scene was dominated by the wing-like movement of the broad white-lace headdresses of the local women.

Maigret didn't notice that something was happening until a part of the market scene took on a different shape; a group had gathered to stare in the same direction. Because his window was closed he heard only a jumbled murmur.

He looked farther off. On the quay, a few

59

fishermen had been loading empty baskets and nets on to their boats. Suddenly they had stopped, and now made way for two local policemen, who were leading a prisoner towards the town hall.

One of the policemen was young, still beardless. His face radiated eager innocence. The other had a large mahogany-coloured moustache, and his heavy eyebrows gave him an almost ferocious look.

In the market, all chatter had stopped, as the crowd watched the three men approach. Some pointed to the handcuffs that bound the prisoner's wrists to those of his captors.

The man was a colossus! His forwards pitch made his shoulders look even broader. As he dragged his feet through the mud, he seemed to be towing the officers along in his wake.

He was wearing an unprepossessing old jacket, and his bare head bristled with thick hair, short and dark.

The waiting reporter darted up the hotel stairs, rattled a door and shouted to his sleeping photographer: 'Benoît! Benoît! Quick, get up! You'll miss a fantastic shot!'

He didn't know how right he was. For as Maigret, his eyes never leaving the square, wiped the last traces of shaving soap from his cheeks and reached for his jacket, a truly extraordinary thing happened.

The crowd had quickly closed around the policemen and their prisoner. Suddenly, the captive, who must have been waiting for the chance, gave a violent jerk of his wrists.

The inspector saw the puny ends of chain dangling from the policemen's hands. The man plunged through the crowd. A woman was sent sprawling. People scattered. Before anyone had recovered from the surprise, the prisoner had darted into an alleyway, twenty metres from the Admiral, that ran alongside the vacant house from which the bullet had spat forth on Friday.

The younger policeman nearly fired, but hesitated, then chased after him, with his gun at the ready. Maigret was afraid there might be an accident. A canopy on wooden struts gave way under the pressure of the escaping throng and its canvas roof collapsed on to the blocks of butter.

The young officer was brave, and he sprinted into the alley alone.

Since Maigret knew the neighbourhood now, he finished dressing without haste. It would take a miracle to catch the fellow. The narrow passage, two metres wide, had two sharp dog-legs. Twenty houses faced on to either the quay or the square and had their back entries on the alley. There were storage sheds as well, a marine supply yard, a cannery warehouse, a whole tangle of odd buildings, nooks and crannies, and roofs within easy reach. They would all make pursuit almost impossible.

The crowd was keeping its distance now. Red with anger, the woman who had been knocked down was shaking her fist in all directions as tears trickled down her chin.

The photographer darted from the hotel, a trenchcoat over his pyjamas, his feet bare.

★ ★ ★

Half an hour later, just after the police lieutenant had sent his men to search the neighbouring houses, the mayor arrived. He found Maigret settled in the café with the young policeman, busily devouring toast. The town's leading magistrate was shaking with indignation.

'I warned you, inspector, that I would hold you responsible for . . . for . . . But you don't seem to care! I'm going to send a telegram to the minister of the interior, to inform him of . . . of . . . and to ask him . . . Have you any idea what's happening out there? People are fleeing their homes. A helpless old man is howling with fear because he's stuck on the second floor. People think they're seeing the criminal everywhere!'

Maigret turned and saw Ernest Michoux huddling close behind him like a frightened child, trying to create as few ripples in the air as a ghost.

'You'll notice that it was the local police — just ordinary policemen — who arrested him, whereas . . . '

'You still insist that I make an arrest?'

'What do you mean? Are you claiming you can lay hands on the fugitive?'

'You asked me yesterday to make an arrest, any arrest . . . '

The reporters were outside, helping the police in their search. The café was practically empty. There had been no time to clean it up, though, and an acrid odour of stale tobacco smoke hung in the air. The floor was covered with cigarette

62

butts, spittle, sawdust and broken glass.

The inspector drew a blank arrest warrant from his wallet. 'Say the word, *Monsieur le Maire*, and I'll — '

'I'd be curious to know whom you would arrest!'

'Emma, pen and ink, please.'

Maigret was drawing short puffs on his pipe. He heard the mayor mutter, just loud enough to be heard, 'Bluffing!'

Unflustered, he wrote, in his usual large angular strokes: 'Ernest Michoux, Director, White Sands Property Company'

★   ★   ★

The scene was more comic than tragic. The mayor read the warrant upside down. Maigret said, 'There you are! Since you insist, I'm arresting the doctor . . . '

Michoux looked at the two of them, gave the sickly smile of a man who cannot decide how to take a joke. But it was Emma the inspector was watching — Emma, who walked towards the till and suddenly turned around, less pale than usual and unable to disguise a surge of joy.

'I suppose, inspector, that you realize the gravity of — '

'It's my trade, *Monsieur le Maire*.'

'And the best you can do, after what's happened, is arrest a friend of mine — an associate, rather — and one of Concarneau's distinguished citizens?'

'Have you got a comfortable jail?'

During this conversation, Michoux seemed to be having a problem swallowing.

'Aside from the police station, in the town hall, there's only the police barracks, in the Old Town . . . '

Leroy had just come in. He gasped when Maigret said to him, in a perfectly natural voice: 'Now, Leroy, be so good as to escort the doctor to the police barracks. Discreetly. No need to handcuff him . . . Lock him up, and make sure he has everything he needs.'

'It's utter madness!' babbled the doctor. 'I don't understand what's going on . . . I . . . It's unheard of . . . It's an outrage!'

'Yes, indeed,' Maigret muttered. Turning to the mayor, he said: 'I have no objection to continuing the search for your vagrant — that keeps the public busy. It might even be useful. But don't attach too much importance to his capture . . . Reassure people.'

'You're aware that when the police caught him this morning they found a flick knife on him?'

'I'm not surprised.'

Maigret was growing impatient. Standing up, he slipped on his heavy overcoat, turned up its velvet collar and brushed his bowler hat on his sleeve.

'I'll see you later, *Monsieur le Maire*. I'll keep you informed. Another word of advice: try to keep people from talking too much to the reporters. When it comes right down to it, there's barely enough in all this to shake a stick at . . . Are you coming?' This question was addressed to the young policeman, who glanced

64

at the mayor as if to say, 'Excuse me, but I have to go along with him.'

Leroy was circling the doctor like a man utterly perplexed by an unwieldy bundle.

Maigret tapped Emma on the cheek as he passed, and then crossed the square, unruffled by the curious stares. 'This way?'

'Yes. We have to go round the harbour. It should take half an hour.'

The fishermen were less interested than the townsfolk in the drama going on around the Admiral café. A dozen boats were making the most of the lull in the storm and sculling out to the harbour mouth to pick up the wind.

The policeman kept looking at Maigret like a pupil eager to please his teacher. 'You know, the mayor played cards with the doctor at least twice a week. This must have given him a shock.'

'What are people saying?'

'That depends. Ordinary folks — workers, fishermen — aren't too upset . . . In a way, they're even kind of glad about what's happening. The doctor, Monsieur Le Pommeret and Monsieur Servières aren't very well thought of around here. Of course, they're important people, and nobody would dare say anything to them . . . Still, they took advantage, corrupting the girls from the canning plant . . . And in the summer it was worse, with their Parisian friends. They were always drinking, making a racket in the streets at two in the morning, as if the town belonged to them. We got a lot of complaints . . . Especially about Monsieur Le Pommeret, who couldn't see anything in a skirt without getting carried away . . . It's sad to say, but things are slow at the cannery. There's a lot of unemployment. So, if a man has a little money . . . all those girls . . . '

'Well, in that case, who's upset?'

'The middle class. And the businessmen who rubbed shoulders with that bunch at the Admiral café . . . That was like the centre of town, you know. Even the mayor went there . . . '

The man was flattered by Maigret's attention.

'Where are we?'

'We've just left town. From here on, the coast is pretty much deserted . . . just rocks, pine woods and a few summer houses used by people from Paris . . . It's what we call Cabélou Point.'

'What made you think of nosing around out here?'

'When you told me and my partner to look for a drifter who might be the owner of the yellow dog, we first searched the old boats in the inner harbour. Now and then we find a tramp there. Last year, a cutter burned up because someone made a fire to get warm and forgot to put it out.'

'Find anything?'

'Nothing. It was my partner who thought of the old watchtower at Cabélou . . . We're just coming to it — that square stone structure on the last rocky point. It dates from the same time as the Old Town fortifications. Come this way . . . watch out for the muck . . . A very long time ago, a caretaker lived here, a kind of watchman, who signalled when boats passed. From it, you can see really far. It overlooks the Glénan Islands channel, the only opening to the sea. But it hasn't been manned for maybe fifty years.'

Maigret stepped through an opening whose door had vanished and entered a space with a beaten-earth floor. On the ocean side, narrow slits gave a view out over the water. On the other side was a single window, without panes or a frame. On the stone walls were inscriptions cut by knifepoint; on the ground were dirty papers and all kinds of rubbish.

'For nearly fifteen years, a man lived here, all alone. Weak in the head — sort of a child of nature. He slept over in that corner. Didn't mind the cold or the damp, or even the storms that flung spray in through the slits. He was a local curiosity. In the summer, the Parisians would come to look at him, give him coins. A postcard pedlar took a picture of him and sold it at the entrance . . . The man finally died, during the War. And no one ever bothered to clean the place up . . . Yesterday, my partner thought that if someone was hiding out around here, this might be the spot.'

Maigret started up the narrow stone stairway cut right into the wall and reached the lookout, a granite tower open on all four sides, giving a view of the whole area.

'This was the watchtower. Before beacon lights were invented, they used to burn a fire here on the terrace . . . Anyhow, this morning very early, we came up here, me and my partner. We moved on tiptoe. And downstairs, right where the halfwit used to sleep, we saw a man snoring away — a giant! You could hear him breathing fifteen metres away. We managed to

67

slip the handcuffs on him before he woke up.'

They went back to the square room below, which was freezing cold from the wind.

'Did he struggle?'

'Not at all! My partner asked for his papers, and he didn't answer . . . You never got a good look at him, did you? . . . He was stronger than the two of us together, so I never took my finger off the trigger of my revolver. What hands! Yours are big, but try to picture hands twice that big, with tattoos on them — '

'Did you see what they were?'

'All I could make out was an anchor, on the left hand, with the letters SS on both. There were some other complicated designs . . . maybe a snake . . . We didn't touch the mess lying around him. Look!'

There were bottles of good wine and expensive liquor, empty tins and about twenty unopened ones. In the centre of the room were the ashes of a fire and, nearby, a stripped lamb bone, chunks of bread, a few fish spines, a big scallop shell and some lobster claws.

'Some feast, eh?' exclaimed the young policeman, who had probably never eaten such food. 'This explains the complaints that have come in lately — a six-pound loaf stolen from the baker's, a basket of whiting that disappeared from a fishing boat and the Prunier warehouse manager's claim that someone was swiping his lobsters during the night. We didn't pay much attention, because it was never very much.'

Maigret was trying to work out how many days it would take a man with a big appetite to consume the amount of food indicated by the debris. 'A week . . . ' he murmured. 'Yes — counting the lamb . . . '

Abruptly he asked, 'What about the dog?'

'Yes. He wasn't here. There are plenty of pawprints on the ground, but we didn't see the animal . . . You know, the mayor must be in a state over the doctor. I'd be surprised if he didn't wire Paris.'

'The man was armed?'

'No. I was the one who searched him, while my partner, Piedbœuf, held on to the handcuffs and kept his gun on him. In one trouser pocket were roasted chestnuts, four or five of them. They must have come from the cart in front of the cinema on Friday and Saturday nights. Then there were a few coins, not even ten francs . . . A knife — but not a dangerous one; the kind sailors use to cut bread.'

'He didn't say anything?'

'Not a word. We thought that he was simple-minded, like the old tenant . . . He stared at us like a bear would. He had a week's growth of beard and two broken teeth, right in the middle.'

'What was he wearing?'

'I didn't notice . . . An old suit? I don't even know now if he was wearing a shirt or a sweater. He came along quietly . . . We were proud of our catch. He could have got away ten times before we made it back to town . . . So our guard was down when he gave that big yank that broke the chain between the cuffs. I thought my right wrist was broken. It still hurts . . . About Dr Michoux . . . '

'What about him?'

'You know his mother's supposed to get back today or tomorrow . . . She's the widow of a deputy. They say she has a lot of influence. And she's a friend of the mayor's wife.'

Maigret was gazing at the grey ocean through the slits. Small boats were tacking between Cabélou Point and a line of rocks marked by breaking surf; they came about and began to lay their nets less than a mile out.

'You really think it was the doctor who — '

'Let's go,' said the inspector.

The tide was coming in. When they left the tower, the water was starting to lap at the base. A hundred metres away, a boy was jumping from rock to rock as he checked lobster pots set in crevices. The young policeman could not keep quiet.

'The strange thing is that anyone would attack Monsieur Mostaguen. He's the best man in Concarneau; they even wanted to make him a district councillor . . . It seems he'll be all right, but they couldn't remove the bullet. So, for the rest of his life he'll be carrying a chunk of lead around in his belly! When you think that if he just hadn't felt like lighting a cigar . . . '

Rather than go around the harbour again, they crossed part of it on a ferry that shuttled to the Old Town.

A short distance from where the boys had been throwing stones at the dog the day before, Maigret noticed a wall with an enormous entryway surmounted by a flag and the words 'National Police Barracks'.

He went in and crossed the courtyard of a

building dating from Colbert's time. In an office there, Leroy was arguing with a police sergeant.

'About the doctor?' asked Maigret.

'Right! The sergeant won't hear of letting him get his meals sent in from outside.'

'Unless you authorize it,' the sergeant told Maigret. 'And I'll need a signed document releasing me . . . '

The courtyard was as tranquil as a cloister. A fountain flowed with a cheerful gurgle.

'Where is he?'

'Down there, to the right. Push open that door. Then it's the second door along the corridor. Do you want me to go with you to open up? The mayor phoned to say we should treat the prisoner with the utmost consideration.'

Maigret scratched his chin. Leroy and the policeman, who were about the same age, watched him with the same bashful curiosity.

A few minutes later, the inspector stepped alone into a whitewashed cell that was no more dismal than any barracks room.

Michoux was seated at a small pine table. He stood up when Maigret entered, hesitated, then, with his eyes averted, began to speak:

'I assume, inspector, that you're just staging this farce to head off another crime, to protect me from . . . from some attack . . . '

Maigret noticed that no one had relieved the doctor of his braces, his scarf or his shoelaces, as regulations required. With the tip of his shoe he drew a chair over, sat down, filled his pipe and said amiably: 'Yes, indeed. But do sit down, doctor!'

6

A Coward

'Are you superstitious, inspector?'

Straddling his chair, his elbows on its back, Maigret pursed his lips in a way that might mean anything at all. The doctor had not sat down.

'I think we all are at certain times, or, if you like, when we're under pressure . . . ' Michoux coughed into his handkerchief, looked at it worriedly, then went on.

'A week ago, I would have said I didn't believe in fortune-telling. And yet . . . It must be about five years ago now that I was having dinner with a few friends at the home of an actress in Paris. Over coffee, one of the guests suggested reading the cards . . . Well, do you know what he told me? Of course I laughed! I laughed all the more because it was so different from the usual line — blonde woman, old man who wishes you well, letter that comes from far away, and so on . . . To me, he said: 'You'll die a hideous death, a violent death. Beware of yellow dogs!''

Michoux had not looked at the inspector so far, but he glanced at him now. Maigret was placid — huge on the little chair, but a monument of placidity.

'That doesn't strike you as odd? . . . Through all the years since, I never heard a word about a yellow dog. Then on Friday there's a shooting. One of my friends is the victim. It could just as easily have been me who ducked into that doorway and got hit by the bullet. And suddenly a yellow dog turns up!

'Another friend disappears under weird circumstances. And the yellow dog is still stalking around.

'Yesterday, it was Le Pommeret's turn . . . The yellow dog again! . . . And you don't think I should be upset?'

He had never talked so much at once, and as he talked he became more confident. The only encouragement the inspector offered was 'Of course . . . of course.'

'Isn't it disturbing? I realize I must have looked like a coward to you . . . Well, yes, I was afraid! It was a vague kind of fear, but it grabbed me by the throat from the minute the first attack . . . And then when the yellow dog came into the picture . . . '

He paced the cell with small steps, his eyes on the floor. Then his face came alive. 'I almost asked you for protection, but I was afraid you would laugh. I was even more afraid of your contempt . . . Because strong men do feel contempt for cowards . . . '

His voice grew shrill. 'And I admit it, inspector: I am a coward! For the past four days I've been frightened — four days I've been sick with fright. It's no fault of mine! I know enough medicine to understand my own case.

'When I was born, they had to put me in an incubator. Growing up, I went through every single childhood disease.

'And when the War broke out, doctors who were examining 500 men a day declared me fit for service and sent me to the front! Well, not only did I have weak lungs, scarred from old lesions, but two years earlier I'd had a kidney removed . . .

'I was terrified. Crazy with terror! Some hospital attendants picked me up after a shell exploded and buried me . . . And finally they realized that I didn't belong in the army.

'What I'm telling you may not be pretty. But I've been watching you. You look like a man who can understand . . .

'It's easy enough for strong people to despise cowards. But they ought to take the trouble to learn where the cowardice comes from . . .

'Look, I could see that you didn't think much of our group at the Admiral café. People told you that I sold land . . . a deputy's son, with a medical degree . . . and then all those evenings at a café table with those other failures.

'But what was I supposed to do? My parents were big spenders even though they weren't rich. That's not so rare in Paris. I was raised in luxury — all the great spas, and so on. Then my father died, and my mother started to dabble in the market and dream up schemes — just as much the great lady as ever, just as arrogant, but with creditors hounding her.

'So I helped her out. That was all I *could* do. This property development — nothing very impressive. And the life here . . . Prominent citizens, oh, yes — but with something not quite solid about them.

'For three days now you've been watching me, and I've been wishing I could talk to you openly . . . I used to be married. My wife asked for a divorce because she wanted a husband with more ambition . . .

'One kidney short — three or four days a week sick, exhausted, dragging myself from my bed to my chair . . . '

He sat down listlessly.

'Emma must have told you we've been lovers — mindlessly, you know? Just because sometimes you need to have a woman . . . Not the sort of thing you tell everyone . . .

'At the Admiral café, I might have wound up going mad. The yellow dog, Servières disappearing, the bloodstains in his car. And the worst was Le Pommeret's miserable death . . .

'Why him? Why not me? We were together two hours earlier, at the same table, with the same glasses in front of us . . . I had a premonition that if I left the hotel I'd be next. I felt the circle tightening around me, that even in the hotel, even locked in my room, danger was tracking me down . . .

'I felt a kind of thrill when I saw you sign the warrant for my arrest. And yet . . . ' He looked at the walls around him, at the window with three iron bars that opened on the courtyard. 'I'll have to move my bunk, push it into that corner . . . How, yes, how in the world could someone tell me about a yellow dog five years ago, when this dog here was probably not even born? . . . I'm afraid, inspector! I admit that. I tell you I'm afraid! I don't care what people think when they hear I'm in jail. The only thing I care about is not dying. And someone's after me, someone I don't know, and who's already killed Le Pommeret, who probably killed Goyard, who shot Mostaguen . . . Why? Tell me! Why? It must be some maniac. And they still haven't managed to wipe him out! He may be lurking nearby right now! He knows I'm here . . . He'll come, with his awful dog that stares like a man!'

Maigret slowly stood up, knocked his pipe against his heel.

And the doctor repeated in a pitiful tone, 'I know you think I'm a coward. It's going to be hell for me tonight, with this kidney . . . '

Maigret stood there like the antithesis of the prisoner — of agitation, fever, sickness — the antithesis of that unwholesome and repellent terror. 'Do you want me to send a doctor?'

'No! If I knew someone was supposed to come here, I'd be even more frightened. I'd be worried that *he* might turn up — the man with the dog, the maniac, the murderer.'

Before long his teeth would start to chatter. 'Do you think you'll arrest him? Or will you just kill him, like a mad dog? Because he is mad! Nobody kills the way he has for no reason!'

In another three minutes the doctor's frenzy would turn into a nervous breakdown. Maigret chose to leave, and the prisoner gazed after him, his head huddled between his shoulders, his eyelids red.

★   ★   ★

76

'Is that perfectly clear, sergeant? No one is to enter his cell except you, and you yourself are to take him his food and whatever else he needs. Meanwhile, take away anything he could use to kill himself with — his shoelaces, his tie. See that the courtyard is under surveillance day and night. And show consideration — the utmost consideration.'

'Such a distinguished man!' sighed the sergeant. 'You think he's the one who — '

'Who might be the next victim, yes. So you'll answer to me for his life!'

Maigret went off down the narrow street, splashing through the puddles. The whole town knew him by now. Curtains parted as he passed. Children broke off their games to watch him with timid respect.

He was crossing the drawbridge between the Old Town and the new when he ran into Leroy, who was looking for him.

'Anything new? I don't suppose they've laid hands on my bear, have they?'

'What bear?'

'The man with the big feet.'

'No. The mayor gave orders to stop the search because it was upsetting the public. He placed a few policemen at strategic spots . . . But that's not what I wanted to talk to you about. It's the newspaperman, Goyard, Jean Servières. A travelling salesman who knows him just got into town, and he says he ran across him yesterday in Brest. Goyard pretended not to see him and walked off.'

Leroy was surprised at how calmly Maigret

took the news. 'The mayor is convinced that the salesman was mistaken. He says there are plenty of short, fat men in any city. And you know what I heard him tell his deputy — talking low but hoping, I think, I'd overhear? Verbatim: 'Watch the inspector take off on this false scent. He'll go to Brest and leave us to deal with the real murderer!''

Maigret walked another twenty paces in silence. In the square, the market stalls were being dismantled.

'I almost told him that . . . '

'That what?'

Leroy blushed and turned his head away. 'Exactly! I don't know . . . I, too, get the feeling that you don't think it's really important to catch the drifter.'

'How's Mostaguen doing?'

'Better. He can't think of any reason he was attacked . . . He asked his wife's pardon, pardon for staying so late at the café. Pardon for being half drunk. He was in tears and swore he'd never touch another drop of alcohol.'

Fifty metres from the Admiral Hotel, Maigret stopped to look at the harbour. Boats were coming in, dropping their brown sails as they rounded the breakwater, sculling slowly along.

At the base of the Old Town's walls, the ebb tide was uncovering banks of mud studded with old pots and other rubbish.

A faint suggestion of sun showed through the almost solid cloud cover.

'Your impression, Leroy?'

The officer grew uneasy again. 'I don't know

. . . I think if we had that fellow . . . Remember that the yellow dog has disappeared again. What could the man have been up to in the doctor's house? There must have been some poisons there. I deduce from that — '

'Yes, of course. But I don't go in for deductions.'

'Still, I'd be curious to see that drifter up close. From the footprints, he must be a giant — '

'Exactly.'

'What do you mean?'

'Nothing.'

Maigret lingered; he seemed delighted by the view of the little harbour: Cabélou Point to the left, with its pines and rocky headlands, the red-and-black tower, the scarlet buoys marking the channel out to the Glénan Islands, which were indistinguishable in the grey light.

Leroy still had a good deal to say. 'I telephoned Paris to get information on Goyard; he lived there for a long time.'

Maigret looked at him with affectionate irony, and, stung to the quick, Leroy recited briskly:'The information is either very good or very bad. I got hold of a fellow who'd been a sergeant in the Vice Squad back then and had known him personally. It seems he dabbled a bit in journalism, first as a gossip columnist. Then he was the manager of a small theatre. Next he ran a cabaret in Montmartre. Went broke twice. For two years he was editor in chief of a provincial newspaper — at Nevers, I believe. Finally, he ran a nightclub. 'A fellow who knows how to stay afloat' — that's what the sergeant said . . . True, he also said, 'Not a bad guy. When he eventually saw that all he'd ever do was eat through his money or make trouble for himself, he decided to reimmerse himself in small-town life.''

'So?'

'So I wonder why he would fake that attack. I went back to look at the car. There are bloodstains, and they're real. If he was actually attacked, why wouldn't he have sent some message, since now he's walking around Brest?'

'Very good!'

Leroy looked sharply at Maigret to see if he was teasing. No. The inspector was gazing seriously at a gleam of sunlight far out at sea.

'As for Le Pommeret — '

'You have a line on him?'

'His brother came to the hotel to speak to you. He couldn't stay. He had nothing but bad things to say about the dead man. As far as he was concerned, his brother was an absolute good-for-nothing. Interested only in women and hunting. And he had a mania for running up bills and for playing the lord of the manor . . . One detail out of the hundreds: the brother is probably the biggest manufacturer in the district, and he told me: 'I'm happy to buy my clothes in Brest. Nothing fancy — just substantial, comfortable clothes. But Yves would go to Paris to order his clothes. And he had to have hand-made shoes signed by a famous bootmaker! Even my wife doesn't wear custom-made shoes.''

'That's a joke!' said Maigret, to his companion's great bewilderment, if not indignation.

80

'Why?'

'All right, then, it's magnificent. To use your own expression, we're immersing ourselves in small-town life. And it's just like it's always been! Knowing whether Le Pommeret wore ready-made or custom-made shoes — that may not seem like much. But, believe it or not, that's the key to the story, right there . . . Let's go and get an aperitif, Leroy — like those fellows did every day at the Admiral café!'

Again Leroy looked at his chief to determine whether the man was making fun of him. He had been hoping for congratulations on his morning's work and for all his enterprise.

Instead, Maigret was behaving as though the whole thing were a joke!

★   ★   ★

The effect was the same as when the teacher enters a classroom where the students are chattering. Conversation stopped. The reporters rushed up to the inspector.

'Can we report the doctor's arrest? Has he confessed?'

'Nothing at all!'

Maigret waved them aside and called to Emma, 'Two Pernods, my dear.'

'But look, if you've arrested Michoux — '

'You want to know the truth?'

They already had their notebooks in hand. They waited, pens at the ready.

'Well then, there is no truth yet. Maybe there will be some day. Maybe not.'

'We hear that Jean Goyard — '

'Is alive. So much the better for him.'

'But still, there's a man in hiding, and they can't find him.'

'Which goes to prove the hunter's not as smart as the prey.'

Taking Emma by the sleeve, Maigret said gently, 'I'll have my lunch in my room.'

He drank his aperitif down straight and got to his feet.

'A piece of advice, gentlemen! No jumping to conclusions. And no deductions, above all.'

'What about the criminal?'

He shrugged his broad shoulders and murmured: 'Who knows?'

He was already at the foot of the stairs. Leroy threw him a questioning look.

'No, my friend. You eat down here. I need a rest.'

He climbed the stairs with heavy tread. Ten minutes later, Emma went up after him with a plate of hors d'œuvres.

Then she carried up a *coquille St Jacques* and roast veal with spinach.

In the dining room, conversation languished. One of the reporters was called to the phone.

'Around four o'clock, yes,' he declared. 'I hope to have something sensational for you . . . Not yet! We've got to wait . . . '

All alone at a table, Leroy ate with the manners of a well-bred boy, regularly wiping his lips with the corner of his napkin.

People outside kept an eye on the Admiral café, hoping vaguely for something to happen.

A policeman leaned against the building at the end of the alleyway where the vagrant had disappeared.

'The mayor is on the phone, asking for Chief Inspector Maigret,' Emma announced.

Leroy jumped. 'Go up and tell him,' he said to her.

The waitress left, but came right back and said, 'He's not there!'

Leroy bounded up the stairs four at a time, returned very pale and snatched the receiver.

'Hello! . . . Yes, *Monsieur le Maire* . . . I don't know. I . . . I'm worried. The inspector is gone . . . No, that's all I can tell you. He had lunch in his room. I didn't see him come down . . . I . . . I'll phone you back.'

Leroy, who had not put his napkin down, used it now to wipe his brow.

7

The Couple by Candlelight

Half an hour later, Leroy went up to his own room. On his table, he found a note in Morse code.

Go up to the roof tonight at eleven. Let no one see you. I'll be there. No noise. Bring gun. Say that I left for Brest and phoned you from there. Don't leave hotel. Maigret.

A little before eleven, Leroy took off his shoes and put on some felt slippers he had bought that afternoon expressly for this expedition. He was somewhat apprehensive.

At the third floor, the staircase ended, but a fixed ladder led to a trapdoor in the ceiling. In the icy, draughty attic above, Leroy took the risk of lighting a match.

A few moments later, he climbed out through a skylight, but he didn't dare move down towards the eaves immediately. It was bitterly cold. His fingers froze on contact with the zinc shingles. And he had decided, unfortunately, not to saddle himself with an overcoat.

When his eyes adapted to the darkness, he seemed to make out a darker, stocky mass, like a huge animal lying in wait. He smelled pipe smoke and whistled softly.

A moment later he was crouched on the ledge next to Maigret. Neither the sea nor the town was visible; they were on the slope of the roof facing away from the quay and over a dark chasm that was the very alleyway through which the big-footed man had escaped.

The view was made up of irregular planes: there were some very low roofs and others at eye level. Some windows were lighted here and there. A few had blinds drawn, and a kind of Chinese shadow play moved across them. In a distant room, a woman was washing a baby in an enamel basin.

The inspector moved, or, rather, shuffled, his large bulk over until his mouth was pressed to his companion's ear.

'Be careful! No sudden movements. The ledge isn't too solid, and right below us there's a gutter pipe that could fall off at any moment and make a racket. What about the reporters?'

'They're downstairs, except for one, who's gone to look for you in Brest. He's convinced you're on Goyard's trail.'

'Emma?'

'I don't know. I wasn't keeping track of her . . . She did serve me coffee after dinner.'

It was unsettling to be up here, unsuspected, on top of a house full of life — people moving around in warmth, in light, with no need to lower their voices.

'Now — turn carefully towards the house that's for sale . . . Careful!'

The house was the second to the right, one of

the few as tall as the hotel. It was part of a block of total darkness, and yet the inspector made out what seemed to be a glint reflecting off a curtainless window on the third floor.

Little by little, he realized that it was not a reflection from outside, but a feeble light inside. He stared at that single point until things began to take shape. A shiny floor . . . a half-consumed candle, its flame burning straight up, ringed by a halo.

'He's there!' Leroy said suddenly, louder than he intended.

'Shh! Yes.'

Someone was lying on the bare floor, half in candlelight, half in shadow. An enormous shoe, a broad torso moulded by a sailor's sweater.

Leroy knew that there was a policeman at the end of the alley, another in the square, and still another patrolling the quay.

'Do you want to arrest him?'

'I don't know. He's been sleeping for three hours now.'

'Is he armed?'

'He wasn't this morning.'

Their words were scarcely audible: an indistinct murmur, almost like breathing.

'What are we waiting for?'

'I'm not sure. I'd like to know why he's kept a candle burning while he's asleep, especially when people are after him . . . Look!'

A yellow square appeared on a wall. 'A light's gone on in Emma's room, right below us. That's the reflection.'

'Have you had any dinner, inspector?'

'I brought some bread and sausage . . . Are you cold?'

The two of them were frozen. They saw the glowing beam from the lighthouse sweep the sky at regular intervals.

'She's turned out the light.'

'Yes. Shh!'

Five minutes of silence, a bleak wait. Then Leroy's hand reached for Maigret's, clasped it meaningfully. 'Look down.'

'I saw.'

A shadow moved on the rough whitewashed wall that separated the garden of the vacant house from the alley.

'She's going to meet him,' whispered Leroy, who could not keep silent.

Up above, the man was still asleep in the light of his candle. A currant bush swayed in the garden. A cat fled along a roof gutter.

'You wouldn't have a lighter with a long wick, would you?'

Maigret had not dared relight his pipe. After hesitating a long time, he finally screened himself with his companion's jacket and scratched a match sharply. Leroy soon smelled the warm odour of tobacco again.

'Look!'

They said nothing more. The man stood up so abruptly he nearly knocked the candle over. He drew back into the darkness as the door opened, and Emma appeared in the light, uncertain and so abject that she looked guilty.

From under her arm, she took a bottle and a package and set them on the floor. The paper, peeled back, showed a roast chicken.

She spoke. That is, her lips moved. She said only a few words, humbly, sadly. Her companion was out of sight of the two watchers.

Was she crying? She still had on her black waitress's dress and the Breton headdress. She had taken off only her white apron, and without it she looked even more woebegone.

Yes, she must have been crying as she said those few halting words. This was confirmed when she suddenly leaned against the door frame and buried her face in the crook of her arm. Her back shuddered fitfully.

The man suddenly appeared, blacking out nearly the whole square of the window, but he freed the view as he strode across the room. His great hand hit the girl's shoulder with such a jolt that she made a complete turn, nearly fell, and raised her poor pale face to him, her lips swollen with sobs.

But the scene was as indistinct, as hazy as a film when the house lights come up. And something was missing: sounds, voices . . . Like a film, a silent film without music.

Now the man was talking, apparently harshly. He was a bear. His head was hunched into his shoulders, and his sweater showed off his chest muscles. With his fists on his hips, he seemed to be shouting reproaches, or insults, perhaps even threats.

He looked so close to hitting the girl that Leroy drew closer to Maigret, as if for reassurance.

Emma was still weeping. Her headdress had

slipped sideways. Her chignon was coming loose. A window slammed shut somewhere and brought a moment's distraction.

'Inspector . . . shouldn't we . . . ' Leroy began.

The scent of tobacco enveloped the two men and gave them an illusion of warmth.

Why was Emma clasping her hands? She was speaking again. Her face was distorted in an expression of fright, of pleading, of pain, and Leroy heard Maigret cock his revolver.

A mere fifteen or twenty metres separated the two pairs. A sharp report, a shattered window-pane, and the giant would be in no condition to do harm.

Now he was striding the length and breadth of the room, his hands behind his back. He seemed shorter, broader. His foot jostled the roast chicken. He nearly slipped and furiously kicked it into the shadow.

Emma looked in that direction.

What could the two of them be saying? What was the subject of their heartbreaking dialogue?

The man seemed to be repeating the same words over again. But was it possible he was saying them more gently?

She fell to her knees, flung herself down in his path and raised her arms towards him. He acted as if she were not there, evaded her grasp. Then she was no longer on her knees, but half sprawled, with one arm stretched out imploringly.

At one moment the man was visible; the next, the darkness swallowed him. When he re-emerged, he stopped short before the pleading girl and looked down at her from on high.

89

Again he paced — came near, moved away — and she no longer had the strength, or the heart, to reach out to him, to entreat. She slipped full length to the floor. The bottle of wine was inches from her hand.

Unexpectedly, the vagrant stooped, seized her dress at the shoulder in one of his huge paws and, in one movement, set Emma on her feet. It was done so roughly that she swayed when she was no longer supported.

And yet, wasn't there some faint hope on her haggard face? Her hair had tumbled loose. The white headdress trailed underfoot.

The man continued pacing. Twice, he strode past his distraught companion.

The third time, he took her in his arms, crushed her to him, tipped back her head and greedily pressed his lips to hers.

All they could see was his back, a back not human, with a small female hand clamped on his shoulder.

Never taking his lips from hers, the creature stroked her straggling locks with his huge fingers, stroked as if he wanted to annihilate his companion, to crush her, to take her into himself.

'My God!' Leroy sounded overcome.

Maigret had been so moved that in reaction he nearly burst out laughing.

★   ★   ★

Had Emma been there a quarter of an hour? The embrace was over. The candle would last only

90

another five minutes. And the atmosphere of relief was almost visible.

Was the waitress laughing? She had apparently found a mirror somewhere. They watched her, in the full light of the candle, roll up her long hair, fasten it with a pin, search the floor for another pin and hold it between her teeth while she put the headdress back in place.

She was almost beautiful. She *was* beautiful! Everything about her was appealing, even her flat figure, her black dress, her red eyelids. The man had picked up the chicken and, without taking his eyes off her, was biting into it lustily, cracking the bones, tearing off strips of meat.

He felt, unsuccessfully, for a knife in his pocket, then snapped the neck of the bottle by knocking it against his heel. He drank. When he urged Emma to drink, she tried to refuse, laughing. Perhaps the jagged glass frightened her. But he made her open her mouth and gently poured in the liquid.

She choked and coughed. He took her by the shoulders and kissed her again, but this time not on the lips. He kissed her gleefully, giving little pecks on her cheeks, on her eyes, on her brow and even on her lace headdress.

She was ready. He pressed his face to the window and once again he almost totally filled the dim rectangle. When he turned away, it was to put out the candle.

Leroy stiffened. 'They're leaving together . . . '

'Yes.'

'They'll be caught . . . '

The currant bush in the garden trembled. A

91

figure was hoisted to the top of the wall. Emma then stood in the alley, waiting for her lover.

'Follow them, but keep your distance. Make sure they don't notice you! . . . Let me know what happens when you get a chance.'

Just as the big man had done for his companion, Maigret helped the inspector hitch himself up the roof tiles to the skylight. Then he leaned over to look down into the alley-way, to see the tops of the fugitives' heads.

They hesitated, whispering. It was Emma who led the man towards a shed. They vanished into it, for the door was only latched.

It was a ship chandler's storage shed, connected to his shop, which would be empty at this hour. Just one lock to force, and the couple could reach the quay.

But Leroy would get there before them.

★   ★   ★

As he climbed down the attic ladder, the inspector realized that something strange was happening. There was a commotion downstairs. And the telephone was ringing amid the clamouring voices.

Among them was Leroy's, louder than usual — he was apparently on the phone.

Maigret hurried down the stairs to the ground floor, where he collided with one of the reporters.

'What's going on?' he asked.

'Another shooting . . . a quarter of an hour ago, in town . . . They took the victim to the pharmacy.'

92

The inspector darted out to the quay and saw a policeman running and brandishing his revolver. The sky was blacker than ever. Maigret caught up with the man and again asked, 'What's going on?'

'A couple just came out of that shop . . . I was on patrol across the way. The man practically fell into my arms . . . It's not worth chasing them now. They must be a long way off!'

'Explain what happened.'

'I heard sounds in the shop, but there were no lights on. So I stood by with my gun ready. The door opened; a man came out . . . But I didn't even have time to take aim. He hit me in the face so hard that I fell down. I dropped my gun, and the one thing that scared me was that he'd grab it . . . But no — he went back to get a woman who was waiting in the doorway. She couldn't run, and he picked her up in his arms . . . By the time I got up, inspector — that was some punch! Look, I'm bleeding! — they'd taken off along the quay. They must have gone around the harbour. And there are lots of little streets off there, and then it's all open country . . . '

The policeman was dabbing his nose with his handkerchief. 'He could have killed me, just like that! He's got a fist like a sledgehammer.'

Voices could still be heard in the hotel, which was all lit up. Maigret left the policeman, rounded the corner and saw the pharmacy. Its shutters were closed, but its open door let out a flood of light.

Fifteen or twenty people were clustered at the door. The inspector elbowed through them.

In the dispensary, a man laid out flat on the floor was emitting rhythmic moans as he stared at the ceiling.

The pharmacist's wife, in her nightgown, was making more noise than all the rest of them together.

And the pharmacist himself, who had slipped a jacket on over his pyjamas, was in a panic, shuffling phials around, tearing open large packages of absorbent cotton.

'Who is it?' Maigret asked.

He didn't wait for the answer; he had already recognized the customs uniform, its trouser leg slit open. And now he recognized the face.

It was the customs guard who had been on duty in the port the Friday before and had witnessed the Mostaguen shooting from a distance.

A doctor arrived in a rush, looked at the wounded man, then at Maigret, and cried, 'What next?'

A little blood had run on to the floor. The pharmacist had washed the guard's leg with hydrogen peroxide, which left streaks of rosy foam.

Outside, a man was telling his tale, perhaps for the tenth time, but in a voice still gasping with excitement nonetheless.

'My wife and I were asleep when I heard a noise that sounded like a gunshot, and a cry! Then nothing more, for maybe five minutes. I didn't dare go back to sleep. My wife wanted me to go and look. Then we heard these moans that sounded as if they were coming from right in front of our door. I opened it — I had a gun — and I saw a dark shape. I recognized the

94

uniform. I shouted, to wake up the neighbours. And the fruitseller — he has a car — helped me bring the fellow here — '

'What time did you hear the shot?'

'Half an hour ago.'

That was just when the scene between Emma and the man of the huge footprints was at its most intense.

'Where do you live?'

'I'm the sailmaker. You've passed my house a dozen times, on the right side of the harbour, past the fish market. My house is at the corner of the quay and a little street . . . After that, the buildings thin out, and there's almost nothing except private houses.'

Four men carried the wounded customs guard into a back room, where they laid him on a couch. The doctor gave instructions. In the shop, the mayor's voice could be heard asking, 'Is the inspector here?'

Maigret went and stood in front of him, his hands in his pockets.

'You must admit, chief inspector . . . '

But Maigret's look was so cold that the mayor was disconcerted for a moment.

'It's our man who did this . . . no?' he asked.

'No.'

'How do you know?'

'I know because at the moment the crime was committed I had just as clear a view of him as I have of you right now.'

'And you didn't arrest him?'

'No.'

'I hear he assaulted a policeman, too.'

'That's correct.'

'Do you realize what repercussions this kind of thing could have? . . . You know, it's since you've been here that — '

Maigret picked up the telephone. 'Give me the police barracks, mademoiselle . . . Yes, thanks . . . Hello! Is this the sergeant? Chief Inspector Maigret here. Dr Michoux is still there, of course? . . . What's that? . . . Yes, go and check anyway. You've got a man posted in the courtyard? . . . Good. I'll wait.'

'You believe it's the doctor who — '

'Not at all! I never believe anything, *Monsieur le Maire* . . . Yes! He hasn't moved? Thank you . . . Asleep, eh? . . . Very good . . . No, nothing special.'

Groans sounded from the back room, and soon a voice called, 'Inspector . . . '

It was the doctor, who was wiping his soapy hands on a towel.

'You can question him now. The bullet only grazed his calf. He's more scared than hurt. Although I should say that he lost a lot of blood.'

The customs man had tears in his eyes. He flushed when the doctor went on: 'He was frightened because he thought we would cut off his leg . . . The fact is, in a week the thing won't even show.'

The mayor stood framed in the doorway.

'Tell me how it happened,' Maigret said gently as he sat on the edge of the couch. 'Don't be afraid . . . You heard what the doctor said.'

'I don't know . . . '

'Well, tell me what you can.'

'I got off duty tonight at ten o'clock. I live a little past the corner where I was wounded — '

'You didn't go directly home?'

'No. The lights were still on at the Admiral. And I wanted to find out the latest . . . I swear my leg is burning up!'

'No, no, it's fine,' the doctor said firmly.

'But I'm telling you . . . Well, as long as it's not serious. I had a beer at the café. Only the reporters were there, and I didn't have the nerve to ask them.'

'Who served you?'

'A chambermaid, I think. I didn't see Emma.'

'And then?'

'I headed for home. I stopped at the booth to light a cigarette off my colleague's pipe. Then I went along the quay, turned right . . . There was no one around. The sea was quite pretty . . . All of a sudden, just as I got a little past a corner, I felt a pain in my leg, even before I heard the shot. It felt like a cobblestone hitting me hard in the calf. I fell down . . . I tried to get up. Someone was running . . . Then my hand touched something hot and wet, and, I don't know how it happened, but I passed out . . . I thought I was dead . . .

'When I came to, the fruitseller at the corner had his door open and was standing there, afraid to come out. That's all I know.'

'You didn't see the person who fired?'

'I didn't see anything. It doesn't happen the way people think . . . There's a moment when you're falling down . . . and then, when my hand felt the blood . . . '

'You don't have any enemies you can think of?'

'No. I've only been here two years . . . I come from inland . . . and in that time I've never spotted any smugglers.'

'Do you always go home by that route?'

'No. That's the longest way . . . But I had no matches, and so I went over to the booth to light my cigarette. Then, instead of cutting through town, I just went along the waterfront.'

'It's shorter through town?'

'A little.'

'So that someone who saw you leave the café and head along the quay would have had time to get in position for an ambush?'

'Oh, yes. But why? I never carry money on me . . . And anyhow, they didn't try to rob me.'

'You're quite sure, inspector, that you never lost sight of your drifter the whole evening?' There was an edge to the mayor's voice.

Leroy came in, holding out a piece of paper.

'A telegram. The post office has just phoned it to the hotel. It's from Paris.'

And Maigret read:

Sûreté Générale to Detective Chief Inspector Maigret, Concarneau. Jean Goyard, alias Servières, per your description, arrested Monday night at eight, Hotel Bellevue, Rue Lepic, Paris, while moving into room 15. Admits arriving from Brest by six o'clock train. Protests innocence and demands presence of counsel at further interrogation. Await instructions.

8

Plus One

'You'll agree perhaps, chief inspector, that it's time we had a serious talk . . . '

The mayor had said this in a tone of icy formality, and Leroy did not know Maigret well enough yet to judge his reaction from the way he blew out his pipe smoke. A slender grey stream emerged slowly from the inspector's half-open lips, and he blinked two or three times. Then he drew his notebook from his pocket and looked around at the pharmacist, the doctor, the bystanders.

'At your service, *Monsieur le Maire* . . . Here is — '

'If you'd like to have a cup of tea at my house,' the mayor interrupted hastily, 'I have my car at the door. I'll wait till you've given the necessary orders.'

'What orders?'

'But . . . the murderer, the drifter . . . that girl . . . ?'

'Oh, yes! Well, if the police have nothing better to do, they can keep an eye on the railway stations round here.' He wore his most ingenuous expression. 'Leroy, wire Paris to send Goyard here. Then go to bed.'

He got in the mayor's car, which was driven by a chauffeur in black livery. As they neared White

Sands, they caught sight of the mayor's house. It was built directly on the cliff, which made it look somewhat like a feudal chateau. Lights shone from several windows.

The two men had barely exchanged two sentences in the course of the drive. 'Allow me to show you a few points of interest,' the mayor had tried.

At the villa, he handed his fur coat to a butler. 'Madame has gone to bed?'

'No, sir. She is waiting for you in the library.'

They found her there. She was about forty years old and looked young next to her husband, who was sixty-five. She nodded to the inspector.

'Well?'

Very much the man of the world, the mayor kissed her hand, which he kept in his as he said, 'Don't worry. A customs guard was slightly wounded . . . And I hope that after the conversation we're about to have, Chief Inspector Maigret and I, this unconscionable nightmare will come to an end.'

She left, with a rustle of silk. A blue plush drape fell back into place at the door.

The huge library had walls lined with fine panelling and exposed ceiling beams, like those in an English manor house. Fairly rich bindings could be seen on the shelves, but more precious ones were apparently kept in a closed bookcase that covered one whole wall.

The setting was one of real luxury, faultless taste, utter comfort. There was central heating, but logs blazed in a monumental fireplace. There was no comparison with the false elegance of the doctor's house.

The mayor selected a box of cigars and held it out to Maigret.

'Thank you! If you'll allow me, I'll smoke my pipe.'

'Please sit down . . . Will you have a whisky?'

He pressed a buzzer, then lit a cigar. The butler came in to serve them. And, perhaps on purpose, Maigret seemed to have the awkward manner of a petit bourgeois visiting an aristocratic house. His features looked heavy, his gaze vague.

His host waited for the butler to leave. 'I'm sure you understand, chief inspector, that this series of crimes cannot go on. It's been . . . let's see . . . three days now since you arrived. And in all that time — '

From his pocket Maigret drew his cheap little oilcloth-covered notebook.

'May I?' he interrupted. 'You mention a series of crimes . . . Now I'd like to point out that all the victims are alive except one. A single death: Monsieur Le Pommeret's . . . As for the customs guard, you'll admit that anyone who really wanted to kill him would not have shot him in the leg. You know the place where the shot was fired. The attacker was hidden, so he could take all the time he needed. Unless he'd never held a revolver before . . . '

The mayor looked at him with astonishment and, seizing his glass, said, 'So you claim — '

'That the assailant meant to wound him in the leg . . . At least until we have proof to the contrary.'

'Did Monsieur Mostaguen's assailant mean to hit him in the leg, too?'

101

The sarcasm was obvious, and the man's nostrils quivered. He was straining to be polite, to keep calm, because he was in his own home. But there was a disagreeable edge to his voice.

His manner that of a proper civil servant reporting to his superior, Maigret went on:

'If you'll allow me, we'll go over my notes one by one . . . I read from the date of Friday, 7 November: *A bullet is fired through the letterbox of a vacant house towards Monsieur Mostaguen.* Remember, to begin with, that no one, not even the victim, could have known that at a given moment Monsieur Mostaguen would get the idea of stopping in a doorway to light his cigar. A little less wind and the crime would never have occurred . . . Of course, there was a man with a revolver behind the door . . . Either he was crazy or he was waiting for *someone who was supposed to come.* Now then, remember what time it was. Eleven o'clock at night. The whole town was asleep, except for the little group at the Admiral café.

'I'm drawing no conclusions, but let's run through the possible guilty parties. Le Pommeret and Jean Servieères, and Emma too, are out of the running, because they were still in the café.

'That leaves Dr Michoux, who had left fifteen minutes earlier, and the vagrant with the enormous footprints. Plus an unknown person we'll call X. Are we in agreement? . . . We should add, parenthetically, that Monsieur Mostaguen did not die and that in two weeks he'll be on his feet again . . .

'Let's go to the second incident. *The following*

day, Saturday, *I enter the café. After introduc-
tions, I am about to drink an aperitif with
Messieurs Michoux, Le Pommeret, and Jean
Servières, when the doctor suddenly becomes
suspicious of something in his glass. Analysis
shows the Pernod bottle to be poisoned.*

'Possible culprits: Michoux, Le Pommeret, Servières;
Emma, the waitress; the vagrant — who might
have entered the café some time during the day
without being seen — and also our unknown
person designated X.

'Let's continue. *Sunday morning, Jean Servières
disappears. His car is found, with bloodstains,
not far from his home. Before this discovery, the
Brest Beacon receives a report of the events
nicely calculated to sow panic in Concarneau.*

'Then *Servières is seen, first in Brest, later in
Paris, where he seems to be hiding and to which
he has apparently gone of his own free will.*

'Only one possible culprit here: Servières
himself.

'*The same day, Sunday, Monsier Le Pommeret has an aperitif with the doctor, returns to
his home, has dinner there and dies afterwards,
from the effects of strychnine poisoning.*

'Possible culprits: at the café, if that's where he
was poisoned, the doctor, Emma and again our
X. This time, the vagrant has to be ruled out,
because the café was never empty for a moment,
and it wasn't the bottle that was poisoned
— only the one glass.

'If the crime was committed in Le Pommeret's
own house, possible culprits: his landlady, the
vagrant and our sempiternal X.

'Bear with me now; we're coming to the end. *Tonight, Monday, a customs guard is shot in the leg as he walks down an empty street. The doctor is still in prison, under close watch. Le Pommeret is dead. Servières is in Paris in the hands of the Sûreté. Emma and the vagrant are at that very moment embracing and then devouring a chicken, before my own eyes.*

'Thus, only one possible culprit: X. That is to say, a person we haven't yet encountered in the course of events. A person who could have committed all the crimes, or only this last one.

'We don't know who this person is. We have no description of him. Just one clue: whoever it is, he was interested in making something happen tonight — had a pressing interest. That bullet wasn't fired by a random prowler.

'Now, don't ask me to arrest X. Because you'll agree, *Monsieur le Maire*, that anyone in town — especially someone who knows the principal characters involved in this business and, in particular, the regular customers at the Admiral café — could be that X.

'Even you.'

These last words were spoken casually as Maigret leaned back in his chair and stretched his legs towards the fire. The mayor gave the merest start. 'I hope that's just a little retaliation . . . '

Then Maigret stood up suddenly, knocked out his pipe on the hearth and declared, as he walked up and down:

'Not at all! You wanted answers? Well, there you are. I just wanted to show you that a case

104

like this is no simple little police operation that can be handled by making a few telephone calls from an armchair . . . And I will add, *Monsieur le Maire*, with all due respect, that when I take charge of an investigation, I insist above all, dammit, on being *left alone!*'

That came out with no premeditation. It had been incubating for days. Perhaps to calm down, Maigret took a swallow of whisky and looked at the door like a man who has said what he has to say and is waiting for permission to leave.

The mayor was silent for a few minutes, contemplating the white ash of his cigar. Finally, he let it fall into a blue porcelain bowl and rose slowly, his eyes seeking Maigret's.

'Listen, chief inspector . . . '

He must have been weighing his words, for they were separated by pauses.

'I may have been wrong, in the course of our brief connection, to show some impatience . . . '

This was rather unexpected — especially in this setting, where the man seemed more aristocratic than ever, with his white hair, his silk-trimmed smoking jacket, his sharply creased grey trousers.

'I am beginning to appreciate your true worth. In these few minutes, by means of a simple summary of the facts, you've made me understand the terrible mystery of this business. It's more complex than I ever suspected. I confess your inertia in the matter of the vagrant did dispose me against you.' He approached the inspector and touched his shoulder. 'I ask you not to hold it against me . . . I have some heavy responsibilities myself.'

It would have been impossible to guess Maigret's thoughts as his thick fingers packed his pipe from a worn tobacco pouch. Through a large window, his gaze wandered over the vast ocean horizon.

'What's that light?' he asked suddenly.

'The beacon.'

'No, I mean that small light to the right.'

'That's Dr Michoux's house.'

'The servant's back, then?'

'No. It's Madame Michoux, the doctor's mother. She came back this afternoon.'

'You've seen her?'

Maigret thought he sensed some discomfort in his host.

'Well, she was surprised not to find her son at home. She came by to ask. I told her about the arrest, explaining that it was mainly a protective measure . . . Because that's what it is, isn't it? She asked my authorization to visit him . . . At the hotel, no one knew where you were. So I took it on myself to permit the visit.

'Madame Michoux came back shortly before dinner to ask for the latest news. My wife invited her to eat with us.'

'They're friends?'

'In a manner of speaking. Good neighbours is more accurate. In the winter, there are very few people in Concarneau.'

Maigret resumed his stroll across the library.

'So the three of you ate together?'

'Yes. That often happens . . . I reassured Madame Michoux as best I could. She was quite

106

upset by the business of the police barracks
. . . She had a difficult time raising her son; his
health has never been very good.'

'Did you discuss Le Pommeret and Jean
Servieères?'

'She never liked Le Pommeret. She claimed he
led her son to drink. The fact is that — '

'And Servières?'

'She didn't know him as well. He didn't move
in her circle. An unimportant newspaperman, a
café acquaintance — merely an amusing fellow.
One couldn't, for example, receive his wife, a
woman whose past is not entirely above reproach
. . . That's small-town life, chief inspector! You've
got to resign yourself to these distinctions. They
partly explain my own short temper. You don't
know what it is to manage a community of
fishermen and at the same time watch out for the
sensibilities of the gentry — and of some
middle-class elements besides — '

'What time did Madame Michoux leave here?'

'About ten. My wife drove her back in the car.'

'That light means that Madame Michoux
hasn't gone to bed yet.'

'That's usual for her . . . For me as well. At a
certain age, we need less sleep. Very late at night
I'm still in here reading, or looking over files — '

'Are the Michoux doing well with their business?'

Uneasiness showed again, though barely percep-
tible.

'Not yet . . . It will take time for the White
Sands project to begin producing a profit. But,
given Madame Michoux's connections in Paris,

that shouldn't be long. A number of plots have been sold already, and construction will start again in the spring. On this recent trip, she practically persuaded a certain banker whose name I can't mention to build a magnificent house on the bluff . . . '

'One more question, *Monsieur le Maire*: who used to own the land they're developing?'

His companion did not hesitate. 'I did. It belonged to my family, as did this house. There was nothing there but heather and broom when the Michouxs got the idea — '

Just then the distant light went out.

'Another whisky, chief inspector? . . . Of course, I'll have my chauffeur drive you back.'

'You're very kind. But I love to walk, especially when I have things to think over.'

'What do you make of this business of the yellow dog? I confess that that may be what upsets me most — that and the poisoned Pernod! Because actually — '

But Maigret was looking around for his hat and coat.

The mayor had no choice but to press the buzzer. 'The chief inspector's things, Delphin.'

The silence was so complete that they could hear the muffled, rhythmic sound of the surf on the rocks below the villa.

'You're sure you don't want my car?'

'Quite sure.'

Wisps of discomfiture hung in the air like the wisps of tobacco smoke coiling about the lamps.

'I wonder what the mood will be in town tomorrow. If the sea is calm, at least we won't have the fishermen on the streets. They'll leap at the chance to set out their lobster pots.'

Maigret took his coat from the butler and put out his big hand. The mayor still had questions, but he was reluctant to ask them in the butler's presence.

'How much longer do you think — '

The clock struck one in the morning. 'I hope it will all be cleared up by tomorrow night.'

'So soon? Despite what you told me earlier? Then you must be counting on Goyard? . . . Unless — '

He was too late. Maigret had started down the stairs. The mayor searched for some last words, but nothing came to mind that expressed his feeling. 'I'm uncomfortable letting you go back on foot — along those roads — '

The door closed. Maigret was on his way, under a fine sky with heavy clouds that raced one another across the moon. The air was sharp. The wind, from off the water, brought the smell of the seaweed strewn in dark masses on the beach.

The inspector walked slowly, his hands in his pockets, his pipe between his teeth. Looking back, he saw the lights go out in the mayor's library, then others going on behind upstairs curtains.

He did not take the road through town, but followed the shore, as the customs guard had, and stopped for a moment at the corner where the man had been shot. All was calm. Street lamps shone here and there into the distance. Concarneau was asleep.

When he reached the square, he saw that the café windows were still shining, violating the nocturnal peace with their poisonous halo. He pushed the door open. A reporter was dictating over the phone.

' . . . By now no one knows whom to suspect. In the streets, people look anxiously at one another. Could this be the killer? Or maybe that one over there? The cloud of mystery and fear has never been so thick . . . '

The proprietor himself stood gloomily at the till. The moment he caught sight of the inspector, he made a move to approach and speak. It was easy enough to guess his complaints.

The café was a shambles, with newspapers and empty glasses on the tables. A photographer was busy drying prints on the radiator.

Leroy walked over to his chief. 'That's Madame Goyard,' he said in an undertone, pointing to a plump woman collapsed on a banquette.

She rose, wiping her eyes.

'Tell me, inspector, is it true? . . . I don't know who to believe any more. They say Jean is alive. But it's impossible — isn't it? — that he would trick us like that. He wouldn't have done that to me. He would never put me through such worry . . . I feel as though I'm going mad! — Why would he have gone to Paris? Tell me! . . . And without me!'

She wept — the way certain women can weep, with great floods of tears pouring down her cheeks, flowing to her chin, while one hand pressed against her plump bosom. She looked for her handkerchief.

'I swear it can't be true!' she insisted. 'I know he ran around a little . . . but he would never do anything like this. Whenever he came home, he asked me to forgive him . . . They're saying' — she pointed to the reporters — 'they're saying he put the bloodstains in the car himself, to make it look like murder. But that would mean he never meant to come back! And I know better. I'm sure he would have . . . He never would have gone gallivanting if the others hadn't dragged him along — Monsieur Le Pommeret, the doctor . . . and the mayor too! That whole bunch, who never even greet me in the street, because I'm not good enough for them . . .

'Someone said he's been arrested . . . I don't believe it. What harm did he ever do? He earned enough for the kind of life we led. We were happy, even if he did treat himself to a fling once in a while . . . '

Maigret looked at her and sighed. Then he picked up a glass from a table, swallowed the contents straight down and murmured, 'You'll have to excuse me, madame. I've got to get some sleep.'

'Do you believe it too — that he's done something wrong?'

'I never believe anything. You should do the same, madame. Tomorrow is another day.'

And as he climbed the stairs heavily, the reporter at the phone turned Maigret's parting words to his own account:

'According to the latest word, Chief Inspector Maigret expects to clear up the mystery by tomorrow.'

111

His tone changed as he finished. 'That's all, mademoiselle. Now be sure to tell the boss not to change one line of my story. He couldn't understand . . . he'd have to be on the scene . . . '

Hanging up, he shoved his notes into his pocket and called to the proprietor, 'Give me a toddy! Lots of rum and just a splash of hot water.'

Meanwhile, Madame Goyard accepted a reporter's offer to drive her back to her house. On the way she began again: 'He did run around a little . . . but you know how it is, monsieur! All men do that!'

9

The Seashell Box

Maigret was in such good spirits in the morning that Leroy felt free to follow him around, chattering and even asking some questions.

In fact, everyone was more relaxed, though it would be hard to say why. It may have been the weather, which had suddenly turned fine. The sky looked freshly laundered. It was blue, a rather pale but vibrant blue, glistening with light clouds. It made the horizon bigger, as if the celestial bowl were hollowed out. The sea sparkled, utterly flat and studded with tiny sails that looked like flags pinned to a military map.

It takes but a single sunbeam to transform Concarneau. Then the Old Town's walls, so gloomy in the rain, turn a joyful, dazzling white.

Exhausted by the comings and goings of the past three days, the reporters sat downstairs, telling each other stories over coffee; one of them had come down in his dressing gown and slippers.

Meanwhile, Maigret had gone into Emma's attic room. The roof sloped, so a person could stand up straight in only half the space. The gable window, which looked over the alleyway, was open. The air was cool, but you could feel the caress of the sun. Across the way, a woman

113

had taken the opportunity to hang her laundry out of her window. The noise of children came up from a school playground somewhere nearby.

Leroy, sitting on the edge of the little iron bed, remarked, 'I still don't quite understand your methods, inspector, but I think I'm beginning to see . . . '

Maigret gave him an amused glance and sent a large cloud of smoke out into the sunshine. 'You're lucky, my friend! Especially in this case, in which my method has actually been not to have one . . . I'll give you some good advice: if you're interested in getting ahead, don't take me for a model, or invent any theories from what you see me doing.'

'Still . . . I do notice that you're getting round to hard evidence now, after — '

'Exactly — after! After everything else! In other words, I ran this investigation from the end, backwards — which doesn't mean I won't go the other way in the next one. It's a question of atmosphere, a question of faces . . . When I first got here, I came across one face that appealed to me, and I never let go of it.'

But he did not say whose face he meant. He lifted aside an old sheet that hid a wardrobe. Inside hung a black velvet Breton costume, which Emma probably saved for special occasions.

On the dressing table were a comb with several teeth missing, some hairpins and a box of too-pink face powder. In a drawer he found what he seemed to be looking for: a box encrusted with shiny seashells, the kind sold in souvenir

114

shops all along the coast. This one, which looked perhaps ten years old and as though it had weathered God knows what travels, bore the words *Souvenir of Ostend.*

A smell of old cardboard, dust, perfume and yellowed paper rose from it. Maigret sat down on the edge of the bed beside his companion and, with his large fingers, lifted out the inventory of tiny items.

There was a rosary of faceted blue glass beads on a flimsy silver chain, a first communion medal and an empty perfume bottle that Emma must have found abandoned in a guest's room and saved for its appealing shape . . .

A paper flower, the keepsake from some dance or festival, struck a lively red note. Beside it was a small gold crucifix, the only object of any value . . .

A whole pile of postcards . . . One showed a large hotel in Cannes. On the back, in a woman's handwriting:

You reely awt to come here, insted of sticking in that awful hole were it rains all the time. And we earn good mony here. We get all we want to eat. Big kiss — Louise.

Maigret passed the card to Leroy and stared attentively at a photograph you get at fairground shooting galleries. Because of the rifle on his shoulder, they could barely see the man taking aim, with one eye shut. He had an enormous build, and a sailor's cap on his head. Emma, grinning into the lens, gripped his arm proudly.

115

At the bottom of the card was the name *Quimper*.

Next was a letter, on paper so tattered that it must have been reread many times:

Darling,

It's done, it's signed: I have my boat. She'll be called the *Pretty Emma*. The priest in Quimper promised he would christen her next week, with holy water, grains of wheat, salt and all, and there will be real champagne, because I want it to be a party people will talk about for a long time around here.

It will be hard to pay for her at first, because I have to hand the bank 10,000 francs a year. But just think, she'll carry over 3,000 square feet of sail and make ten knots. There's good money in carrying onions to England. What I mean is that it won't be too long before we can get married. I've already found a cargo for the first trip, but they're trying to bargain me down, because I'm new.

Your boss ought to give you two days off for the launch because everyone will be drunk and you won't be able to get back to Concarneau. I've had to treat everyone in the cafés round here to celebrate the boat, which is already in port and flying a brand-new flag.

I'll get my picture taken on board and send you one. I kiss you with all my love, waiting for the day when you'll be the

beloved wife of your
    Léon.

Gazing dreamily at the drying laundry on the other side of the alley, Maigret slipped the letter into his pocket. There was nothing else in the shell box but a pen holder carved of bone; a little glass lens in the base showed a view of the crypt at Notre-Dame de Lourdes.

'Is there anyone in the room the doctor generally uses?' he asked.

'I don't think so. The reporters are on the third floor.'

Out of duty, the inspector searched the room again, but he found nothing else of interest. A little later, down on the second floor, he opened the door to Michoux's room, the one with the balcony overlooking the port and the roadstead.

The bed was made, the floor polished. There were clean towels on the washstand.

Leroy watched his chief with a mixture of curiosity and scepticism. But Maigret whistled a quiet tune as he looked around, then headed for a small oak table in front of the window. On it lay a promotional writing folder and an ash tray.

Inside the folder were white paper with the hotel's letterhead and a blue envelope to match. But there were also two large sheets of blotting paper — one nearly black with ink, the other barely marked with sketchy characters.

'Go and get a mirror, son!'

'A big one?'

'Doesn't matter. Just one I can set up on the table.'

When Leroy returned, he found Maigret planted on the balcony, his thumbs hooked in the armholes of his waistcoat, smoking his pipe with obvious satisfaction.

'Will this do?'

The balcony window was closed again. Maigret stood the mirror on the table and, using two candlesticks from the mantel, he set the sheet of blotting paper upright in front of it.

The characters reflected in the mirror were far from easy to read. Letters, even whole words, were missing. Others were so distorted that he could only guess at them.

'I see what you're doing!' said Leroy, looking sly.

'Good! Now go and ask the proprietor for one of Emma's account books, or anything else with her hand-writing on it.'

With a pencil he transcribed words on a sheet of paper:' . . . see you . . . o'clock . . . vacant . . . absolutely . . . '

By the time Leroy returned, Maigret had filled in the blanks roughly and pieced together the following note:

I need to see you. Come tomorrow night at eleven to the vacant house on the square, a few doors past the hotel.

I'm absolutely counting on you. Just knock and I'll open the door.

'Here's the book Emma keeps for the laundry,' Leroy announced.

'It's the same writing. And look — the letter is

signed. An initial E ... And the letter was written here in this room.'

'Where she spent nights with the doctor?' Leroy was aghast.

Maigret could understand his repugnance at accepting this idea, especially after the scene they had witnessed the night before from their perch on the roof.

'In that case, then she's the one who — '

'Easy! Easy, my boy! No jumping to conclusions. And no deductions, remember? . . . What time does Jean Goyard's train get in?'

'Eleven thirty-two.'

'Here's what you're going to do, my friend. First, tell our two colleagues with him to bring the fellow to me at the police barracks . . . He'll get there at about noon. Telephone the mayor that I'd like to see him at the same time, same place . . . Wait! Same message for Madame Michoux — phone her at home . . . Then, at some point, the local police or others will probably be bringing in Emma and her sweetheart. Same place, same time for them . . . Am I forgetting anyone? . . . Good! Just one thing: Emma's not to be questioned in my absence. In fact, stop her from talking if she tries.'

'The customs guard?'

'I don't need him.'

'Monsieur Mostaguen?'

'Hmm . . . no. That's all.'

In the café, Maigret ordered the local brandy and sipped it with visible pleasure as he remarked to the newspapermen: 'We're winding up, gentlemen. You should be getting back to Paris tonight.'

119

His walk through the Old Town's twisting streets added to his good humour. And when he reached the gateway to the police barracks, with the bright French flag above it, he noticed that, by some magical effect of the sunlight, the three colours and the wall rippling with light, there was a kind of Bastille Day gaiety to the atmosphere.

An elderly policeman was sitting inside the gate, reading a humour magazine. The courtyard, with green moss growing between its small paving stones, was still as serene as a cloister.

'The sergeant?'

'They're all out — the lieutenant, the sergeant and most of the men — looking for that drifter.'

'The doctor hasn't budged?'

The man smiled and looked at a barred prison window to the right. 'No danger of that.'

'Open the door for me, will you?'

As soon as the bolts were drawn, Maigret exclaimed, in a bright, cordial voice: 'Hello there, doctor! Slept well, I hope!'

But all he saw was a pale, knife-sharp face emerging from the grey blanket on the bunk. The eyes were feverish, sunk deep into their sockets.

'Well now, what's the problem? Something wrong?'

'Very wrong,' mumbled Michoux, raising himself with a sigh. 'My kidney . . . '

'They're giving you whatever you need, I hope?'

'Yes . . . Good of you . . . '

He had gone to bed fully dressed, which was apparent when he slid his legs from under the

120

blanket. He sat up and wiped his hand over his forehead.

Meanwhile, Maigret, bursting with health and vigour, straddled a chair and planted his elbows on its back.

'Well now! I see you ordered yourself a nice bottle of Burgundy!'

'My mother brought it yesterday . . . I would just as soon have skipped that visit. She must have got wind of something in Paris . . . She came back.'

The dark circles under his eyes seemed to cover half of his unshaven hollow cheeks. The lack of a tie and his crumpled suit added to his aura of distress.

He cleared his throat and spat conspicuously into his handkerchief, which he then examined like a man worried about tuberculosis and keeping an anxious watch on himself.

'Is there anything new?' he asked warily.

'The police must have told you about last night.'

'No! What hap . . . Who's been . . . ?' He cowered against the wall as if afraid of being attacked.

'Nothing serious. Someone was shot in the leg.'

'Did they get the . . . whoever did it? . . . I can't take any more, inspector! You have to admit it's enough to drive a person crazy . . . Someone else from the Admiral café. Am I right? We're the ones he's after! And I'm racking my brain to work out why . . . Yes, why? Mostaguen! Le Pommeret! And the poison — that was meant for all of us together . . . You'll see, they'll get me, no

121

matter what, even in here! . . . But why? Tell me!'

He was no longer just pale. He was livid. It was painful to see such a picture of panic at its most pathetic and repellent.

'I don't even dare fall asleep . . . That window — look! There are bars, yes, but someone could shoot between them, at night. Suppose a guard fell asleep, or let his mind wander . . . I'm not made for this kind of life. Yesterday I drank that whole bottle, in hopes of getting to sleep, but I never closed an eye. I just felt sick. If they'd only kill that drifter, with his yellow dog . . . Did he turn up again, the dog? Is he still prowling around the café? . . . I don't understand why nobody's put a bullet into his hide. His and his master's both!'

'His master left Concarneau last night.'

'Oh!' The doctor seemed to have some trouble believing that. 'Right after — after his latest attack?'

'Before.'

'But — that's impossible! That would mean — '

'Correct. That's what I was telling the mayor, last night . . . Odd character, the mayor. Just between you and me, what do you think of him?'

'Me? I don't know . . . I . . . '

'Well, he sold you the land for the development. You're involved with him. You were friends, so to speak.'

'We did some business together and we are neighbours, that's all . . . out here in the country, you know . . . '

Maigret noticed that the doctor's voice was

growing firmer, his gaze less distracted.

'What was it you were telling him?' Michoux asked.

Maigret pulled his notebook from his pocket. 'I was saying that the series of crimes — or murder attempts, if you like — couldn't have been committed by any of the persons now known to us. I won't go over the events one by one; I'll just summarize: objectively, you understand, like a technician . . . Well, obviously you were in no position last night to fire at the customs guard, which could be enough to rule you out altogether. Le Pommeret couldn't have shot him either, since they're burying him tomorrow morning. Neither could Goyard; he's just been found in Paris . . . And they couldn't, any of them, have been the person behind the letterbox in the vacant house last Friday . . . Nor could Emma.'

'What about the drifter with the yellow dog?'

'I considered him. Not only is he probably not the one who poisoned Le Pommeret, but last night he was a long way from where the shooting occurred . . . That's why I told the mayor that it might be some unknown person, some mysterious X, who committed all these crimes. Unless . . . '

'Unless?'

'Unless it's not one person. Instead of some sort of unilateral offensive, suppose there's actually a battle going on between two groups, or between two individuals.'

'But what happens to me then, inspector? If there are unknown enemies prowling around, I . . . ' And his face went dull again. He put his head in his hands. 'When I think how sick I am, and how the doctors tell me I need absolute calm! . . . Oh, there's no need for any bullet or poison to do me in. You'll see — my kidney will take care of that.'

'What do you think of the mayor?'

'I don't know! I don't know anything about him! . . . He comes from a very rich family. When he was young, he lived the high life in Paris, had his own racing stable. And then he settled down. He had managed to save some of his money and came to live here, in the house built by his grandfather, who used to be mayor of Concarneau himself . . . He sold me the land he didn't need. I think he'd like to be appointed to the departmental council, and then move on to the Senate.'

The doctor had stood up, and anyone would have sworn he had lost fifteen pounds in the last few days. It would have been no surprise, moreover, to see him burst into nervous tears.

'What do you think is going on? . . . What about Goyard, turning up in Paris when everyone thinks . . . What could he have been doing there? And why?'

'We'll soon find out, because he's about to arrive in Concarneau. In fact, he should be here by now.'

'Is he under arrest?'

'He was asked to come along with two gentlemen. That's not the same thing.'

'What did he say?'

'Nothing. But then, no one asked him anything.'

The doctor suddenly looked the inspector square in the face. A quick flush rose to his cheeks.

'What does that mean? . . . I get the impression that something crazy is going on. You come in here and chat about the mayor, about Goyard . . . and meanwhile I'm sure — you hear me? — I'm convinced, more and more, that I'm about to be killed! In spite of those bars. Never mind that big idiot policeman on duty out in the courtyard! . . . And I don't want to die! I don't! Just give me a revolver to defend myself. Or else lock up the people who are after me, the ones who killed Le Pommeret, who put poison in the bottle . . . '

He was breathing heavily.

'I'm no hero! Facing death isn't my job. I'm just a man. A sick man! And I've got enough to do just fighting this disease . . . You talk and you talk, but what exactly are you doing?'

In a rage, he knocked his forehead against the wall. 'This whole thing looks like a conspiracy to me . . . unless people are trying to drive me crazy! That's it — they want to commit me! . . . Who knows? Maybe it's my mother. She's probably had enough of me. Because I've always hung on to my share of my father's legacy. But I won't let them get away with this!'

Maigret had not moved. He sat there quietly — his elbows on the back of the chair, his pipe in his teeth — in the middle of the white cell with one wall drenched in sunlight.

The doctor moved back and forth, his agitation close to delirium.

Then suddenly there was the sound of a cheerful voice, a touch ironic, imitating a child's. 'Coocoo!'

Ernest Michoux jumped and looked into all four corners of the cell before he turned to stare hard at Maigret. The inspector had taken his pipe from his mouth and was looking at Michoux with a wide grin.

It was as if a switch had been flipped. Michoux stopped short, went limp. His substance seemed to fade to a ghostly mist.

'Was that you?' he asked.

The voice might have come from anywhere, like a ventriloquist's, springing from the ceiling or out of a china vase.

Maigret's eyes were still laughing as he rose and, in a tone entirely at odds with his expression, said: 'Pull yourself together, doctor! I hear footsteps in the courtyard. In a few moments, I expect the murderer to be right here within these four walls.'

It was the mayor the guard brought in first. But there were sounds of others in the courtyard.

10

The *Pretty Emma*

'You asked me to come, inspector?'

Before Maigret had time to answer, he saw two officers enter the courtyard with Jean Goyard between them; out in the street, an excited crowd had gathered around the gate.

The journalist looked smaller, plumper, between his two bodyguards. He had pulled his soft hat down over his eyes and, probably worried about photographers, held a handkerchief over the lower part of his face.

'This way!' Maigret told the policemen. 'You might get us some chairs, since I hear a female voice.'

'Where is he?' a shrill voice demanded. 'I want to see him immediately! And I'll have you demoted, young fellow — you hear me? I'll have you demoted . . . '

It was Madame Michoux, in a mauve dress and wearing her jewels, powder and rouge, and seething with anger.

'Ah! You're here, dear friend,' she simpered, addressing the mayor. 'Can you imagine such a thing? This little man arrives at my house before I'm even dressed — my maid is away — and I tell him, through the door, that I cannot receive him. He insists, he demands, he waits while I get

127

ready, claiming he has an order to bring me here. It's simply outrageous! When I think that my husband was a deputy, practically prime minister, and that this . . . this lout — yes, lout . . . '

She was too indignant to register what was going on around her. Suddenly, she saw Goyard, averting his face, and her son sitting on the edge of his bunk with his head in his hands.

A car drove into the sunny courtyard at that point. Police uniforms gleamed. And a clamour rose from the crowd.

A guard had closed the gate, to keep the throng from forcing its way into the courtyard. For the first person to be pulled out of the car, literally, was none other than the drifter. Not only did he have handcuffs on his wrists, but his ankles were shackled with sturdy rope and he had to be dragged in like a sack.

Behind him came Emma, her limbs free but her movements dazed, as though she were in a dream.

'Untie his legs!' Maigret commanded.

The police were full of themselves, still elated at having captured him. It couldn't have been easy, to judge by their dishevelled uniforms and, especially, by the prisoner's face, which was smeared with the blood still running from his split lip.

Madame Michoux gave a frightened cry and recoiled against the wall. The man let himself be freed without a word, lifted his head and gazed slowly around.

'Easy there, eh, Léon?' growled Maigret.

The man started and looked around again, to see who had spoken.

'Someone give him a chair and a handkerchief.'

Maigret noticed that Goyard had sidled to the farthest reach of the cell, behind Madame Michoux, and that the doctor was trembling and looking at no one. The police lieutenant was wondering uncomfortably what his role should be in this unusual assembly.

'Please close the door. Will everyone kindly be seated . . . Lieutenant, can your sergeant take down the proceedings? . . . Very good! He can sit at that little table. I'll ask you to have a seat too, *Monsieur le Maire*.'

The crowd outside was no longer shouting, but it was unmistakably present — a sense of tightly packed humanity, an intense air of expectancy out in the street.

Maigret stuffed his pipe as he paced the cell. Turning to Leroy, he said: 'Before we start, I'd like you to telephone the seamen's association at Quimper to ask what happened four or five years ago — maybe six — to a boat called the *Pretty Emma*.'

As Leroy headed for the door, the mayor coughed and indicated that he had something to say.

'I can tell you about that, inspector. Everyone knows the story around here.'

'Go on.'

The vagrant tensed in his corner like an attack dog. Emma, sitting on the very edge of her chair, never took her eyes off him. By chance she had ended up beside Madame Michoux, whose perfume, a sugary scent of violet, had begun to permeate the air.

'I never saw the boat,' the mayor said casually, his tone perhaps slightly forced. 'It belonged to a fellow named Le Glen, or Le Glérec, who was said to be an excellent seaman but hot-headed. Like all the coasters in this area, the *Pretty Emma* mainly carried early vegetables to England . . . One fine day she apparently sailed on a longer voyage. There was no news for two months. Eventually, we heard that the *Pretty Emma* had been searched when it had arrived at a small port near New York. Its crew was sent to prison, and the cargo — cocaine — was seized. The boat, too, of course . . . That was at the time when most freighters, especially those that carried salt to Newfoundland, were involved in smuggling liquor.'

'Thank you . . . Stay where you are, Léon. Answer me from there . . . And answer the questions I ask you exactly, and *nothing more*! You hear me? . . . First, where did they arrest you just now?'

The vagrant, wiping at the blood on his chin, said in a hoarse voice, 'At Rosporden . . . in a railway station, where we were waiting till dark to jump on to a train.'

'How much money did you have?'

It was the lieutenant who answered: 'Eleven francs and a little change.'

Maigret looked at Emma, whose cheeks were wet with tears, then at the brute, now silent and withdrawn. He sensed that the doctor, though quiet, was intensely agitated, and he signed to one of the policemen to station himself near Michoux, ready for any eventuality.

The sergeant was still writing. His pen scratched on the paper with a metallic sound.

'Tell us, exactly, the circumstances of this cocaine cargo, Le Glérec.'

The man raised his eyes. His gaze locked on to the doctor and grew hard. His mouth bitter, his heavy fists clenched, he muttered, 'The bank had lent me money to get my boat built . . . '

'I know that. Go on.'

'It was a bad year. The franc was rising. The English were buying less produce. I was worried about paying the interest . . . I wanted to get most of the loan paid off before I married Emma . . . Then this newspaperman looked me up. I knew him because he hung around the port a lot . . . '

Astonishing everyone, Ernest Michoux dropped his hands from his face. It was pale, but infinitely calmer than anyone had expected. He drew a notebook and a pencil from his pocket and wrote a few words.

'Did Jean Servières offer you a cocaine shipment?'

'Not right away. He only talked about doing some business. He told me to meet him in a café in Brest. He was waiting there with two other men — '

'Dr Michoux and Monsieur Le Pommeret?'

'That's right.'

Michoux jotted down some more notes, his expression disdainful. At one point he even gave a sardonic smile.

'Which of the three actually gave you the job?'

The doctor waited, his pencil poised.

131

'None of them . . . That is, they just talked about the big money I could make for a month or two's work . . . An American turned up an hour later. I never heard his name, and I saw him only twice. He obviously knew the sea, because he asked me the specifications of my boat, the number of men I'd need on board and how much time it would take to install an auxiliary engine . . . I figured what they had in mind was bootlegging liquor. Everyone was doing some of that, even officers on the liners . . . The next week, workmen came to install a semi-diesel engine on the *Pretty Emma* . . .'

He spoke slowly, his gaze fixed. But the slow, spasmodic movements of his huge fingers were more eloquent than his face, and it was affecting to watch them.

'They gave me an English chart that showed Atlantic wind patterns and routes for sailing vessels, because I'd never made the crossing . . . Being cautious, I took only two men with me, and I never told anyone about it but Emma. She was on the jetty the night we left . . . The three Frenchmen were there too, standing next to a car with its lights out . . . We'd taken on the cargo that afternoon. And at that moment, as we set out, I got scared . . . Not so much about the contraband. But I never had much schooling. As long as I can use the compass and the plumb line, I'm all right; I can do as well as anyone. But out there on the open ocean . . . An old sea captain had tried to teach me how to use the sextant to take bearings. And I bought logarithm tables and all that. But I was sure to get tangled up in the calculations . . . Still, if I made it, the boat would be paid for and I'd have about 20,000 francs left . . . There was a terrible wind that night. We lost sight of the car and the three men. Then Emma, her dark shape at the end of the jetty . . . Two months at sea . . . '

Michoux was still taking notes, but he avoided looking at the man speaking.

'I had landing instructions. Finally — God knows how — we got to the little port they'd told us about . . . But before we even threw out the anchors, we were surrounded — three police launches with machine guns and men carrying rifles. They jumped on deck, held us at gun-point and shouted things in English. They hit us with the rifle butts till we put our hands up . . .

'All we saw was the gunfire — it happened so fast . . . Somehow my boat was tied up to the pier, and we got shoved into a van. An hour later, we were each locked up in a separate cell, at Sing Sing . . .

'We were ill. Nobody spoke any French. The other prisoners made jokes and yelled insults at us . . .

'Things move fast over there. The next day, we went before some kind of tribunal, and the lawyer who was supposed to be defending us never said a word to us! . . .

'Afterwards, he told me that I was sentenced to two years of hard labour and a 100,000-dollar fine, that my boat was confiscated . . . and a lot I didn't understand. A hundred thousand dollars! I swore I didn't have any money. That meant I don't know how many extra years in prison . . .

133

'I stayed at Sing Sing. My men must have been put in another prison, because I never saw them again . . . They shaved my head . . . They put me in a road gang, smashing rocks . . . There was a chaplain who tried to give me Bible lessons . . .

'You can't imagine what it was like. There were rich prisoners who went off into town almost every night . . . and they used the rest of us as their servants! . . .

'It doesn't matter. After a whole year of that, one day I ran into the American from Brest. He was visiting another prisoner. I recognized him and called to him. It took him a while to remember. Then he burst out laughing and had me brought to the visiting room.

'He was very cordial . . . treated me like an old friend. He told me he'd been a Prohibition agent. He worked abroad mostly, in England, in France, in Germany; he'd send the American police information on shipments leaving from there.

'But at the same time he occasionally did some trafficking for himself. That was the case with that cocaine shipment, which was supposed to bring in millions, because there were ten tons aboard at who knows what price per ounce . . . So he'd got together with some Frenchmen, who were to supply the boat and part of the investment — that was my three men — and naturally they would split the profits among the four of them . . .

'But listen! The best part is coming . . . The very day we were loading at Quimper, the American got word from back home: there was a new Prohibition chief, and surveillance was going

134

to be stepped up. Buyers in the United States were holding off, and for that reason the merchandise might not find a taker . . .

'At the same time, a new order said anyone who informed on prohibited cargo would get a bounty, as much as a third of its value . . .

'There I was in prison hearing this! . . . He told me that, at the moment I was casting off — worried sick about whether we would even reach the other side of the Atlantic alive — he was in the car, and my three men were arguing with him, there on the quay.

'Should they gamble on getting through, for the whole stake? . . . I know now that it was the doctor who held out for informing on me. At least that way they'd be sure of getting a third of the money, with no complications.

'Not counting that the American had made a deal with a colleague to skim off part of the impounded cocaine. An unbelievable racket, I know! . . .

'The *Pretty Emma* sailed out into the dark water of the harbour . . . I took one last look at my fiancée, telling myself I'd be back to marry her in a few months . . .

'And they knew — those men watching us leave — they knew we'd be picked up when we got there! They'd even figured that we'd put up a fight, that we'd probably be killed in the struggle. It was happening every day in American waters at the time . . .

'They knew that my boat would be confiscated, that it was not entirely paid for, and that I had nothing else in the world. They knew my one dream was to marry Emma. And they watched us go!

'That's what the American told me at Sing Sing, where I'd turned into an animal, among those other animals . . . He proved it to me. He laughed and slapped his thigh, and said, 'Some bastards, those friends of yours!' '

Suddenly, there was absolute silence. And in that silence could be heard the startling sound of Michoux's pencil sliding over a fresh page.

Maigret looked at the initials *SS* tattooed on the giant's hand and understood: 'Sing Sing.'

'I probably had ten years more to go . . . In that country, you never know. You break the smallest rule, and the sentence gets longer, and meanwhile they go on hitting you with their clubs . . . I got hundreds of those beatings — from the other prisoners, too . . . Then my American took steps to help me. I think he was disgusted by the behaviour of those men he kept calling my 'friends' . . . The only company I had was a dog. I raised him on board, and he'd saved me from drowning once. In spite of all their rules over there, they let him stay in the prison — they have different ideas from us about that kind of thing . . . Oh, it was hell! They'll play music for you on Sundays, and then beat you to a pulp afterwards . . . Finally, I didn't even know if I was still a man. I broke down in tears a hundred times, a thousand times . . .

'And then, one morning, they suddenly opened the door, rammed a rifle butt in to my back to send me off into the civilized world, and I passed out on the pavement like an idiot . . . I

136

didn't know how to live any more; I had nothing left . . .

'No! I did have one thing left!'

His wounded lip still bled, but he forgot to wipe it. Madame Michoux was hiding her face in her lace handkerchief, with its sickening scent. And Maigret smoked placidly, never taking his eyes off the doctor, who went on writing.

'One thing — the determination to put them through the same hell, those men who had brought the whole catastrophe down on me. Not to kill them — no! Dying is nothing. At Sing Sing, I tried it a dozen times, but I couldn't do it. I'd stop eating, and they'd force-feed me . . . No, no! I wanted to make them live in prison! I wanted it to be an American jail, but that's not possible . . .

'I dragged around Brooklyn, doing any kind of job, to pay my way home . . . I even bought passage for my dog . . .

'I'd had no news of Emma . . . I didn't set foot in Quimper; people might have recognized me, even if I am a wreck.

'Here, I heard that she was a waitress, and Michoux's mistress now and then . . . Other people too, maybe? A waitress, after all . . .

'It wouldn't be easy to send those three bastards to prison, but I was determined! That was the only thing I still wanted . . . I lived with my dog on an abandoned boat, and later in the old watchtower at Cabélou Point . . .

'I began to let Michoux see me around — just see me. See my hideous face, my brutish body! You understand? I wanted to scare him. I wanted to stir up such fear in him that he'd be driven to shoot at me. I might wind up dead, but he'd go to prison. He'd get it all; he'd be kicked and beaten, with clubs and gun butts! And the terrible people in there with you — so strong they can make you do anything they want . . . I prowled around Michoux's house. I put myself in his path. Three days. Four days. He finally recognized me. Then he went out less . . . But still, life here hadn't changed in all that time. They still had their daily aperitif together, the three of them; people tipped hats to them in the streets . . . And I was stealing food from stalls! . . . I wanted things to happen fast.'

A curt voice spoke: 'I beg your pardon, inspector. This hearing, without an examining magistrate present — I don't suppose it has any legal standing?'

It was Michoux — white as a sheet, his features drawn, nostrils pinched, lips drained of colour, but he was speaking with a curtness that was almost threatening.

A glance from Maigret sent another policeman to take up a position between the doctor and the vagrant. Just in time! Drawn by that voice, Léon Le Gleérec rose slowly, his fists clenched and as heavy as clubs.

'Down! Sit down, Léon!'

And the creature obeyed, breathing hoarsely as the inspector shook out his pipe and said, 'Now it's my turn to talk.'

11

Fear

His quiet voice and his rapid, even delivery were a sharp contrast to the impassioned speech of the sailor, who watched him suspiciously.

'First, a word about Emma, gentlemen: she learns that her fiancé has been arrested; she hears nothing more from him . . . One day, for some trivial reason, she loses her job and becomes a waitress at the Admiral Hotel. She's a poor girl, with no family. Men flirt with her, the way rich customers do with servant girls. Two years, three years go by. She has no idea Michoux had a hand in Léon's fate. One night she goes to his room. Time goes by, life rolls on. Michoux has other mistresses. From time to time, he decides to sleep at the hotel. Or sometimes, when his mother is away, he has Emma come to his house . . . Dreary love-making, with no love to it. And Emma's life is dreary. She's no heroine. She has a shell-covered box, where she keeps a letter, a snapshot, but that's just an old dream that fades a little more each day . . .

'She doesn't know that Léon has come back.

'She doesn't recognize the yellow dog that prowls around her — it was four months old when the boat left.

'One night, Michoux dictates a letter to her, without saying who it's for. It's about an appointment with someone in an empty house at eleven o'clock at night.

'She writes it down, signing it 'E' — for Ernest, she thinks. A waitress! You understand? . . . Léon Le Glérec was right: Michoux is frightened; he's afraid for his life . . . He wants to do away with the enemy who's haunting him.

'But he's a coward. He couldn't help telling me that himself. He sends his victim the letter by tying it around the dog's neck. He figures he'll hide behind the door in the empty house the next night.

'Will Léon be suspicious? Well, there's a chance the sailor might want to meet with his old fiancée again, no matter what's happened. When he knocks at the door, Michoux will just shoot through the letterbox and slip away through the back alley.

'But Léon does suspect something. Maybe he was lurking around the square, watching. Maybe he was even thinking of going to the appointment. By chance, Monsieur Mostaguen comes out of the café just then, with a few drinks in him, and stops in that doorway to light his cigar. He's a little unsteady; he stumbles against the door. That's the signal, and a bullet hits him right in the belly.

'That's the first incident . . . Michoux bungled his attempt. He goes home. Goyard and Le Pommeret are terrified. They know what's going on and they have the same interest in getting rid of the man — he's a threat to all three of them.

'Emma understands the trick she was made to play. She may have caught sight of Léon . . . or perhaps she put two and two together and finally identified the yellow dog.

'The next day, I arrive on the scene. I see the three men, I sense their terror. *They're expecting some trouble!* And I want to find out where they think it will come from. I want to be sure I'm not wrong.

'So I'm the one who put the poison in the aperitif bottle, in my clumsy way . . . I'm ready to step in if someone should start to drink. But there's no need! Michoux is on guard. Michoux is suspicious of everything — of the people going by, of what he drinks . . . By now he doesn't even dare leave the hotel.'

Emma was frozen, the very picture of stupefaction. Michoux had lifted his head for a moment, to look squarely at Maigret. Now he was writing feverishly again.

'That was the second incident, *Monsieur le Maire.* And our trio lives on, still in fear . . . Goyard is the most excitable of the three, and probably also the least bad. This business of the poisoning throws him into a panic. He's convinced something will happen to him one day or another. He sees I'm on the trail — and he decides to run off. Without a trace — run off in such a way that no one will be able to accuse him of running away. He'll fake an attack, let people think he's been killed and that his body was thrown into the harbour.

'But before that, something leads him to take a look around Michoux's house, maybe out of

141

curiosity, maybe to look for Léon and offer to make peace. He finds signs that the big man has been there. He knows it won't take me long to discover the same signs myself.

'Remember, he's a newspaperman! He knows very well how easy it is to stir up a mob. He knows he won't be safe anywhere as long as Léon is alive. So he thinks up a really brilliant move: he writes an article, in a disguised hand, and sends it to the *Brest Beacon*.

'The piece talks about the yellow dog, the drifter. Every sentence is calculated to spread terror in Concarneau. In those circumstances, if people spot the man with the big feet, there's a good chance he'll get a shot of lead in his chest.

'And that's nearly what happened! They started by shooting the dog; they would just as easily have shot the man. A panicky crowd is capable of anything.

'On Sunday, terror *does* take over the town. Michoux sticks to the hotel, sick with fright. But he's still determined to defend himself to the end — *by any means*.

'I leave him alone with Le Pommeret. I don't know what goes on between the two of them then. Goyard's gone. Le Pommeret, who belongs to a respectable local family, is probably tempted to turn to the police, to tell the whole story rather than go on living through this nightmare . . . After all, what's the risk for him? A fine, a little stint in prison. If that! The major crime, the only one he had any part in, had been committed abroad, in America.

'And Michoux, who sees him weakening, who

142

has the Mostaguen attack on his conscience, wants to save his own skin at any cost. He doesn't hesitate to poison him . . .

'Emma is there in the café. Maybe they'll suspect her instead . . .

'I'd like to talk to you a little more about fear, because that's what underlies this whole business. Michoux is afraid. Michoux is more obsessed with conquering his fear than with conquering his enemy.

'He knows Léon Le Glérec. He knows that the man won't be stopped without a struggle. He's counting on a bullet fired by the police or by some terrified townsman to take care of that problem.

'He stays put . . . I bring the wounded dog, barely alive, into the hotel. I want to see if the vagrant will come to get him, and he does. We've never seen the dog since, and that probably means he's dead.'

There was a small catch in Léon's throat. 'Yes.'

'Did you bury him?'

'On Cabélou. There's a little cross, made of two fir branches.'

'The police find Léon Le Glérec. He breaks away, because his one goal is to incite Michoux to attack him. He's said it: *he wants to see him in prison* . . . My job is to prevent any further harm, and that's why I arrest Michoux, even though I tell him that my purpose is to protect him. It's not a lie. But, by the same move, I keep Michoux from committing other crimes. He's reached the point of being capable of anything. He feels threatened from all sides.

'Nonetheless, he's still capable of doing his little act, talking to me about his poor health, blaming his panic on some mystical idea about a fortune-teller years back — a story he invented out of whole cloth.

'What he needs desperately is for the public to decide to slaughter his enemy.

'He knows that he could quite logically be suspected of everything that's happened up till then. Alone in his cell, he racks his brain. Isn't there some way of turning those suspicions around once and for all? For instance, if some new crime were to occur while he's under lock and key, that would provide him with the most wonderful alibi for everything, by implication.

'His mother comes to see him. She knows the whole story. She's got to stay clear of suspicion, of investigation. But she's got to save him! . . .

'She dines at the mayor's. She gets herself driven home after dinner and leaves her light burning for the next few hours. Meanwhile, she returns to town on foot. Is everyone asleep? Everyone except those in the Admiral café. All she has to do is wait, at some street corner, for someone to leave the café. Then aim at his leg, to be sure he doesn't chase her.

'That crime, that completely gratuitous crime, would be the worst of the charges against Michoux, if we didn't already have others. The next morning, when I get here, he's feverish. He doesn't know that Goyard is under arrest in Paris. Most important, he doesn't know that at the very moment the shot hit the customs guard, I had the vagrant under my very eyes.

144

'For, with the police after him, Léon had stayed right in the same neighbourhood where they'd lost him. He was anxious to finish his business, so he didn't want to get too far from Michoux.

'He goes to sleep in a room in the vacant building. From her window, Emma sees him. And she goes over to join him. She swears that she's not guilty, that she never meant to help Michoux. She throws herself down, clings to his knees . . .

'This is the first time he's seen her face to face, heard the sound of her voice again . . . She's been with another man, a few others.

'But there isn't much he hasn't been through, himself. His heart melts. He seizes her in a brutal grip, as if to crush her, but then, instead, his lips crush hers.

'He is no longer all alone, the man with nothing to live for but a single goal, a single idea. Through her tears, she speaks to him — about a chance for happiness, a life they might begin again . . .

'And they leave together, without a sou, into the night. They'll go anywhere; it doesn't matter! . . . They leave Michoux to his terrors.

'They'll try to be happy somewhere . . . '

Maigret fills his pipe, slowly, looking at each person in the room, one after the other.

'You'll excuse me, *Monsieur le Maire*, for not letting you know what I was up to. But when I arrived here, I felt sure the drama had just begun . . . To figure out its pattern, I had to let it develop, heading off further damage as best I

145

could . . . Le Pommeret is dead, murdered by his accomplice. But from what I know of him, I'm convinced he would have killed himself the moment he was arrested. A customs guard was shot in the leg; in a week, it won't even show. On the other hand, I can now sign a new arrest warrant for Ernest Michoux, for attempted murder and assault on the person of Monsieur Mostaguen, and for the wilful poisoning of his friend Le Pommeret. Here's another warrant, against Madame Michoux, for last night's assault . . . As to Jean Goyard, called Servières, I don't believe he can be cited for anything more than obstruction of justice with that hoax he set up.'

That was the only comic moment. The plump journalist heaved a sigh, an elated sigh. Then he had the nerve to babble: 'In that case, I presume I can be released on bail? I'm prepared to put up 50,000 francs.'

'The public prosecutor will determine that, Monsieur Goyard.'

Madame Michoux had collapsed in her chair, but her son was more resilient.

'You have anything to add?' Maigret asked him.

'I will answer only in the presence of my lawyer. Meanwhile, I formally protest the legality of this proceeding.'

And he stretched out his neck, a thin chicken neck with a prominent, sallow Adam's apple. His nose looked more crooked than ever. He was gripping his notepad.

'And those two?' murmured the mayor as he rose.

'I have absolutely no charge against them. Léon Le Glérec has stated that his goal was to provoke Michoux to shoot him. To that end, he did nothing but put himself in the man's path. There's no law against — '

'Except vagrancy,' put in the police lieutenant.

But Maigret shrugged in a way that made the man blush at his own suggestion.

★ ★ ★

Lunchtime was long past, but there was still a crowd outside. So the mayor agreed to lend his car, which had curtains that could be sealed tight shut.

Emma climbed in first, then Léon Le Glérec and, last, Maigret, who sat on the rear seat with the young woman, leaving the sailor to arrange himself awkwardly on the jump seat.

They cut quickly through the crowd. A few minutes later, they were on the road to Quimperlé. Uncomfortable and averting his gaze, Léon asked Maigret, 'Why did you say that?'

'What?'

'That you're the one who put the poison in the bottle?'

Emma was very pale. She didn't dare lean back against the cushions; it was doubtless the first time in her life that she had ridden in a limousine.

'It just came to me!' muttered Maigret, clamping his pipe stem in his teeth.

Then the girl cried out in distress:

'I swear to you, inspector, I didn't know what I

147

was doing any more! Michoux made me write that letter. I'd finally recognized the dog. And on Sunday morning I saw Léon lurking around . . . Then I understood. I tried to talk to him, but he walked off without looking at me, and he spat on the ground . . . I wanted to get revenge for his sake . . . I wanted . . . oh, I don't even know! I was nearly crazy. I knew they were trying to kill him . . . I still loved him . . . I spent the whole day turning over ideas in my head. At noon, before lunch, I ran over to Michoux's house to get the poison. I didn't know which one to pick . . . He showed them to me once, and said there was enough there to kill everyone in Concarneau . . .

'But I swear I would never have let you drink . . . At least, I don't think so.'

She was sobbing. Léon awkwardly patted her knee to calm her.

'I can never thank you, inspector,' she said through her sobs. 'What you've done is . . . is . . . I can't think of the word . . . It's so wonderful!'

Maigret looked at each of them, at him with his split lip, his cropped hair and his face of a beast trying to become human; at her with her poor little face faded white from living in that aquarium, the Admiral café.

'What are you going to do?'

'We don't know yet . . . Leave this place. Maybe head for Le Havre . . . I managed to earn a living on the New York docks . . . '

'Did anyone give you your twelve francs back?'

Léon flushed but did not answer.

148

'What's the train fare to Le Havre?'

'No! Don't do that, inspector. Because then . . . we couldn't . . . You see what I mean?'

They were passing a small railway station. Maigret tapped on the glass separating them from the driver. Drawing two hundred-franc notes from his pocket, he said: 'Take this. I'll put it on my expense account.'

He practically pushed them out of the car and closed the door while they were still looking for words to thank him.

'Back to Concarneau. Fast!'

Alone in the car, he shrugged his shoulders three times, like a man with a strong urge to make fun of himself.

★   ★   ★

The trial lasted a year. During that whole year, as often as five times a week, Dr Michoux went to see the examining magistrate, carrying a morocco briefcase crammed with documents.

At each court session he argued over something else. Every item in the dossier set off new controversies, investigations and counter-investigations.

Michoux grew steadily thinner, yellower, sicklier, but he never gave up.

'I'm sure you'll allow a man with only three months to live . . . '

That was his favourite expression. He fought every inch of the way, with underhanded manoeuvres, unpredictable responses. And he had found a lawyer even nastier to back him up.

Sentenced to twenty years' hard labour by the

149

Finistère Criminal Court, he spent six months trying to appeal his case to the higher court.

But a month ago, a photograph printed in all the newspapers showed him, still skinny and yellow, with his crooked nose, a bag on his back and a forage cap on his head, embarking from the Ile de Ré on the *Martinière*, which was carrying 180 convicts to Devil's Island.

Madame Michoux served her three-month sentence in prison and is in Paris pulling strings in political circles. She hopes to get her son's case reheard.

Léon Le Glérec fishes for herring in the North Sea, aboard the *Francette*, and his wife is expecting a baby.

Night at the Crossroads

Translated by LINDA COVERDALE

1

The Black Monocle

Detective Chief Inspector Maigret was sitting with his elbows on the desk, and when he pushed his chair back with a tired sigh, the interrogation of Carl Andersen had been going on for exactly seventeen hours.

Through the bare windows he had observed at first the throng of salesgirls and office workers storming the little restaurants of Place Saint-Michel at noon, then the afternoon lull, the mad six o'clock rush to the Métro and train stations, the relaxed pace of the aperitif hour . . .

The Seine was now shrouded in mist. One last tug had gone past with red and green lights, towing three barges. Last bus. Last Métro. At the cinema they'd taken in the film-poster sandwich boards and were closing the metal gates.

And the stove in Maigret's office seemed to growl all the louder. On the table, empty beer bottles and the remains of some sandwiches.

A fire must have broken out somewhere: they heard the racket of fire engines speeding by. And there was a raid, too. The Black Maria emerged from the Préfecture at around two o'clock, returning later to drop off its catch at the central lock-up.

The interrogation was still going on. Every

hour — or every two hours, depending on how tired he was — Maigret would push a button. Sergeant Lucas would awaken from his nap in a nearby office and arrive to take over, glancing briefly at his boss's notes. Maigret would then go and stretch out on a cot to recharge his batteries for a fresh attack.

The Préfecture was deserted. A few comings and goings at the Vice Squad. Towards four in the morning, an inspector hauled in a drug pusher and immediately began grilling him.

The Seine wreathed itself in a pale fog that turned white with the breaking day, lighting up the empty quays. Footsteps pattered in the corridors. Telephones rang. Voices called. Doors slammed. Charwomen's brooms swished by.

And Maigret, setting his overheated pipe on the table, rose and looked the prisoner up and down with an ill humour not unmixed with admiration. Seventeen hours of relentless questioning! Before tackling him, they had taken away his shoelaces, detachable collar, tie and everything in his pockets. For the first four hours they had left him standing in the centre of the office and bombarded him with questions.

'Thirsty?'

Maigret was on his fourth beer, and the prisoner had managed a faint smile. He had drunk avidly.

'Hungry?'

They'd asked him to sit down — and stand up again. He'd gone seven hours without anything to eat and then they had harassed him while he devoured a sandwich.

154

The two of them took turns questioning him. Between sessions, they could each doze, stretch, escape the grip of this monotonous interrogation.

Yet they were the ones giving up! Maigret shrugged, rummaged in a drawer for a cold pipe and wiped his damp brow.

Perhaps what impressed him the most was not the man's physical and psychological resistance, but his disturbing elegance, the air of distinction he'd maintained throughout the interrogation.

A gentleman who has been searched, stripped of his tie and obliged to spend an hour completely naked with a hundred malefactors in the Criminal Records Office, where he is photographed, weighed, measured, jostled and cruelly mocked by other detainees, will rarely retain the self-confidence that informs his personality in private life.

And when he has endured a few hours of questioning, it's a miracle if there's anything left to distinguish him from any old tramp.

Carl Andersen had not changed. Despite his wrinkled suit, he still possessed an elegance the Police Judiciaire rarely have occasion to appreciate, an aristocratic grace with that hint of reserve and discretion, that touch of arrogance so characteristic of diplomatic circles.

He was taller than Maigret, broad-shouldered but slender, lithe and slim-hipped. His long face was pale, his lips rather colourless.

He wore a black monocle in his left eye.

Ordered to remove the monocle, he had obeyed with the faintest of smiles, uncovering a glass eye with a disconcerting stare.

'An accident?'

'A flying accident, yes.'

'So you were in the war?'

'I'm Danish. I did not have to fight. But I had a private aeroplane, back home.'

The artificial eye was so disturbing in this young face with pleasant features that Maigret had muttered, 'You can put your monocle back.'

Andersen had not made a single complaint, either about them leaving him standing or their forgetting for so long to give him anything to eat or drink. He could see the street traffic out of the window, the trams and buses crossing the bridge, the reddish sunlight as evening had fallen and now the bustle of a bright April morning.

And he held himself as straight as ever, as if it were only natural, and the sole sign of fatigue was the thin dark shadow underlining his right eye.

'You stand by everything you've said?' Maigret asked.

'I do.'

'You realize how improbable this all sounds?'

'Yes, but I cannot lie.'

'You're expecting to be released, for lack of conclusive evidence?'

'I'm not expecting anything.'

A trace of an accent, more noticeable now that he was tired.

'Do you wish me to read you the official record of your interrogation before I have you sign it?'

He gestured vaguely, like a gentleman

156

declining a cup of tea.

'I will summarize the main points. You arrived in France three years ago, accompanied by your sister, Else. You spent a month in Paris. Then you rented a country house on the main road from Paris to Étampes, three kilometres from Arpajon, at the place called Three Widows Crossroads.'

Carl Andersen nodded slightly in agreement.

'For the last three years, you have lived there in isolation so complete that the local people have seen your sister only a few times. No contact with your neighbours. You bought an old 5CV that you use to do your own shopping at the market in Arpajon. Every month, in this same car, you come to Paris.'

'To deliver my work to the firm of Dumas and Son, Rue du Quatre-Septembre, that's correct.'

'You work designing patterns for upholstery fabrics. You are paid five hundred francs for each pattern. You produce on average four patterns a month, earning two thousand francs . . . '

Another nod.

'You have no male friends. Your sister has no female friends. On Saturday evening, you both went to bed as usual at around ten o'clock. And, as usual, you also locked your sister in her bedroom, which is near yours. You claim this is because she is nervous and easily frightened . . . We'll let that pass for the moment! At seven o'clock on Sunday morning, Monsieur Émile Michonnet, an insurance agent who lives in a house almost a hundred metres from your place, enters his garage to find that his car, a new six-cylinder model of a well-known make, has

157

vanished and been replaced by your rattle-trap . . . '

Showing no reaction, Andersen reached automatically for the empty pocket in which he must ordinarily have kept his cigarettes.

'Monsieur Michonnet, who has talked of nothing but his new car ever since he bought it, believes he is the victim of an unpleasant prank. He goes to your house, finds the gate closed and rings the bell in vain. Half an hour later he describes his predicament to the local police, who go to your house, where they find neither you nor your sister. They do, however, discover Monsieur Michonnet's car in your garage and in the front seat, draped over the steering wheel, a dead man, shot point-blank in the chest. His identity papers have not been stolen. His name is Isaac Goldberg, a diamond merchant from Antwerp.'

Still talking, Maigret put more fuel in the stove.

'The police promptly question the employees of the station at Arpajon, who saw you and your sister take the first train for Paris . . . You are both picked up when you arrive at Gare d'Orsay . . . You deny everything . . . '

'I deny having killed anyone at all.'

'You also deny knowing Isaac Goldberg . . . '

'I saw him for the first time, dead, at the wheel of a car that does not belong to me, in my garage.'

'And instead of phoning the police, you made a run for it with your sister.'

'I was afraid . . . '

'You have nothing to add?'

'Nothing!'

'And you insist that you never heard anything that Saturday night?'

'I'm a heavy sleeper.'

It was the fiftieth time that he had given precisely the same answers and Maigret, exasperated, rang for Sergeant Lucas, who swiftly appeared.

'I'll be back in a moment!'

★ ★ ★

The discussion between Maigret and Coméliau, the examining magistrate to whom the matter had been referred, lasted about fifteen minutes. The magistrate had essentially given up in advance.

'You'll see, this will be one of those cases we get only once in ten years, luckily, and which are never completely solved! And it lands in my lap! Nothing about it makes any sense . . . Why this switching of cars? And why didn't Andersen use the one in his garage to flee instead of walking to Arpajon to take the train? What was that diamond merchant doing at Three Widows Crossroads? Believe me, Maigret — this is the beginning of a whole string of headaches, for you as well as me . . . Let him go if you want. Perhaps you're right to feel that if he can withstand seventeen hours of interrogation, we'll get nothing more out of him.'

The inspector's eyes were red-rimmed from lack of sleep.

'Have you seen the sister?'

159

'No. When they brought me Andersen, the young woman had already been taken back to her house by the local police, who wished to question her at the scene of the incident. She's still there. Under surveillance.'

They shook hands. Maigret returned to his office, where Lucas was idly watching the prisoner, who stood with his forehead pressed against the windowpane, waiting patiently.

'You're free to go!' announced Maigret from the doorway.

Calmly, Andersen gestured towards his bare neck and unlaced shoes.

'Your personal effects will be returned to you at the clerk's office. You remain, of course, at the disposition of the authorities. At the slightest attempt to flee, I'll have you sent to La Santé Prison.'

'My sister?'

'You will find her at home.'

The Dane must have felt some emotion after all as he left the room, for he removed his monocle to pass his hand over what had once been his left eye.

'Thank you, chief inspector.'

'You're welcome.'

'I give you my word of honour that I'm innocent . . . '

'Don't mention it!'

Andersen bowed, then waited for Lucas to take him along to the clerk's office.

After witnessing this scene with astonished indignation, a man in the waiting room rushed over to Maigret.

160

'What? So you're letting him go? That's not possible, chief inspector . . . '

It was Monsieur Michonnet, the insurance agent, the owner of the new six-cylinder car. He walked into Maigret's office as if he owned the place and set his hat down on a table.

'I am here, above all, about the matter of my car.'

A small fellow going grey, carefully but unprepossessingly dressed, constantly turning up the ends of his waxed moustache.

He spoke with pursed lips, weighing his words and trying to appear imposing.

He was the plaintiff! He was the one whom the forces of justice had to protect! Was he not in some way a hero? No one was going to intimidate him, oh no! The entire Préfecture was at his personal service.

'I had a long talk last night with Madame Michonnet, whose acquaintance you will soon make, I trust . . . She agrees with me . . . Mind you, her father was a teacher at the Lycée de Montpellier and her mother gave piano lessons . . . I mention this so that . . . In short . . . '

That was his favourite expression, which he pronounced in a manner both cutting and condescending.

'In short, a decision must be made with all possible speed. Like everyone, even the richest among us, including the Comte d'Avrainville, I bought my new car on the instalment plan. I must make eighteen payments. Mind you, I could have paid cash, but there is no point in tying up one's capital. The Comte d'Avrainville,

161

of whom I just spoke, purchased his Hispano-Suiza in the same fashion. In short . . . '

Breathing heavily, Maigret did not move.

'I cannot do without a car, which is absolutely necessary for me in the exercise of my profession. When you consider that my territory covers everywhere within a thirty-kilometre radius of Arpajon . . . Now, Madame Michonnet agrees with me on this: we wish to have nothing further to do with a vehicle in which a man has been killed. It is up to the authorities to take the necessary steps and to procure a new car for us, the same model as the other one, and I would like it to be of a burgundy colour, which would not affect the price . . . Mind you, my car was already broken in and running smoothly, and I shall be obliged to — '

'Is that all you have to tell me?'

'I beg your pardon!'

That was another expression he often used.

'I beg your pardon, chief inspector! It's understood that I am prepared to draw upon all my accumulated knowledge and experience of this locality to assist you, but regarding the urgent matter of this car . . . '

Maigret brushed his hand over his forehead.

'Well! I will come to see you soon at your house . . . '

'What about the car?'

'Yours will be returned to you when the investigation has been concluded.'

'But I just finished telling you that Madame Michonnet and I . . . '

'Then do give my regards to Madame

162

Michonnet! Good day, monsieur.'

It was over so quickly that the insurance man had no time to protest. He found himself back on the landing holding his hat, which had been shoved into his hands, and the office boy was calling to him.

'This way, please! First staircase on the left . . . Exit's straight ahead . . . '

As for Maigret, he locked his door and set water to boil on the stove for some good strong coffee.

His colleagues thought he was working, but he had to be woken up an hour later when a telegram arrived from Antwerp.

Isaac Goldberg, 45, diamond broker, rather well known in the trade. Medium-sized business. Good bank references. Travelled weekly by train or plane to Amsterdam, London and Paris to solicit orders.

Luxurious house Rue de Campine, Borgerhout. Married. Two children, 8 and 12.

Madame Goldberg informed, has taken Paris train.

At eleven in the morning the telephone rang: it was Lucas.

'Hello! I'm at Three Widows Crossroads. I'm calling you from the garage a little more than a hundred metres from the Andersens' house. The Danish fellow has gone home. The gate's locked again. Nothing much to report . . . '

'The sister?'

'Must be inside, but I haven't seen her.'

'Goldberg's body?'

'At the hospital morgue in Arpajon . . . '

★ ★ ★

Maigret went home to his apartment in Boulevard Richard-Lenoir.

'You look tired!' was all his wife said in welcome.

'Pack a bag with a suit and a spare pair of shoes.'

'Will you be away long?'

There was a ragout in the oven. The bedroom window was open and the bed unmade, to air out the sheets. Madame Maigret hadn't had time yet to comb out her hair, still set in lumpy little pin curls.

'Goodbye . . . '

He kissed her. As he left, she remarked, 'You're opening the door with your right hand . . . '

That was unlike him; he always opened it with his left hand. And Madame Maigret wasn't shy about being superstitious.

'What is it? A gang?'

'I've no idea.'

'Are you going far?'

'I don't know yet.'

'You'll be careful, won't you?'

But he was already going downstairs and hardly turned around at all to wave to her. Out on the boulevard, he hailed a taxi.

'Gare d'Orsay . . . Wait . . . How much to

drive to Arpajon? . . .Three hundred francs, with the return trip? . . . Let's go!'

He almost never did this. But he was exhausted. He could barely fight off the drowsiness stinging his eyelids.

And wasn't he — just perhaps — a little perplexed, even uneasy? Not so much because of that door he'd opened with his right hand, nor because of that bizarre business of Michonnet's stolen car turning up in Andersen's garage with a dead man at the wheel.

It was rather the Danish fellow's personality that was bothering him.

'Seventeen hours of grilling!'

Hardened criminals, crooks who'd traipsed through all the police stations in Europe hadn't stood up to that ordeal.

Maybe that was even why Maigret had let Andersen go.

That didn't prevent him from falling asleep in the back of the taxi after they'd gone through Bourg-la-Reine. The driver woke him up at Arpajon, in front of the old market with its thatched roof.

'What hotel do you want?'

'Take me to Three Widows Crossroads.'

It was uphill along the oil-slicked paving stones of the main road, lined on both sides by billboards advertising Vichy, Deauville, fancy hotels, brands of automotive fuel.

A crossroads. A garage with its five fuel pumps, painted red. To the left, the road to Avrainville, marked with a signpost.

All around, fields as far as the eye could see.

165

'This is it!' announced the driver.

There were only three houses. First, the garage owner's, a stuccoed affair hastily erected when business was booming. A big sports car with aluminium coachwork was filling up at the pump. Mechanics were working on a butcher's van.

Across the way, a small villa of millstone grit with a narrow garden, surrounded by a six-foot-high fence. A brass plate: *Émile Michonnet, Insurance.*

The last house was a good hundred metres away. The wall around the grounds hid all but the second storey, a slate roof and a few handsome trees. This building was at least a century old. It was a fine country residence of times gone by, with a cottage for the gardener, outbuildings, poultry houses, a stable and a flight of front steps flanked by bronze *torchères.*

A small concrete pond had dried up. A wisp of smoke rose straight into the air from a carved chimney cap.

That was all. Beyond the fields, a belfry . . . farmhouse roofs . . . a plough abandoned at the edge of some tilled land.

And along the smooth road cars streamed by in both directions, passing one another and honking their horns.

Maigret got out of the taxi with his suitcase and paid the driver, who filled up at the garage before heading back to Paris.

2

The Moving Curtains

Emerging from the roadside, where some trees had concealed him, Lucas walked over to Maigret, who set his suitcase down by his feet. Just as they were about to shake hands, they heard an increasingly loud whistling sound — and suddenly a racing car whipped past so close to them that the suitcase went flying three metres away.

There was nothing left to see. The turbo-charged car had swung around a hay cart and vanished over the horizon.

Maigret made a face.

'Do many of those go by?'

'That's the first one . . . And I could have sworn it was aiming at us!'

It was a grey afternoon. A curtain twitched in a window of the Michonnet villa.

'Is there any place to stay around here?'

'At Arpajon or Avrainville . . . Arpajon's three kilometres away; Avrainville is closer but has only a country inn . . . '

'Take my suitcase there and get us some rooms. Anything to report?'

'Not a thing . . . They're watching us from the villa . . . It's Madame Michonnet. I got a look at her a little while ago. A largish brunette who doesn't appear to be too pleasant.'

'Do you know why this place is called Three Widows Crossroads?'

'I asked: it's because of the Andersen house, which dates from the revolution. In the old days it was the only house here. In the end, it seems that fifty years ago three widows lived in it, a mother and two daughters. The mother was ninety years old, a helpless invalid. The elder daughter was sixty-seven, the other at least sixty. Three old fusspots, so stingy they bought nothing locally and lived off their kitchen garden and poultry yard . . . The shutters were never opened. Weeks would go by without a glimpse of them. The elder daughter broke her leg at some point, but people learned about it only after she was dead. Quite a strange story! When a long time had passed without anyone hearing the slightest noise from the Three Widows house, people got to talking . . . The mayor of Avrainville decided to come and see for himself — and he found all three of them dead. They'd been dead for at least ten days! There was a lot of newspaper coverage at the time, apparently. A local schoolteacher, fascinated by this mystery, even wrote a booklet in which he claims that the daughter with the broken leg hated her still-active sister so much that she poisoned her, and the mother wound up poisoned as well . . . The elder sister supposedly starved beside the two corpses because she couldn't get herself anything to eat!'

Maigret stared at what he could see of the house's top storey. Then he considered the

Michonnets' new villa, the even newer garage, the cars going by on the main road at eighty kilometres an hour.

'Go and get those rooms, then come back and join me.'

'What are you going to do?'

The inspector shrugged, then walked to the gate of the Three Widows house. It was a good-sized building, surrounded by three or four hectares of grounds graced by a few majestic trees.

A sloping lane ran alongside a lawn and up to the front steps, then on to a garage that had once been a stable, its roof still bearing a pulley.

Nothing stirred. Aside from a thread of smoke, there was no sign of life behind the faded curtains. In the gathering dusk, some farm horses in a distant field were plodding back home.

Maigret noticed a little man taking a walk along the road, his hands stuck deep into the pockets of his flannel trousers, a pipe between his teeth, a cap on his head. The man came right up to him the way neighbours do out in the countryside.

'You're the one in charge of the investigation?'

He was wearing slippers and had no collar on, but his jacket was of fine grey English cloth and he sported an enormous signet ring on one finger.

'I own the garage at the crossroads . . . I saw you from my place . . . '

Definitely a former boxer: he'd had his nose broken. His face looked as battered as an old copper pot. His drawling voice was husky, coarse, but very self-assured.

'What do you make of this business with the cars?'

The man laughed, revealing some gold teeth.

'If there weren't a stiff involved, I'd find the whole thing hilarious. You can't possibly understand — you don't know the guy across the way, Milord Michonnet, as we call him. A stand-offish fellow who wears collars *this* high and patent-leather shoes . . . Then there's Madame Michonnet! You haven't seen her yet? Huh! Those people complain about anything and everything, go running to the police because the cars make too much noise when they stop at my garage pumps . . . '

Maigret didn't encourage or discourage the man. He simply stared at him in a way that disconcerted most talkative people but had no effect on the garage owner.

A baker's van drove by and the man in slippers yelled, 'Hey there, Clément! . . . Your horn's been fixed! Just ask Jojo for it!'

Turning back to Maigret, he offered him a cigarette and carried on.

'Michonnet had been talking about getting a new car for months, was pestering all the car dealers, myself included! He wanted discounts, ran us ragged . . . The coachwork was too dark, too light; he wanted a burgundy colour — not *too* burgundy, but definitely *burgundy* . . . Well, he ended up buying the car from a colleague of mine in Arpajon. You've got to admit, it was a damn fine joke to have the car turn up a few

170

days later in the Three Widows garage! I'd have given anything to see our gentleman's face that morning when he found the old jalopy instead of the six-cylinder job! . . . Pity about the dead man, which spoils everything. Because a corpse is a corpse, after all, and such matters deserve our respect . . . Say! You'll drop by the garage, won't you, and have a drink? No watering holes at the crossroads, but we'll get some yet! If I can just find the right fellow to run a place, I'll back him for it . . . '

The man must have noticed that Maigret wasn't responding to his patter, because he held out his hand.

'See you later, then . . . '

He strolled off at the same pace, stopping to talk to a farmer passing by in a one-horse cart. Over at the Michonnet villa, there was still a face behind the curtains.

In the evening the surrounding countryside had a monotonous, stagnant air about it, and sounds carried a long distance: a horse neighing, a church bell pealing perhaps ten kilometres away . . .

The first car with its headlamps on went by, but they could hardly be seen in the twilight.

Maigret reached for the bell-pull hanging to the right of the gate. Rich, mellow tones rang through the garden, followed by a long silence. At the top of the steps, the front door did not open, but from behind the house came the crunch of gravel. A tall form appeared; a pale face, a black monocle.

Carl Andersen showed no emotion as he

171

approached and he bowed his head slightly when he opened the gate.

'I knew you would come . . . I suppose you want to see the garage. The prosecutor's office has sealed the premises, but you must have the necessary authority . . . '

He was wearing the same clothes as at Quai des Orfèvres, an elegantly cut suit that was beginning to show signs of wear.

'Is your sister here?'

It was already too dark to notice any change in his expression, but Andersen did feel the need to resettle the monocle in his eye-socket.

'Yes . . . '

'I would like to see her.'

A brief hesitation. Andersen nodded again.

'Please follow me.'

They walked around to the back of the house, where all the ground-floor rooms had tall French windows that opened directly on to a terrace overlooking a fairly large lawn.

There were no lights in any of the upstairs bedrooms. At the far end of the grounds, veils of mist twined around the tree trunks.

'Allow me to show you the way . . . '

Andersen led Maigret from the terrace into a large drawing room all draped in shadow. The cool yet heavy evening air followed them in, bringing with it the smell of wet grass and leaves. A single log shot a few sparks up the chimney.

'I will call my sister.'

Andersen had not lighted any lamps or even appeared to notice that night was falling. Left alone, Maigret walked slowly up and down the room, stopping before an easel on which sat a sketch in gouache. It was a modern design for a fabric pattern, with bold colours and a strange motif.

But not as strange as the way the room conjured up for Maigret the memory of the three widows of long ago . . .

Some of the furniture must have been theirs. There were Empire armchairs with flaking paint and threadbare silk, and rep curtains that had hung there for fifty years.

Some pine bookshelves had been built along one wall, however, and were piled with paper-bound books in French, German, English and no doubt Danish as well.

And the white, yellow or multicoloured covers were in stark contrast to an old-fashioned hassock, some chipped vases and a carpet worn almost through in the centre.

The twilight was darkening. A cow lowed in the distance. From time to time, a faint humming pierced the silence, intensifying until a car whizzed by on the road and the engine's rumbling at length died away.

In the house, nothing! Perhaps just a few creaks or scratching sounds. Perhaps just some tiny undecipherable noises suggesting the possibility of life.

Carl Andersen came in first. His white hands betrayed a certain nervous anxiety. He stood still and mute for a moment by the door.

A faint movement on the stairs.

'My sister Else,' he announced at last.

She stepped forwards, her silhouette slightly

blurred in the dim light. She stepped forwards like a film star, or rather, like the perfect woman in an adolescent's dream. Was her dress of black velvet? It was darker than anything else, in any case, and made its deep, magnificent mark on the dusk. And what little light still drifted in the air seemed to settle on her fine blonde hair and matte complexion.

'I hear you wish to speak to me, chief inspector. But first, please do sit down.'

Her accent was stronger than Carl's and her voice melodious, dropping gently at the ends of words.

And her brother stood by her as a slave stands near the sovereign he is sworn to protect.

She advanced a few steps and only when she was quite close did Maigret realize that she was as tall as Carl. Her slim hips emphasized her willowy silhouette. She turned to her brother.

'A cigarette!'

Nervously, clumsily, he hurried to offer one. She picked up a lighter and the flickering red of the flame fought, for an instant, with the dark blue of her eyes.

Afterwards the darkness weighed more heavily, so heavily that the inspector, feeling uneasy, looked around for a light switch and, finding none, murmured, 'May I ask you to light a lamp?'

He had to call on all his self-possession, for this scene was too theatrical for him. Theatrical? Disorienting, rather, like the perfume that had invaded the room with Else's entrance.

Above all, a scene too estranged from normal

174

life. Perhaps just too strange altogether! That accent . . . Carl's perfect manners and his black monocle . . . That mixture of sumptuous luxury and distressing old relics . . . Even Else's dress, which wasn't the sort of dress one sees in the street, at the theatre, or in society . . .

Why was that? It had to be the way she wore it. Because the style — the cut — was simple. The dress clung to her figure, covering even her neck, revealing only her face and hands.

Andersen was leaning over a table, removing the glass chimney from an oil lamp dating back to the three old ladies, with a tall porcelain base decorated with faux bronze. It cast a circle of light two metres wide in its corner of the drawing room. The lampshade was orange.

'Excuse me . . . I hadn't noticed that all the chairs have things piled on them.'

Andersen removed books from the seat of an Empire armchair and set them down in a heap on the carpet. Else was smoking, standing perfectly straight, a statue sheathed in velvet.

'Your brother, mademoiselle, has told me that he heard nothing unusual last Saturday night. He seems to be a very heavy sleeper.'

'Very,' she repeated, exhaling a wisp of smoke.

'You heard nothing either?'

'Nothing particularly unusual, no.'

She spoke slowly, like a foreigner who must translate her thoughts from her native language.

'You know that we are on a main road. The traffic hardly slows down at all at night. Every evening from eight o'clock on, market lorries driving to Les Halles in Paris go past and they

175

make a lot of noise. On Saturdays we also have tourists heading for Sologne and the Loire. Our sleep is interrupted by the sounds of engines and brakes, loud voices . . . If this house were not so cheap . . . '

'Had you ever heard of Isaac Goldberg?'

'Never.'

Outside, it was not yet completely dark. The lawn was intensely green and each blade of grass stood out so distinctly that it seemed possible to count them all.

Although the grounds had not been kept up, they were still as picturesque as a stage set at the opera. Every clump of bushes, every tree, even every branch was in just the right place. And the background of fields with a farmhouse roof put the finishing touch to this harmonious vision of the French heartland.

On the other hand, in the drawing room with its old furniture were books with foreign titles, words that Maigret didn't understand. And these two foreigners, the brother and sister . . . Especially the sister, who struck a discordant note . . .

A note that was too voluptuous, too lascivious? Yet she herself was not provocative. Her gestures were unaffected, and she held herself in a natural way.

But this simplicity did not suit such a décor. The inspector would have felt more at home with the three old ladies and their monstrous passions!

'Will you allow me to have a look around the house?'

Neither Carl nor Else seemed to mind. She sat

down in an armchair, while he picked up the lamp.

'If you'll just follow me . . . '

'I suppose you use the drawing room, for the most part?'

'Yes, that's where I work and where my sister spends most of her day.'

'You have no servant?'

'You already know how much I earn. It isn't enough for me to hire any help.'

'Who prepares the meals?'

'I do.'

He said this easily, without any embarrassment or shame, and as the two men entered a corridor, Andersen pushed open a door and held the lamp just inside the kitchen, murmuring, 'Please excuse the clutter.'

The place was worse than cluttered. It was sordid. A spirit stove encrusted with boiled milk, sauces, grease, on a table covered with a scrap of oilcloth. Tag ends of bread. The remains of an escalope in a frying pan sitting right on the table and dirty dishes in the sink.

Out in the corridor again, Maigret glanced back at the drawing room, where the only light was now the glow from Else's cigarette.

'We don't use the dining room or the morning room at the front of the house. Would you like to see them?'

The lamp shone on some piled-up furniture and a rather nice parquet floor, on which potatoes lay spread out. The shutters were closed.

'Our bedrooms are up there . . . '

177

The staircase was wide; one step creaked. The smell of perfume grew stronger as they went upstairs.

'Here is my room.'

A simple box mattress set on the floor, as a divan. A rudimentary dressing table. A large Louis XV wardrobe. An ashtray overflowing with cigarette butts.

'You smoke a lot?'

'In the morning, in bed . . . Perhaps thirty cigarettes, while I read.'

In front of the door opposite his, he said quickly, 'My sister's bedroom.'

But he did not open the door, and when Maigret did, Anderson scowled.

He was still holding the lamp and did not bring it into the room. The perfume was now so cloying that the inspector almost gagged.

The entire house lacked style, order, luxury. A campsite furnished with old odds and ends.

But here in the dim light the inspector had the feeling of a warm, cosy oasis. The floor was completely covered with animal skins, including a splendid tiger pelt serving as a bedside rug.

The bed itself was of ebony, covered with black velvet, on which lay some rumpled silk underwear.

Andersen was edging down the hall with the lamp, and Maigret followed him.

'The three other bedrooms are empty.'

'Which means that your sister's is the only one overlooking the road . . . '

Without answering, Carl pointed out a narrow staircase.

178

'The service staircase. We don't use it. If you'd care to see the garage . . . '

They went downstairs single file in the dancing light of the oil lamp.

In the drawing room, the red dot of a cigarette remained the only illumination. As Andersen advanced, the lamplight invaded the room, revealing Else lounging in an armchair, gazing with indifference at the two men.

'You haven't offered the chief inspector any tea, Carl!'

'Thank you, but I never drink tea.'

'Well, I want some! Would you like a whisky? Or perhaps . . . Carl! Please . . . '

Carl, self-conscious and a little on edge, set down the lamp and lit a small spirit stove on which sat a silver teapot.

'What may I offer you, inspector?'

Maigret could not put his finger on what was bothering him. The atmosphere was intimate and yet haphazard. Up on the easel, large flowers with crimson petals were in full bloom.

'So,' he said, 'first someone stole Monsieur Michonnet's car. Goldberg was murdered in that car, which was then placed in your garage. And your car was driven to the insurance agent's garage.'

'Unbelievable, isn't it!'

Else spoke in a soft, lilting voice as she lit another cigarette.

'My brother insisted that because the dead man was found at our place, we would be accused . . . He tried to run away . . . As for me, I didn't want to. I was sure that people would

179

understand that if we had really killed anyone, it would not have been in our interest to — '

She broke off, looking for Carl, who was rummaging around in a corner.

'Well, aren't you going to offer the inspector anything?'

'Sorry . . . I . . . We don't seem to have any more . . . '

'It's always the same with you! You never think of anything . . . You must excuse us, monsieur . . . ?'

'Maigret.'

' . . . Monsieur Maigret. We drink very little alcohol and — '

There was the sound of footsteps outside, where Maigret now saw that Sergeant Lucas was looking for him.

3

Night at the Crossroads

'What is it, Lucas?'

Maigret was standing at the French windows, with the uneasy atmosphere of the drawing room at his back and, before him, the face of Lucas in the cool shadows of the grounds.

'Nothing, chief . . . I wanted to know where you were . . . '

And a slightly sheepish Lucas tried to see inside the house over the inspector's shoulder.

'You booked me a room?'

'Yes. And there's a telegram for you. Madame Goldberg is arriving tonight by car.'

Maigret turned around: Andersen was waiting with bowed head; Else was smoking and wiggling one foot impatiently.

'I will probably return to question you again tomorrow,' he told them. 'My respects, mademoiselle.'

Else nodded to him with gracious condescension. Carl offered to walk the policemen back to the gate.

'You're not going to look at the garage?'

'Tomorrow . . . '

'Listen, chief inspector . . . This may seem somewhat strange to you . . . I'd like you to make use of me if I can be helpful in any way. I

181

know that I am not only a foreigner, but your prime suspect as well. Yet another reason for me to do my utmost to find the guilty man. Please don't hold my awkwardness against me.'

Maigret looked him right in the eye. He saw the sadness in that eye, which slowly turned away. Carl Andersen relocked the gate and went back to the house.

★ ★ ★

'What came over you, Lucas?'

'Something was bothering me . . . I got back from Avrainville a while ago. I don't know why, but this crossroads suddenly gave me such a bad feeling . . . '

The two men were walking in the dark along one side of the road. There weren't many cars.

'I've tried to reconstruct the crime in my mind,' continued Lucas, 'and the more you think about it, the more bewildering it becomes.'

They were now abreast of the Michonnet villa, which formed one point of a triangle, the other two of which were the garage and the Three Widows house, all more or less equidistant from one another. Connecting them all, the smooth, shining ribbon of the road, running like a river between two rows of tall trees.

No light could be seen over at the Three Widows house. Two windows were illuminated at the insurance agent's villa, but dark curtains allowed only a thin streak of light to escape, an uneven line, revealing that someone was peeking through the curtains to look outside.

182

Over by the garage: the milk-white globes atop the pumps, plus a rectangle of harsh light streaming from a workshop resounding with hammer blows.

The two policemen had stopped, and Lucas, who was one of Maigret's oldest colleagues, explained his reasoning.

'First thing: Goldberg had to have come here. You saw the corpse in the morgue at Étampes? You didn't? A man of forty-five, definitely Jewish-looking. A short, stocky guy with a tough jaw, a stubborn brow, curly hair like sheep's wool . . . Showy suit . . . Nice linen, and mono-grammed. Someone used to living well, giving orders, spending freely . . . No mud, no dust on his patent-leather shoes, so even if he came to Arpajon by train, he did not cover the three kilometres to get here on foot! My theory is that he arrived from Paris, or maybe Antwerp, by car.

'The doctor says that his dinner had been completely digested at the time of death, which was instantaneous. And yet a large quantity of champagne and toasted almonds was found in his stomach. No hotel proprietor in Arpajon sold any champagne on Saturday night or early Sunday morning, and I defy you to find a single toasted almond anywhere in that town.'

With a screech of rattling iron, a lorry went by at fifty kilometres an hour.

'Consider the Michonnets' garage, sir. The insurance agent has had a car for only one year. His first one was an old wreck that he simply kept in the padlocked wooden shed that opens on to the road. He hasn't had time to have another garage built, so the new car was stolen

183

from the shed. Someone had to drive it to the Three Widows house, open the gate, then the garage, take out Andersen's old heap and leave Michonnet's car in its place . . . And to top it off, stick Goldberg behind the wheel and shoot him dead point-blank. Nobody saw or heard a thing! . . . *Nobody has an alibi!* . . . I don't know if you've got the same feeling I have about this, but when I was coming back from Avrainville a little while ago, while it was growing dark, I was completely at sea . . . I get the sense that there's something wrong with this case, something weird, almost malignant . . .

'I went up to the gate of the Three Widows house . . . I knew you were in there. The façade was dark, but I could make out a halo of yellow light in the garden.

'It's idiotic, I know! But I was afraid! Afraid for you, understand? . . . Don't turn around too quickly . . . It's Madame Michonnet, lurking behind her curtains . . .

'I must be wrong about this, but I'd swear that half the drivers going by are giving us odd looks . . . '

Maigret glanced from one point to another of the triangle. The fields had vanished, flooded in darkness. To the right of the main road, across from the garage, the road to Avrainville branched off, not planted with trees like the highway but lined on one side by a string of telegraph poles.

Eight hundred metres away, a few lights: the outlying houses of the village.

'Champagne and toasted almonds!' grumbled the inspector.

184

He began walking slowly, stopping in front of the garage as if out for a stroll. In the glare of an arc lamp, a mechanic in overalls was changing a tyre on a car.

It was more of a repair shop than a garage. About a dozen cars were there, all old models, and one of them, stripped of its wheels and engine, was just a carcass hanging in the chains of a pulley.

'Let's go and have dinner! When is Madame Goldberg due to arrive?'

'I don't know. Sometime this evening.'

★ ★ ★

The inn at Avrainville was empty. A zinc counter, a few bottles, a big stove, a small billiard table with rock-hard cushions and torn felt, a dog and cat lying side by side . . .

The proprietor was the waiter; his wife could be seen in the kitchen, cooking escalopes.

'What's the name of the garage owner at the crossroads?' asked Maigret, swallowing a sardine served as an appetizer.

'Monsieur Oscar,' replied the inn-keeper.

'How long has he been in this area?'

'Maybe eight years . . . Maybe ten . . . Me, I've a horse and cart, so . . . '

And the man continued serving them half-heartedly. He was not a talker. He even had the shifty look of someone on his guard.

'And Monsieur Michonnet?'

'He's the insurance agent.'

That was it.

'Will you have red or white?'

He spent a long time trying to fish out a piece of cork that had fallen into the bottle and in the end just decanted the wine.

'And the people in the Three Widows house?'

'I've never seen them . . . Not the lady, anyway, since it seems there's one there . . . The highway's not really part of Avrainville.'

'Well done?' called his wife from the kitchen.

Maigret and Lucas fell silent, lost in their own thoughts. At nine o'clock, after a synthetic calvados, they went back out to the road, paced up and down for a while, then finally headed for the crossroads.

'She's not coming . . . '

'I'd like to know what Goldberg was doing out here. Champagne and toasted almonds! . . . Did they find any diamonds in his pockets?'

'No. Just a bit over two thousand francs in his wallet.'

The garage was still lit up. Maigret noticed that Monsieur Oscar's house was not by the side of the road but behind the workshop, which meant its windows could not be seen.

Dressed in overalls, the mechanic sat eating on the running board of a car. And suddenly, just a few steps away from the policemen, the garage owner himself came out of the darkness on the road.

'Good evening, gentlemen!'

'Good evening,' grunted Maigret.

'A lovely night! If this keeps up, we'll have wonderful weather for Easter.'

'Tell me,' the inspector asked bluntly, 'does

your place stay open all night?'

'Open, no! But there's always a man there who sleeps on a cot. The door's locked. Regular customers ring the bell when they need something.'

'Do you get much traffic on the road at night?'

'Not a lot, no, but it never stops. Lorries on their way to Les Halles . . . This region's known for its early fruits and vegetables, especially its watercress. The drivers sometimes run out of petrol, or need some little repair made . . . Would you like to join me for a drink?'

'No, thanks.'

'Your loss . . . but I won't insist. So! You haven't sorted out this business with the cars yet? You know, Monsieur Michonnet is going to worry himself sick over it. Especially if he isn't issued another six-cylinder car right away!'

A headlamp gleamed in the distance, growing larger. A rumbling sound. A shadow went past.

'The doctor from Étampes!' murmured the garage owner. 'He went to see a patient in Arpajon. His colleague must have invited him for dinner . . . '

'You know every vehicle that goes past here?'

'Many of them . . . Look! Those two side-lamps: that's watercress for Les Halles. Those fellows can never bring themselves to use their headlamps . . . And they take up the entire road! . . . Evening, Jules!'

A voice replied from up in the cab of the passing lorry, and then the only thing to see was the small red tail-light, which soon dissolved into the night.

Somewhere, a train, a glowing caterpillar that stretched out into chaos of the night.

187

'The 9.32 express . . . Listen, you're sure you won't have anything? . . . Say, Jojo! When you've finished your supper, check the third pump, it's jammed.'

More headlamps. But the car went on by. It was not Madame Goldberg.

Maigret was smoking constantly. Leaving Monsieur Oscar in front of his garage, he began to walk up and down, trailed by Lucas, who kept talking softly to himself.

Not a single light in the Three Widows house. The policemen went past the gate ten times. Each time Maigret automatically looked up at the window he knew was Else's.

Then came the Michonnet villa, brand new, nondescript, with its varnished oak door and silly little garden.

Then the garage, the mechanic busy repairing the petrol pump, Monsieur Oscar dispensing advice, both hands stuck in his pockets.

A lorry from Étampes on its way to Paris stopped to fill up. Lying asleep atop the heap of vegetables was the relief driver, who made this same journey every night at the same hour.

'Thirty litres!'

'How's it going?'

'Can't complain!'

The clutch growled and the lorry moved off, down the hill to Arpajon at sixty kilometres an hour.

'She won't be coming now,' sighed Lucas. 'Probably decided to spend the night in Paris . . . '

After they'd covered the 200 metres up and down from the crossroads three more times,

188

Maigret veered off abruptly towards Avrainville. When they reached the inn, there was only one lamp still burning and no one in the café.

'I think I hear a car . . . '

They turned around. And two headlamps were indeed shining in the direction of the village. A car was turning slowly in front of the garage. Someone was talking.

'They're asking for directions.'

The car came towards them at last, illuminating the telegraph poles one after another. Maigret and Lucas were caught in the light, standing across the road from the inn.

The sound of brakes. The driver got out and opened a door to the back seat.

'Is this the right place?' asked a woman's voice from inside.

'Yes, madame. This is Avrainville. And there's the traditional branch of fir over the front door of the inn.'

A leg sheathed in silk. A foot placed on the ground. An impression of fur . . .

Maigret was about to walk towards the woman.

At that moment there was a loud bang, a cry — and the woman fell headlong, literally crashing to the ground, where she lay curled up in a ball while one of her legs kicked out spasmodically.

★ ★ ★

Maigret and Lucas looked at each other.

'Take care of her, Lucas!' shouted the inspector.

189

But already a few seconds had been lost. The chauffeur stood stunned, rooted to the spot. A window opened on the second floor of the inn.

The shot had come from the field to the right of the road. As he ran, the inspector drew his revolver from his pocket. He could hear something, footsteps thudding softly on clayey soil . . . But he couldn't see a thing: the car's headlamps were shining so brightly straight ahead that they flooded everywhere else with darkness.

Turning around he yelled, 'The headlamps!'

When nothing happened, he yelled it again. And then there was a disastrous misunderstanding: the driver, or Lucas, turned one of the headlamps towards the inspector.

Now he was spotlit, a huge figure in black against the bare ground of the field.

The murderer had to be farther on, or more to the left — or the right — but in any case, outside that circle of light.

'God almighty, the headlamps!' yelled Maigret one last time.

He was clenching his fists in rage, running in zigzags like a hunted rabbit. That glare was disrupting even all perception of distance, which is why he suddenly saw the garage's pumps less than a hundred metres away.

Then there was a human figure, quite close, and a voice saying hoarsely, 'What's going on?'

Furious and humiliated, Maigret stopped short, looked Monsieur Oscar up and down and saw there was no mud on his slippers.

'Did you see anyone?'

'Just a car asking the way to Avrainville.'

The inspector noticed a red light on the main road heading towards Arpajon.

'What's that?'

'A lorry for Les Halles.'

'He stopped?'

'Long enough to take twenty litres . . . '

They could hear the commotion going on over by the inn and the headlamp was still sweeping the deserted field. Maigret suddenly noticed the Michonnet villa, crossed the road and rang the bell.

A small spy hole opened.

'Who's there?'

'Detective Chief Inspector Maigret. I would like to speak with Monsieur Michonnet.'

A chain and two bolts were undone. A key turned in the lock. Madame Michonnet appeared, anxious, even upset, impulsively darting furtive glances up and down the main road.

'You haven't seen him?' she asked.

'He's not here?' replied Maigret gruffly, with a glimmer of hope.

'I mean . . . I don't know . . . I . . . I just heard a shot, didn't I? . . . But do come in!'

She was about forty, plain, with prominent features.

'Monsieur Michonnet stepped out for a moment to . . . '

On the left, the door to the dining room was open. The table had not been cleared.

'How long has he been gone?'

'I don't know . . . Perhaps half an hour . . . '

Something moved in the kitchen.

'Do you have a servant?'

191

'No. It might be the cat . . . '

The inspector opened the kitchen door and saw Monsieur Michonnet himself, coming in through the garden door, mopping his face. His shoes were caked with mud.

There was a moment of surprised silence as the two men looked at each other.

'Your weapon!' said the inspector.

'My . . . ?'

'Your weapon, quickly!'

The insurance agent handed him a small revolver he'd pulled from a trouser pocket. All six of its bullets were still there, however, and the barrel was cold.

'Where have you been?'

'Over there . . . '

'What do you mean by 'over there'?'

'Don't be afraid, Émile! They wouldn't dare touch you!' exclaimed Madame Michonnet. 'This is too much, really! And when I think that my brother-in-law is a judge in Carcassonne . . . '

'Just a moment, madame: I am speaking to your husband . . . You were at Avrainville just now. What did you go there to do?'

'Avrainville? Me?'

He was shaking, trying in vain to put up a front, but seemed genuinely dumbfounded by his predicament.

'I swear to you, I was over *there*, at the Three Widows house! I wanted to keep an eye on them myself, since — '

'You didn't go into the field? You didn't hear anything?'

'Wasn't there a shot? Has anyone been killed?'

His moustache was drooping. He looked at his wife the way a kid looks at his mother when he's in a tight spot.

'I swear, chief inspector! . . . I swear to you . . . '

He stamped his foot, and two tears rolled down his cheeks.

'This is outrageous!' he cried. 'It's my car that was stolen! It's my car they found the body in! And no one will give my car back to me, when I'm the one who worked fifteen years to pay for it! And now I'm the one accused of — '

'Be quiet, Émile! I'll talk to him!'

But Maigret didn't give her the chance.

'Are there any other weapons in the house?'

'Only this one revolver, which we bought when we had the villa built . . . And the bullets are even the same ones the gunsmith put in himself.'

'You were at the Three Widows house?'

'I was afraid my car would be stolen again . . . I wanted to conduct my own investigation . . . I entered the grounds — or rather, I climbed up on the wall.'

'You saw them?'

'Who? Those two? The Andersens? Of course! . . . They're in the drawing room. They've been quarrelling for an hour now.'

'You left when you heard the shot?'

'Yes. But I wasn't sure it was a gunshot . . . I only thought so . . . I was worried.'

'You saw no one else?'

'No one.'

Maigret went to the door and, opening it, saw Monsieur Oscar coming towards him.

'Your colleague has sent me, chief inspector, to tell you that the woman is dead. My mechanic has gone to inform the police in Arpajon. He'll bring back a doctor . . . And now, will you excuse me? I can't leave the garage unattended.'

At Avrainville, the pale headlamp beams could still be seen, illuminating a section of wall at the inn and some shadowy figures moving around a car.

4

The Prisoner

Head down, Maigret was walking slowly in the field, where the growing corn was beginning to dot the earth with pale green.

It was morning. The sun was out and the air was vibrant with the songs of invisible birds. In Avrainville, Lucas was standing outside the inn door, waiting for representatives of the prosecutor's office and keeping an eye on the car Madame Goldberg had hired in Paris on Place de l'Opéra for her journey.

The wife of the diamond merchant from Antwerp was laid out upstairs on an iron bed. A sheet had been thrown over her corpse, which the doctor had partly unclothed the night before.

It was early on a fine April day. In the very field where Maigret, blinded by the headlamps, had chased the murderer in vain and now advanced step by step, following the traces left in the darkness, two farm workers loaded a cart with beets they were harvesting from a hillock while their horses waited quietly.

The double row of trees along the main road sliced through the countryside. The red petrol pumps at the garage sparkled in the sunlight.

Slow, stubborn, quite possibly in a bad mood, Maigret was smoking. The footprints found in the field seemed to prove that Madame Goldberg had been shot dead with a rifle, for the murderer had not come within thirty metres of the inn.

The footprints were unremarkable: smooth soles, average size. The trail curved around to wind up at the Three Widows Crossroads, keeping a more or less equal distance from the Andersens' house, the Michonnet villa and the garage.

In short, this trail proved nothing! It introduced no new lead and Maigret, stepping out on to the road, was biting down on his pipe stem rather grimly.

He saw Monsieur Oscar at his door, his hands in the pockets of his baggy trousers and a smug expression on his common-looking face.

'Up already, chief inspector?' he shouted across the road.

At that same moment someone pulled up between Maigret and the garage: it was Carl Andersen in his little old car.

He was wearing gloves and a fedora and had a cigarette between his lips. He doffed his hat.

'May I have a word with you, chief inspector?'

After rolling down his window, he went on in his usual polite manner.

'I did want to ask your permission to go to Paris, and was hoping to find you here . . . I'll tell you why I must go: today is the 15th of April, the day I am paid for my work for Dumas and Son. It's also the day when the rent is due . . . '

He smiled apologetically.

'Quite ordinary errands, as you see, but urgent ones all the same. I'm low on funds.'

196

When he removed his monocle for a moment to resettle it more securely, Maigret turned his head away because he did not like looking into that staring glass eye.

'And your sister?'

'Precisely . . . I was about to bring this up: would it be too much to ask you to have someone look in on the house from time to time?'

Three dark, official-looking cars came up the hill from Arpajon and turned left towards Avrainville.

'What's going on?'

'They're from the public prosecutor's office. Madame Goldberg was killed last night as she was getting out of a car at the inn.'

Maigret watched his reaction. Across the street, Monsieur Oscar was strolling idly up and down in front of his garage.

'Killed!' repeated Carl. Suddenly nervous, he said, 'Listen, chief inspector: I must get to Paris! . . . I can't stay here without any money, especially on the day when I have to pay all my local bills, but as soon as I get back I want to help find the murderer. You will allow me to do this, won't you? I don't know anything for certain, but I feel . . . I don't know how to put this . . . I'm beginning to see some kind of pattern here . . . '

He had to pull in closer to the pavement because a lorry driver coming back from Paris was honking his horn to get by.

'Off you go, then!' exclaimed Maigret.

Carl tipped his hat and took a moment to light

197

another cigarette before letting in the clutch, whereupon the jalopy went down the hill and puttered up the next one.

People were moving around over by the three cars that were parked just outside Avrainville.

'Sure you wouldn't like a little something?'

Maigret frowned at the smiling garage owner, who just wouldn't stop offering him a drink.

Filling a pipe, he walked off towards the Three Widows house, where the tall trees were alive with the fluttering and chirping of birds. The Michonnet villa was on his way.

The windows were open. Wearing a dust cap, Madame Michonnet was upstairs in the bedroom, shaking out a rug.

Unshaven, his hair uncombed, wearing no collar, her husband was downstairs smoking a meerschaum with a cherry-wood stem and looking out at the road with a glum, abstracted air. When he noticed the inspector, he avoided greeting him by making a show of cleaning out his pipe.

A few minutes later Maigret was ringing the bell at the Andersens' front gate, where he waited in vain for ten minutes. All the shutters were closed. The only sound was the constant twittering of the birds, which transformed every tree into a bustling little world.

In the end Maigret shrugged, examined the lock and let himself in with a passkey. As on the previous day, he walked around the house to the drawing room.

He knocked but, again, without success. Then, grumbling and obstinate, he went inside, where his eye fell upon the open phonograph. There was a record on the turntable.

Why did he start the machine? He would have been at a loss to explain. The needle was scratchy. An Argentinean orchestra played a tango as the inspector started up the stairs.

The door to Carl Andersen's bedroom stood open. Near a wardrobe Maigret saw a pair of shoes that seemed to have recently been cleaned, for the brush and tin of polish sat beside them and the floor was dotted with crumbled, dried mud.

The inspector had made paper tracings of the footprints found in the field. He compared them with the shoes. A perfect match.

And yet he never so much as blinked. He didn't seem the least bit pleased. He went on smoking, as grumpy as he'd been all morning.

'Is that you?' a woman's voice inquired.

Maigret hesitated . . . He could not see who was speaking: the voice had come from Else's room, but the door was closed.

'It's me,' he finally replied, as indistinctly as he could.

Then, a long silence.

'Who's there?' the voice asked abruptly.

It was too late to fool her.

'Detective Chief Inspector Maigret. I was here yesterday. I'd like to speak to you for a moment, mademoiselle.'

More silence. Maigret tried to guess what she could possibly be doing behind that door, beneath which gleamed a thin line of sunlight.

'I'm listening,' she said at last.

'If you'd be good enough to open the door

. . . I can certainly wait, if you need time to dress.'

That annoying silence again.

A little laugh, and then, 'What you ask of me is somewhat difficult, chief inspector!'

'Why is that?'

'Because I'm locked in. So you will have to speak without seeing me.'

'Who locked you in?'

'My brother Carl . . . I am the one who asks him to, whenever he goes out, because I'm so terribly afraid of prowlers.'

Without saying anything, Maigret pulled out his passkey and quietly inserted it in the lock. His throat felt tight; was he troubled by any untoward thoughts?

And when the bolt shifted, he decided not to open the door before announcing first, 'I'm going to come in, mademoiselle . . . '

A strange sensation: he was in a dark, drab corridor — and stepped immediately into a setting alive with light.

Although the shutters were closed, the horizontal slats admitted great beams of sunshine.

The entire room was thus a jigsaw puzzle of darkness and light. The walls, objects, even Else's face were as if striped in luminous bands. Then there was the young woman's heavy perfume, plus such incidental details as the silk underwear tossed on to a bergère, the Turkish cigarette smouldering in a china bowl on a lacquered pedestal table, and finally there was Else, lounging on the black velvet couch in a deep red peignoir.

Eyes wide open, she watched Maigret come towards her with amused astonishment and, just perhaps, a tiny tremor of fear.

'What are you doing?'

'I wanted to talk to you. Please forgive me if I'm disturbing you . . . '

She laughed like a little girl. When her peignoir slipped off one shoulder, she pulled it up again but remained lying on or, rather, nestled in the low couch striped with sunlight like the rest of the room.

'You see? . . . I wasn't doing much of anything. I never do!'

'Why didn't you go to Paris with your brother?'

'He doesn't want me to. He says having a woman around gets in the way when men discuss business.'

'You never leave the house?'

'But I do! I take walks around the property.'

'That's all?'

'We have three hectares here, enough for me to stretch my legs, don't you think? . . . But do sit down, chief inspector. It's rather funny, having you here in secret . . . '

'What do you mean?'

'That my brother will have a fit when he gets back. He's worse than any mother. Worse than a jealous lover! He is the one who looks after me and he takes this responsibility seriously, as you can see.'

'I thought you were the one who wanted to be locked in, because of your fear of burglars.'

'There's that, too . . . I've grown so used to

solitude that now I am afraid of people.'

Maigret had sat down in a large upholstered armchair and placed his bowler on the rug. And whenever Else looked at him he turned his face away, still unable to meet her gaze with his usual composure.

The previous day, she had simply seemed mysterious to him. In the dim light, a formal, almost regal figure, she'd had the presence of a film star, and their first meeting had taken on a theatrical air.

Now he was trying to discover her human side, but something else was bothering him: the very intimacy of their encounter.

Else relaxing in her peignoir, dangling a slipper from the tip of a bare foot in that perfumed bedchamber, while the middle-aged Maigret sat slightly flushed, his hat on the rug . . .

Wasn't that a perfect illustration for *La Vie Parisienne*?

Rather clumsily, the inspector put his pipe away in his pocket even though he hadn't cleaned it out.

'So, you find it boring here?'

'No . . . Yes . . . I don't know . . . Do you smoke cigarettes?'

She waved towards a pack of Turkish cigarettes, the price of which was marked on the band: 20 francs 65 centimes. Maigret recalled that the Andersens lived on 2,000 francs a month, and that Carl had been obliged to hurry and collect his wages so as to pay the rent and local bills on time.

'Do you smoke a lot?'

'A pack or two a day . . . '

She held out a delicately engraved lighter, then heaved a sigh that caused the neckline of her peignoir to open a little more revealingly.

The inspector did not immediately hold it against her, though. Among the clientele of luxury hotels he had seen showily dressed foreign women whom the average citizen would have taken for tarts.

'Your brother went out, last night?'

'You think so? . . . I have no idea . . . '

'Didn't you spend the evening arguing with him?'

She showed her perfect teeth in a big smile.

'Who told you that? Did he? We sometimes squabble, but nicely. As a matter of fact, I scolded him yesterday for not receiving you properly. He's so unsociable! And he was already like that as a boy . . . '

'Did you live in Denmark?'

'Yes. In a big castle beside the Baltic . . . A very dreary castle, all white amid dusty green foliage . . . Do you know the country? So gloomy! And yet, it is beautiful . . . '

As her gaze grew distant with nostalgia, she felt a shiver of pleasure.

'We were rich, but our parents were quite strict, like most Protestants. Personally, I pay no attention to religion, but Carl is still a believer . . . Less so than his father, who lost all his fortune through clinging stubbornly to his principles. We left Denmark, Carl and I . . . '

'That was three years ago?'

'Yes . . . Just imagine! My brother was

destined to become an important dignitary of the Danish court — and here he is, forced to earn his living designing dreadful fabrics . . . In Paris, in the second-and third-class hotels where we had to stay, he was horribly unhappy. He had the same tutor as our crown prince! But he preferred to bury himself out here.'

'And bury you at the same time.'

'Yes . . . I'm used to it. I was a prisoner in our parents' castle, too. I was kept away from all the girls who might have become my friends, supposedly because they weren't my social equals.'

Her expression changed with striking abruptness.

'Do you think that Carl has become . . . I'm not sure how to put it . . . abnormal?'

And she leaned forwards, as if to hear the inspector's reply as quickly as possible.

'You're afraid of . . . ?' exclaimed Maigret in surprise.

'I didn't say that! I didn't mean anything! Please excuse me . . . You've started me talking . . . I don't know why I trust you like this . . . So . . . '

'Does he behave oddly at times?'

She shrugged wearily, crossed and uncrossed her legs, then stood up, uncovering for an instant a flash of skin between the folds of the peignoir.

'What do you want me to say to you? I don't know any more. Ever since that business with the car . . . Why would he have killed a man he didn't know?'

'You're sure you have never seen Isaac Goldberg?'

'Yes . . . As far as I know . . . '

'You and your brother never went to Antwerp?'

'We stayed there one night, three years ago, when we arrived from Copenhagen . . . No, Carl could not do such a thing! If he has become somewhat strange, I'm sure that his accident is more to blame than our financial ruin. He was handsome! He still is, when he wears his monocle. But otherwise . . . Can you see him kissing a woman without that bit of black glass? That staring eye in its red-rimmed socket . . . '

She shuddered.

'That has to be the main reason my brother hides himself away . . . '

'But he's keeping you hidden along with him!'

'What difference does that make?'

'You're being sacrificed.'

'That's the lot of every woman, especially a sister. It isn't quite the same thing here in France. In our country, as in England, only the eldest male counts in the family, the son who will carry on the name.'

She was growing agitated, puffing hard on her cigarette. She paced up and down through the patterns of sunshine and shadow in the shuttered room.

'No! Carl could not have killed him. That was all a mistake. Wasn't it because you realized this that you let him go? . . . Unless . . . '

'Unless?'

'But you would never admit this! I know that when the police haven't enough proof, they sometimes release a suspect so that they can catch him for good later on . . . That would be despicable!'

She stubbed out her cigarette in the china bowl.

'If only we hadn't chosen this awful crossroads . . . Poor Carl, who wanted to be left alone . . . But we're less on our own here, chief inspector, than in the most crowded neighbourhood in Paris! Across the way are those impossible, ridiculous, narrow-minded people who spy on us, especially her — with that white dust cap every morning and her crooked chignon in the afternoon . . . Then that garage, a little farther on . . . Three groups, three camps is more like it, and all at about the same distance from one another . . . '

'Did you ever have any contact with the Michonnets?'

'No! The man came once, peddling insurance. Carl showed him the door.'

'And the garage owner?'

'He has never set foot here.'

'Was it your brother who wanted to make a run for it on Sunday morning?'

She was quiet for a moment, hanging her head, her cheeks pink.

'No,' she sighed at last, almost inaudibly.

'It was you?'

'Yes, me . . . I hadn't thought things through. The idea that Carl could have committed a crime almost drove me crazy. I'd seen him in such distress the day before . . . So I dragged him along after me . . . '

'Didn't he swear to you he was innocent?'

'Yes.'

'You didn't believe him?'

'Not at first . . . '

'And now?'

She took her time, pronouncing each syllable distinctly.

'I believe that, in spite of all his misfortunes, Carl is incapable of deliberately doing anything evil . . . But listen, chief inspector, he'll probably be getting back home soon and if he finds you here, God knows what he'll think!'

And yet, there was something almost flirtatious, if not provocative, about her smile.

'You will defend him, won't you? You'll get him out of all this? I would be so grateful!'

She held out her hand to him and, as she did so, the peignoir fell slightly open once again.

'Goodbye, chief inspector.'

He picked up his hat and sidled from the room.

'Could you lock the door again, so that he won't notice anything?'

A few moments later, Maigret was going downstairs, crossing the drawing room with its motley collection of furniture, stepping out on to the terrace bathed in sunshine that was already warm.

Cars were humming along the road. The front gate did not creak when he locked it behind him.

As he passed the garage, a mocking voice called out, 'Good for you! You're a brave one, that's for sure!'

It was Monsieur Oscar, in a jovial, man-of-the-people mood.

'Come on!' he added. 'Take the plunge and have a drop with me! Those fellows from the prosecutor's office have already left, so you can easily spare a minute . . . '

The chief inspector hesitated, wincing as a mechanic scraped his file across a piece of steel clamped in a vice.

'Ten litres!' called a motorist waiting by one of the pumps. 'Anyone around, in there?'

Monsieur Michonnet, as yet unshaven and without his shirt collar, was standing in his tiny garden looking over the fence at the road.

'Finally!' exclaimed Monsieur Oscar when Maigret made a move to join him. 'Plain and simple, that's how I like folks. Not like that snob at the Three Widows!'

5

The Abandoned Car

'This way, inspector! . . . Nothing fancy, eh! This is just a working man's home here . . .'

He pushed open the door of the house behind the garage and they walked directly into a kitchen that must also have served as a dining room, for the breakfast dishes still sat upon the table.

A woman in a pink housecoat of heavy crêpe stopped polishing a copper tap.

'Come over here, honey, and meet Detective Chief Inspector Maigret . . . My wife, inspector! She could afford her own maid, mind you . . . but then there'd be nothing left to do and she'd be bored!'

The woman was neither ugly nor pretty. She was about thirty. Her housecoat was cheap-looking and unflattering, and she stood awkwardly before Maigret, watching her husband.

'Well, go and fetch us an aperitif! . . . An Export Cassis, chief inspector? . . . You'd rather we went into the drawing room? No? That's fine! I never stand on ceremony, myself. Right, honey? . . . No, not those ones — get some highball glasses!'

He leaned back in his chair. He was wearing a pink shirt, no waistcoat, and he slipped his hands inside his belt, cradling his ample belly.

'Exciting, isn't she, the lady over at the Three Widows house . . . Mustn't make a point of it in front of my wife, but between ourselves, she's certainly easy on a man's eyes. Only problem is, she has a brother . . . or so *he* says! A 'knight of doleful countenance' that one is — and he spends his time spying on her . . . I've even heard it said around here that when he goes off for an hour, he locks her in — and does the same every night! That sound to you anything like a brother and sister, hmm? . . . Cheers! . . . Say, honey, go and tell Jojo not to forget he's to fix the lorry for that fellow from Lardy.'

Hearing a noise that sounded like a 5CV engine, Maigret turned towards the window.

' 'Tisn't him, inspector! I can tell you exactly from here, blindfolded, what's passing on the road. That old heap belongs to the power-house engineer. You're waiting for our snob to come back?'

According to an alarm clock on a shelf, it was eleven o'clock. Through an open door Maigret could see a telephone on the wall out in the corridor.

'You haven't touched your drink . . . Well, here's to your investigation! Listen, don't you find something comical in this whole affair? The idea of switching the cars, and especially the bit about pinching the six-cylinder beauty from that stuffed shirt across the way . . . Because that's just what he is — a stuffed shirt! I swear to you, we've got the bottom of the barrel here for neighbours . . . But I've enjoyed watching you coming and going since you arrived yesterday.

Particularly when you squint at people as though you suspect the whole lot of them . . . Mind you, I've a cousin on my wife's side who was in the police, too. Gambling Squad. He spent every afternoon at the races, and the best part of the joke? He passed me tips! Well, down the hatch! . . . So, honey, all taken care of?'

'Yes . . . '

For a moment the young woman, who had just come in, stood wondering what she should do next.

'Come on, have a drink with us. The chief inspector isn't snooty, he won't refuse to drink your health because you've got your hair in curlers . . . '

'Would you mind if I make a phone call?' said Maigret abruptly.

'Be my guest! You turn the handle . . . If it's for Paris, they'll connect you right away.'

The inspector looked in the directory for the number of Dumas and Son, the fabric manufacturers to whom Carl Andersen had gone to receive some money.

The phone call was brief. The cash clerk who spoke to Maigret confirmed that Andersen had two thousand francs coming to him that day but had not yet shown up at the premises in Rue du Quatre-Septembre.

When Maigret returned to the kitchen, Monsieur Oscar was rubbing his hands together with great relish.

'You know, I'd rather come right out and say how much fun I'm having. Because I know the score! Something happens at the crossroads

211

. . . there are just three households here . . . it's only natural to suspect us all. Oh yes you do! Don't pretend otherwise. I saw how you were looking at me and how you didn't want to come and have a drink here! . . . Three houses! The insurance agent seems too big a fool to be capable of committing a crime. The snob is an imposing gentleman . . . And that leaves yours truly, a poor working guy who's clawed his way up to being his own man but doesn't know how to talk proper. A former boxer! If you ask after me at police headquarters in Paris, they'll tell you I was picked up a few times in raids, because I used to like dancing the Java in the Rue de Lappe music halls, especially when I was a boxer. Another time I had a go at a cop who was picking on me . . . Bottoms up, chief inspector!'

'No, thanks.'

'You're not going to refuse! A fizzy Export Cassis never hurt anyone . . . You see, I like to put my cards on the table. It bothers me to see you skulking around my garage as if you were watching me on the sly. Right, honey? . . . Didn't I say so last night? 'The chief inspector's here! Well, then, let him come in! Let him rummage around everywhere! Let him search me! And then admit that I'm a stand-up guy and innocent as a baby.' What really interests me about this whole thing is the cars — because when you get right down to it, the case revolves around cars . . . '

Half past eleven! Maigret stood up.

'Another phone call to make.'

With a worried frown, he asked for police

headquarters and told an inspector to send the description of Andersen's little car out to all police stations as well as the border posts.

The four aperitifs Monsieur Oscar had put away had brought a gleam to his eyes and roses to his cheeks.

'Oh, I know you'll refuse to join us for some veal ragout. Especially seeing as we eat in the kitchen here . . . Ah! Here's Groslumeau's lorry back from Les Halles: you must excuse me, chief inspector . . .'

He went outside. Maigret was left alone with the young woman, who was tending to her ragout with a wooden spoon.

'Quite a card, your husband!'

'Yes . . . He's a cheerful sort.'

'And gets tough at times, right?'

'He doesn't like being contradicted. But he's a good fellow.'

'Chases a few skirts?'

No reply.

'I bet he goes out on the town now and again.'

'Like all men . . .'

Her voice had turned bitter. They could hear snatches of conversation over by the garage.

'Put that over there! . . . Good! . . . Yes . . . We'll change your back tyres tomorrow morning.'

Monsieur Oscar returned in a fine humour, as if he felt like singing and playing the fool.

'Come on! Sure you won't tuck into some lunch with us, chief inspector? We could bring up a bottle from the cellar! . . . Why are you making that face, Germaine? . . . Women! Moody things, always changing on you.'

213

'I've got to get back to Avrainville,' announced Maigret.

'Should I drive you back? Wouldn't take a minute . . . '

'No, thank you. I'd rather walk.'

Maigret stepped outside into a bath of warm sunshine, and on the road to Avrainville a yellow butterfly led the way.

A hundred metres from the inn he encountered Sergeant Lucas, who had come out to meet him.

'Well?'

'You called it! The doctor extracted the bullet, which did come from a rifle.'

'Nothing else?'

'Yes, there's information from Paris. Isaac Goldberg arrived there in a Minerva sports car he used for travelling and which he drove himself. That's the car he must have driven here from Paris.'

'And that's all?'

'We're still waiting for replies from the Belgian police.'

The driver of the hired car that had delivered Madame Goldberg to her own death had left in his vehicle.

'The body?'

'They took it to Arpajon. The examining magistrate is worried and asked me to tell you to work quickly. His main concern is that the papers in Brussels and Antwerp might splash this affair all over their front pages.'

Humming to himself, the inspector went inside the inn and sat down at his assigned table.

214

'Do you have a telephone here?'

'Yes! But there is no service between noon and two o'clock, and it's now half past twelve.'

The inspector ate in silence. Seeing that he was preoccupied, Lucas tried a few times to strike up a conversation, but in vain.

It was one of the first lovely days of spring. After lunch Maigret dragged his chair into the inn courtyard and sat down by a wall, in the company of the ducks and chickens, where he dozed in the sun for half an hour.

At two on the dot, however, he was standing at the telephone, clinging to the receiver.

'Hello! Police Judiciaire? . . . You haven't located that car we're looking for yet? . . . '

The inspector began walking around and around the courtyard. Ten minutes later he was called back to the phone: Quai des Orfèvres was on the line.

'Detective Chief Inspector Maigret? . . . We have just this moment received a call from Jeumont . . . The car has been found there, abandoned across from the train station. We assume that the driver preferred to cross the border on foot or by train.'

Maigret hung up only for an instant, then asked for the offices of Dumas and Son. He was informed that Carl Andersen had still not shown up to collect his two thousand francs.

★ ★ ★

When Maigret and Lucas walked past the garage at around three o'clock, Monsieur Oscar popped

215

out from behind a car to ask brightly, 'How's it going, chief inspector?'

Maigret merely waved at him and continued on to the Three Widows house.

The doors and windows of the Michonnet Villa were shut but, yet again, the policemen noticed the dining-room curtains twitching.

The garage owner's cheerfulness seemed once more to have aggravated the ill humour of the inspector, who was puffing furiously on his pipe.

'Now that Andersen has made a run for it — ' began Lucas quietly.

'Stay here!'

The inspector entered the grounds and house of the Three Widows property just as he had that morning. In the drawing room he sniffed the air, looked quickly around and noticed wisps of smoke hovering in the corners of the room, which smelled strongly of freshly smoked tobacco.

Without even thinking about it he grasped the butt of the revolver in his pocket before going upstairs, where he could hear phonograph music and recognized the tango he had played that morning.

The music was coming from Else's room. When he knocked, it ceased immediately.

'Who's there?'

'The inspector.'

A short laugh.

'In that case, you know what to do. I can't let you in . . . '

The passkey did its job again. The young woman was wearing the same clinging black

216

dress as the day before.

'Are you the one who has kept my brother from coming home?'

'No. I have not seen him since early this morning.'

'Then they must not have had his payment ready at Dumas. Sometimes he has to go back there in the afternoon . . . '

'Your brother has tried to cross the border into Belgium. As far as I know, he has succeeded.'

She stared at him in astonishment — and some disbelief.

'Carl?'

'Yes.'

'This is some kind of test, isn't it?'

'Can you drive?'

'Drive what?'

'A car.'

'No! My brother has never been willing to teach me.'

Maigret had not taken the pipe from his mouth and was still wearing his hat.

'Have you left this room?'

'Me?'

She laughed. A merry, musical laugh. And more than ever, she was wreathed in what American movies portray as sex appeal.

For a woman can be lovely without being alluring, while other, less classically beautiful women unfailingly inspire desire or sentimental feelings.

Else aroused both: she was at once woman and child, creating her own aura of voluptuous attraction. And yet, whoever looked into her eyes was astonished to find her gaze as limpid as a little girl's.

'I don't understand what you mean . . . '

'Someone has been smoking downstairs in the drawing room within the last half-hour.'

'But who?'

'That's what I'm asking you.'

'And how do you expect me to know that?'

'This morning, that phonograph was downstairs.'

'Impossible! . . . How could that . . . Wait, inspector! I hope you don't suspect me of anything! You seem different, strange . . . Where is Carl?'

'I'm telling you, he has left the country.'

'That's not true! It can't be! Why would he do that? Besides, he would never leave me alone here! . . . That's crazy! What would happen to me, all on my own?'

It was bewildering. Without any warning, without making grand gestures or even raising her voice, she had become touching, pitiable. It was in her eyes . . . Dismay beyond words. An expression of helplessness, of supplication.

'Tell me the truth, chief inspector! Tell me Carl isn't guilty! If he were, then it would mean he had gone mad! I refuse to believe that! . . . It frightens me . . . His family . . . '

'Do you know of any insanity there?'

She turned her head away.

'Yes, his grandfather died in a fit of madness. And one of his aunts is in an asylum. But no, not Carl! I know him . . . '

'Have you eaten any lunch?'

Startled, she looked around her and replied in surprise, 'No!'

'Aren't you hungry? It's three o'clock.'

'I think I am hungry, yes.'

'In that case, go and have lunch. There is no longer any reason for you to remain locked in. Your brother will not be coming back.'

'That's not true! He will come back! He would never leave me all alone.'

'Come on . . . '

Maigret was already out in the corridor, still frowning and still smoking his pipe. He did not take his eyes off the girl, but when she brushed past him it had no effect on him.

Downstairs she seemed even more disoriented.

'It was always Carl who served our meals . . . I don't even know if there's anything to eat.'

A loaf of bread turned up in the kitchen, at least, and a tin of condensed milk.

'No, I can't, I'm too upset. Go away! . . . No, wait — don't leave me! . . . Oh, this horrible house. I have never liked . . . What's that? Out there!'

She pointed to an animal outside, curled up in a ball on one of the paths through the grounds. It was only a cat.

'I hate animals! I hate the countryside! It's full of creaking and snapping sounds that make me jump . . . At night — every night — there's an owl somewhere that gives ghastly hooting cries . . . '

The French windows seemed to frighten her as well, because she was staring at them as if she expected to see enemies pour through them from all sides.

'I will not sleep here alone in the house! I won't!'

'Is there a telephone?'

'No . . . My brother thought about getting one, but we cannot afford it. Can you imagine? Living in such a big house, with I don't know how many hectares, and not being able to pay for a telephone, or electricity or even a cleaning woman for the hard work! That's Carl all over! He's like his father . . . '

And she burst out laughing, but with an edge of hysteria.

It was a difficult situation, because she could not manage to compose herself and although she was still shaking with laughter, there was desperation in her eyes.

'What is it? What's so funny?'

'Nothing! You mustn't be angry with me . . . I'm thinking of when we were children, in our castle back home, with Carl's tutor and all the servants, the visitors, the carriages pulled by four horses . . . and *here* . . . '

Knocking over the tin of milk, she went to lean her forehead against a windowpane, staring out at the front steps baking in the sun.

'I'll arrange for a policeman to keep an eye on the house tonight.'

'Yes, good . . . No! I don't want a policeman, I want you to come yourself, chief inspector! Otherwise I'll be frightened . . . '

Was she laughing? Crying? She was panting: her entire body was trembling from head to toe.

She might have been putting on a show to make a fool of someone — but she might just as well have been on the verge of a breakdown.

'Don't leave me by myself!'

'I have work to do.'

'But if Carl has run away . . . '

'You think he's guilty?'

'I don't know! I don't know any more. If he has run off . . . '

'Do you want me to lock you in your room again?'

'No. What I want, as soon as possible, tomorrow morning, is to get away from this house, from this crossroads! I want to go to Paris, where the streets are full of people, where life goes on . . . The countryside scares me . . . I just don't know . . . '

And suddenly, 'Will they arrest Carl in Belgium?'

'There will be a warrant for his extradition.'

'It's unbelievable. When I think that only three days ago . . . '

She clasped her head in both hands, mussing her blonde hair.

Maigret stood outside on the front steps.

'I will see you later today, mademoiselle.'

He strode off with relief and yet he was sorry to leave her. Lucas was walking up and down the road.

'Anything new?'

'Nothing! The insurance agent came over to ask me if he was going to get a car back soon.'

Monsieur Michonnet had chosen to ask Lucas rather than Maigret. And they could see him in his little garden, watching them.

'He has nothing to keep himself busy?'

'He claims he can't visit his clients out in the country without a car. He's talking about suing us for damages.'

A van and a touring car carrying an entire family were waiting by the pumps at the garage.

'One fellow who's not working himself to death,' remarked the sergeant, 'is that Monsieur Oscar! He seems to earn money hand over fist. That place is hopping day and night . . . '

'Have you got any tobacco?'

The spring sunshine bathing the countryside was surprisingly strong, and Maigret mopped his brow.

'I'm going to nap for an hour,' he murmured. 'We'll see what happens tonight . . . '

Monsieur Oscar called out to him as he walked by.

'Take a drop, chief inspector? Just a quick one, since you're in the neighbourhood!'

'Some other time!'

Judging from the loud voices coming from the millstone villa, Michonnet was arguing with his wife.

6

Back from the Dead

It was five that afternoon when Maigret was awakened by Lucas bringing him a telegram from the Belgian police.

Isaac Goldberg under surveillance for several months as standard of living exceeded visible income Stop Suspected trafficking mainly stolen jewels Stop No proof Stop Trip to France coincided theft 2,000,000 in jewels London two weeks ago Stop Anonymous letter affirms jewels surfaced Antwerp where two international thieves seen spending freely Stop Believe Goldberg bought jewels then entered France to fence Stop Request description jewels Scotland Yard Stop

Still half-asleep, Maigret stuffed the telegram into his pocket and asked, 'Anything else?'

'No. I've kept an eye on the crossroads. When I saw the garage owner all dressed up I asked him where he was going. Seems he and his wife visit Paris once a week for dinner and a show. On those evenings they stay over in a hotel and return the next day.'

'Has he left?'

'By this time, he must have, yes!'

'You asked him which restaurant he was going to?'

'L'Escargot, Rue de la Bastille. Then he's off to the Théâtre de l'Ambigu and will stay at the Hôtel Rambuteau, Rue de Rivoli.'

'That about covers it,' muttered the inspector, who was combing his hair.

'The insurance fellow had his wife tell me that he'd like to talk to you, or rather, 'have a chat with you', as he put it.'

'Nothing else?'

Maigret went into the kitchen, where the innkeeper's wife was preparing the evening meal. He cut himself a thick hunk of bread, moved on to a terrine of pâté, and asked for a mug of white wine.'

'You're not waiting for supper?'

The inspector began devouring his huge sandwich in reply.

The sergeant watched him, obviously eager to talk.

'You're expecting some important development tonight, is that it?'

'Humpf . . . '

But why deny it? Standing there eating, wasn't he like a soldier about to go into battle?

'I've been going over things,' began Lucas, 'trying to organize my ideas. It's not easy . . . '

Chewing away, Maigret looked placidly at his colleague.

'It's still the girl who puzzles me the most. At times I feel that everyone around her — garage owner, insurance man, Carl Andersen — is guilty, but not her. At other times I'd swear instead that she's the only poisonous thing here . . . '

There was a twinkle of amusement in the inspector's eyes that seemed to say, 'Keep going!'

'There are moments when she really does seem like a girl from an aristocratic family, but again, at others she reminds me of when I was with Vice. You know what I mean, those girls who coolly reel off the most outrageous nonsense in the world, as bold as brass! Yet the details are so disturbing that you just can't believe such a girl could make them up. So you fall for her story . . . But later you find an old novel under her pillow and discover that she got everything from that book . . . Women who lie as easily as they breathe, and maybe even wind up believing all those stories they tell!'

'That's it?'

'You think I'm wrong?'

'I have no idea!'

'Remember, I believe different things at different times, and mostly it's Carl Andersen who worries me. Imagine an intelligent, cultivated, well-bred man like him, running a gang . . . '

'We'll see him tonight!'

'Him? But he's crossed the border.'

'Well . . . '

'You think that . . . '

'That this business is a whole lot more complicated than you imagine, Lucas. And that we'd be better off concentrating on a few important elements instead of getting lost in details.

'For instance,' continued Maigret, 'Monsieur Michonnet was the first person to file a complaint and he's the one who wants me to go and see him this evening.

'An evening, in fact, when the garage owner will *quite obviously* be off in Paris!

'And where is Goldberg's Minerva? Think about that, too! As there aren't many of them in France, it's not an easy car to make disappear.'

'You think that Monsieur Oscar . . . '

'Not so fast! . . . But if you feel like it, play around with those three little things.'

'But what about Else?'

'Her again?'

And wiping his mouth, Maigret went out to the main road. Fifteen minutes later he rang the Michonnets' bell and was welcomed by the woman's surly face.

'My husband is waiting for you upstairs!'

'So good of him . . . '

Oblivious to the irony of his words, she led him upstairs. Michonnet was in his bedroom, seated in a low-slung Voltaire armchair near the window. The shade was pulled down and he had a tartan blanket tucked around his legs.

'Well, now!' he began aggressively. 'When will I be getting a car back? You think it's a good idea, do you, to deprive a man of his livelihood? And meanwhile, you're paying calls on that creature across the way, when you're not off having aperitifs with the garage owner! Fine police work that is! I'll not mince words with you, chief inspector! Yes, a fine state of affairs! Never mind the murderer! The top priority is to torment honest citizens! . . . I have a car: does it belong to me, yes or no? . . . I put it to you.

Answer me! Is it mine? . . . Well, what gives you the right to keep my car locked up?'

'Are you ill?' Maigret asked quietly, looking at the blanket around the man's legs.

'Who wouldn't be! I'm fretting myself into an attack of gout! It always goes to my legs . . . I'm looking at two or three nights sitting sleepless in this chair. I asked you here to tell you this: look at the state I'm in! You can see for yourself that I'm unable to work, especially without a car! . . . Enough . . . I will call you as a witness when I sue for damages. And now, I bid you goodnight, monsieur!'

He had made his speech with the exaggerated bravado of a small-minded prig confident of being in the right.

'But while you seem to be skulking around spying on us,' added Madame Michonnet, 'the murderer himself is still out there! That's our justice! Attacking ordinary folks, but leaving the big shots free!'

'Is that all you have to say to me?'

Michonnet glared and sat back in his armchair while his wife led the way to the door.

The interior of the house was of a piece with its façade: spotless suites of furniture, gleaming with polish but seemingly frozen in place, unused.

Out in the corridor Maigret stopped at an old-fashioned wall-telephone and promptly turned the crank, as Madame Michonnet looked on in outrage.

'Hello, operator? This is the Police Judiciaire! Can you tell me if there have been any calls this afternoon for the Three Widows Crossroads?

227

. . . There are two numbers, you say, the garage and the Michonnet villa? . . . Good, and when? . . . A call for the garage from Paris at around one o'clock and another towards five? . . . And the other number? . . . Only one call . . . From Paris? . . . At five past five? . . . Thank you, mademoiselle.'

His eyes alight with mischief, he bowed to Madame Michonnet.

'I wish you a pleasant evening, madame.'

He opened the gate of the Three Widows house with practised ease, walked around the back to the drawing room and on upstairs.

Else Andersen met him in a state of great agitation.

'I'm sorry to make such demands of you, chief inspector; you'll think I'm presumptuous, but I am so restless, on edge . . . I'm frightened and I don't know why! Ever since our conversation this morning I've felt that you are the only one who can protect me from harm . . . You now know this sinister crossroads as well as I do, these three houses that seem to defy one another . . . Do you believe in premonitions? I do, like all women — and I sense that something bad will happen before this night is over . . . '

'And you're asking me again to watch over you?'

'It's too much to ask, isn't it — but I can't help being afraid!'

Maigret's eye had been caught for a moment by a painting of a snowy landscape, which hung crookedly on a wall, but he turned immediately to the girl, who stood waiting for his reply.

'Aren't you afraid for your reputation?'

'What does that matter to someone who's frightened?'

'In that case, I will return in one hour. A few orders to give . . . '

'Really? You'll come back? That's a promise? . . . Besides, I have all sorts of things to tell you, things I've remembered only in bits and pieces . . . '

'About?'

'My brother . . . But they may not be important . . . Well . . . For example, I remember, after that plane crash, the doctor taking care of him told Father that he could vouch for his patient's physical health, but not his mental health. I'd never really thought about what he meant . . . And other things . . . His insistence on living far from any city, hiding away . . . I'll tell you about all that when you return.'

She smiled at him with gratitude and only a flicker of lingering fear.

★   ★   ★

Walking past the millstone villa, Maigret looked up automatically at the first-floor window, which shone bright yellow in the darkness. Framed in the glowing shade was the silhouette of Monsieur Michonnet, sitting in his armchair.

At the inn, the inspector simply gave Lucas a few orders without any explanation.

'See to it that half a dozen inspectors are posted around the crossroads. Once an hour make sure that Monsieur Oscar is still in Paris by phoning the restaurant, then the theatre and the hotel. Have everyone who leaves any of the three houses here followed.'

'Where will you be?'

'At the Andersens' place.'

'You think that . . . '

'I don't think anything, old friend! I'll see you later, or tomorrow morning.'

Night had fallen. As he went back to the main road, the inspector made sure that his revolver was loaded and that he had sufficient tobacco.

The moustachioed profile of the insurance agent and the shadow of his armchair were still visible in the Michonnets' upstairs window.

Else Andersen had changed her black velvet dress for the peignoir she had worn that morning and Maigret found her stretched out on the divan, smoking a cigarette, calmer than he had last seen her but frowning thoughtfully.

'If you only knew how relieved I am to know you're here, chief inspector! Some people inspire confidence from the moment you meet them . . . but they are rare. In any case, I personally have met few people with whom I felt an instinctive, sympathetic bond . . . Do smoke, if you like . . . '

'Have you eaten?'

'I'm not hungry. I don't know any more what's keeping me going . . . For four days, from the horrible instant that body was found in the car, I've been thinking, thinking . . . Trying to understand, to make up my mind . . . '

'And you conclude that your brother is the guilty one?'

'No. I do not want to accuse Carl. Especially as, even if he actually were guilty, it would only be due to a moment of uncontrollable madness . . . You've chosen the worst armchair. If you would like to lie down at any point, there is a cot in the next room.'

She was calm and anxious at the same time. A seeming calm, deliberate, painfully achieved. An anxiety that still managed to surface at certain moments.

'Something terrible has already happened in this house, a long time ago, hasn't it? Carl has spoken about it, but only vaguely . . . He was afraid of frightening me. He always treats me like a little girl.'

Her whole body leaned forwards, in a supple movement, as she flicked her cigarette ash into the china bowl on the lacquered table. Her peignoir fell open, as it had that morning, revealing a small, round breast. Only for an instant. And yet Maigret had had time to notice a scar, and he frowned.

'You were wounded some time ago!'

'What do you mean?'

Blushing, she instinctively drew the edges of her peignoir closed over her chest.

'You have a scar on your right breast.'

She was deeply embarrassed.

'Excuse me,' she said. 'I'm used to dressing casually here, I never thought . . . As for that scar . . . There! Another thing I've suddenly recalled, but it's certainly just a coincidence . . . When we were still children, Carl and I used to play on the castle grounds and I remember that one day he was given a rifle, for Saint Nicholas's Day. Carl must have been fourteen . . . It's all so silly, you'll see. At first he shot at a target. After an evening at the circus, the next day he wanted to play at being William Tell. I held out a cardboard target in each hand. The first bullet hit me in the chest.'

Maigret had stood up. He walked over to the divan with a face so impassive that Else grew uneasy as he approached, and she clutched the neck of her peignoir.

But he was not looking at her. He was staring at the wall behind the divan, where the snowy landscape painting was now perfectly level.

Slowly he swung the frame to one side and discovered a niche in the wall, neither large nor deep, where two bricks had been removed. Within the niche were an automatic loaded with six bullets, a box of cartridges, a key and a tube of veronal.

Else had watched his every move but seemed hardly to react at all. A slight rosiness in the cheeks; her eyes a bit more bright . . .

'I would probably have got around to showing you that hiding place myself, chief inspector . . .'

'Really?'

As he spoke he was pocketing the revolver and noting that half the veronal tablets in the tube were gone. He went over to the bedroom door and stuck the key into the lock: it fitted perfectly.

The young woman had risen from the divan. She no longer cared about covering her chest and moved her hands awkwardly and abruptly as she spoke.

'What you just discovered confirms what I've already told you, but you must understand my position! How could I accuse my brother? . . . If I had confessed to you, when you first came here, that I have for a long time now considered him insane, you would have been shocked by my behaviour. And yet, it's the truth . . . '

Her accent, which grew stronger whenever she became emotional, imparted a peculiar quality to every word she said.

'The revolver?'

'How can I explain . . . We left Denmark as paupers, but my brother was convinced that, with his education, he would find a brilliant position in Paris . . . He did not. And became even more distressingly strange. When he resolved to bury us out here, I understood that he was seriously ill. Especially as he insisted on locking me in my bedroom every night under the pretext that enemies might attack us! You can imagine my situation, imprisoned within these walls, unable to escape in case of fire, for example, or any other catastrophe . . . I couldn't sleep! I was as frantic as if I'd been underground in a tunnel . . .

'One day when he was in Paris, I had a locksmith come to make me a key to the bedroom door. Since I was locked in here, I had to climb out of the bedroom window . . .

'Now I could move around freely, but it wasn't enough. There were days when Carl was half mad . . . He often talked about destroying us both to avoid complete ruin.

'I bought a revolver in Arpajon on another day

233

when my brother was in Paris. And as I was sleeping poorly, I got myself some veronal.

'You see how simple it is! He's so distrustful . . . No one is more wary than a deranged man who's still lucid enough to realize that he is disturbed . . . I made this hiding place one night.'

'Is that it?'

She was surprised by his brutal bluntness.

'Don't you believe me?'

Without answering, he went to the window, opened it, then the shutters — and was bathed in the cool freshness of the night.

The road below was like a stream of ink that shone as if by moonlight whenever cars went by. The headlamps would gleam in the distance, perhaps ten kilometres away. Then suddenly there'd be a sort of cyclone, a roaring whoosh of air, a single red tail light fading into the darkness.

The petrol pumps were lit up. In the Michonnets' villa, one light still outlined the silhouette of the insurance agent in his armchair on the pale blind upstairs.

'Close the window, chief inspector!'

Maigret turned around. He saw Else shivering, drawing her peignoir tightly around her.

'Do you understand now why I'm worried? You've persuaded me to tell you everything — but I wouldn't want anything to happen to Carl, not for the world! He's told me many times that we would die together . . . '

'Would you please be quiet!'

He was straining to hear the noises of the night, so he drew his armchair over to the

234

window and put his feet up on the railing.

'But I'm cold, I tell you . . . '

'Put some clothes on!'

'You don't believe me?'

'Be quiet, dammit!'

And he began smoking. Vague sounds came from a distant farm: a lowing cow, shifting, indistinct noises of movement . . . Off in the garage, though, as steel objects were banged about, the electric tyre-pump began vibrating.

'And I trusted you! . . . But now — '

'Once and for all, are you going to be quiet?'

He had spotted a shadow behind a tree by the road, close to the house, and assumed it was one of the inspectors he had requested.

'I'm hungry . . . '

He turned around angrily to face the young woman, who looked pathetic.

'Go and get something to eat!'

'I don't dare go; I'm afraid . . . '

Maigret shrugged, made sure that everything was quiet outside and abruptly decided to go downstairs. He knew his way around the kitchen. Near the stove were some leftover cold meat, bread and part of a bottle of beer.

He took everything upstairs and placed it on the lacquered table, near the cigarette bowl.

'You're being mean to me, chief inspector.'

She looked like such a little girl . . . She seemed about to burst into tears!

'I don't have time to be mean or nice. Eat!'

'You're not hungry? . . . Are you angry that I told you the truth?'

But he was already turning his back on her to

look out of the window. Behind the shade, Madame Michonnet was bending over her husband, probably giving him some medicine, for she was holding a spoon to his face.

Else had picked up a piece of cold veal with her fingertips and now nibbled on it glumly. Then she poured herself a glass of beer.

'It tastes terrible!' she exclaimed, and gasped convulsively. 'But why won't you close that window? I'm scared . . . Don't you ever feel sorry for people?'

Exasperated, Maigret suddenly shut the window and looked over at Else like a man about to lose his temper.

Then he saw her turn white, saw her blue eyes glaze over and her hand reach out for some support . . . He reached her just in time to slip an arm around her waist as she collapsed.

He lowered her gently to the floor, raised her eyelids to check her pupils and sniffed the empty glass, which had an acrid smell.

There was a spoon on the table. He used it to pry Else's jaws open and immediately thrust the spoon into her mouth, repeatedly touching it to her palate and the back of her throat.

Her face twitched a few times. Her chest heaved in spasms.

She was lying on the rug. Tears trickled from beneath her eyelids, and when her head fell to one side, she was shaken by a huge hiccup.

The contractions caused by the spoon were clearing her stomach: a yellowish liquid stained the rug; some drops glistened on her peignoir.

Taking the water pitcher from the dressing

table, Maigret moistened her face.

He kept turning impatiently towards the window.

And Else was taking a long time to come around. She moaned weakly. Finally she raised her head.

'What . . . ?'

She got to her feet, disoriented and still shaky, and saw the spoon, the empty glass, the stained rug.

Then she began sobbing, her head in her hands.

'You see, I was right to be afraid: they've tried to poison me! And you didn't want to believe me . . . You — '

She started at the same instant as Maigret. Both of them froze for a few moments, listening intently.

A shot had been fired near the house, probably in the garden, and been followed by a hoarse cry.

Now a long, shrill whistle was sounding over by the road. People were running. Someone was shaking the front gate. Through the window Maigret could see his inspectors' flashlights searching in the darkness. Not quite a hundred metres away, in the villa's window, Madame Michonnet was settling a pillow behind her husband's head . . .

The inspector opened the bedroom door. He heard noise below.

Then Lucas yelled up the stairs: 'Chief!'

'Who was it?'

'Carl Andersen . . . He isn't dead . . . Are you coming?'

Maigret turned and saw Else sitting hunched on the edge of the divan with her elbows on her knees, staring straight ahead, with her chin cupped in her hands and her jaws clenched. She was shivering uncontrollably.

7

The Two Wounds

Carl Andersen was carried up to his bedroom. An inspector followed, bringing the lamp from the drawing room. The wounded man neither moved nor groaned. Only after he had been laid on his bed did Maigret lean over him and see that his eyes were half open.

Andersen recognized him, seemed somewhat comforted and reached for the inspector's hand, murmuring, 'Else?'

She was standing in the doorway in an attitude of anxious waiting, looking bleakly into the bedroom.

It was a striking tableau. Carl had lost his black monocle, and next to the healthy but blood-shot, half-closed eye, the glass one still stared vacantly.

The glow of the oil lamp made everything seem mysterious. The police could be heard searching the grounds and raking the gravelled paths.

As for Else, when Maigret told her firmly to go over to her brother, she went rigid and hardly dared advance towards him at all.

'I think he's badly wounded,' whispered Lucas.

She must have heard. She looked at him but

hesitated to go any closer to her brother, who gazed at her intently, struggling to sit up in bed.

In a sudden storm of tears, she turned and ran to her own room, where she threw herself, weeping, on to the divan.

Maigret motioned to the sergeant to keep an eye on her and attended to the wounded man, removing Andersen's jacket and waistcoat with the ease of someone familiar with this sort of incident.

'Don't be afraid . . . We've sent for a doctor. Else is in her room.'

Andersen was silent, like someone crushed by some mysterious misgiving. He looked around him as if he were anxious to resolve an enigma or discover a solemn secret.

'Later on I will question you, but — '

Examining the man's bare torso, the inspector frowned.

'You've been shot twice . . . This wound in your back is far from fresh . . . '

And it was a terrible injury: ten square centimetres of skin had been torn away. The flesh was literally cut up, burned, swollen, encrusted with scabs of dried blood. This wound had stopped bleeding, which showed that it was a few hours old, whereas the latest bullet had fractured the left shoulder blade. As Maigret was cleaning the wound, the deformed bullet spilled out of it.

He picked it up. The bullet was not from a revolver, but from a rifle, like the one that had killed Madame Goldberg.

'Where is Else?' murmured the wounded man, who was bearing his pain without grimacing.

'In her room. Don't move . . . Did you see who just shot you?'

'No.'

'And the other shooter? Where was that?'

Andersen frowned, opened his mouth to speak, but gave up, exhausted. With a faint motion of his left arm he tried to explain that he could not talk any more.

★   ★   ★

'Well, doctor?'

It was irritating trying to function in the semi-darkness. There were only two oil lamps in the house, one currently in the wounded man's bedroom, the other in Else's.

Downstairs, one candle burned, without lighting even a quarter of the drawing room.

'Unless there are unexpected complications, he'll pull through. The first wound is the more serious one. He must have received it early in the afternoon, if not late this morning. A bullet from a Browning fired point-blank into the back. Absolutely point-blank! I even think it possible that the muzzle of the weapon was right against the flesh. The victim made a sudden movement, deflecting the shot, so the ribs are basically all that were hit. Bruises on the shoulder, the arms, some scratches on the hands and knees — these must have occurred at the same time . . . '

'And the other bullet?'

'The shoulder blade is shattered. He must be seen to by a surgeon tomorrow. I can give you the address of a clinic in Paris . . . There is one

241

in the area, but if the wounded man can afford it, I recommend Paris.'

'Was he able to get about after the first incident?'

'Probably . . . No vital organ was hit . . . It would have been a question of stamina, of will-power. Although I do fear that he'll have a stiff shoulder for the rest of his life.'

The police had found nothing out in the grounds, but they had taken up positions so as to be ready for a thorough search at first light.

Maigret then went to check on Andersen, who was relieved to see him.

'Else?'

'In her bedroom, I've already told you twice.'

'Why . . . '

Always that morbid anxiety, betrayed by the man's twitching face and by his every glance.

'Do you know of any enemies you might have?'

'No.'

'Don't upset yourself. Simply tell me how you got shot that first time. Go slowly . . . Take it easy . . . '

'I was on my way to Dumas and Son . . . '

'You didn't get there.'

'I tried! At the Porte d'Orléans, a man signalled to me to pull over.'

Andersen asked for some water and drained a large glass, then looked up at the ceiling and continued.

'He told me he was a policeman. He even showed me a card, which I didn't really look at. He ordered me to drive across Paris and take the road to Compiègne, claiming that I was going to be brought face to face with a witness. He got into the passenger seat beside me.'

'What did he look like?'

'Tall, wearing a grey fedora. Shortly before Compiègne, the main road goes through a forest. At a turning, I felt a violent impact on my back . . . A hand grabbed the steering wheel from me while I was pushed out of the car. I lost consciousness. I came to in the roadside ditch. The car was gone.'

'What time was it?'

'Perhaps eleven in the morning . . . I'm not sure. The clock in my car doesn't work. I walked into the forest, to recover from the shock and have time to think. I was having dizzy spells . . . I heard trains going by . . . Finally I came to a small station. By five o'clock I was in Paris, where I got a room. There I took care of myself, brushed off my clothes . . . And I came here.'

'In secret . . . '

'Yes.'

'Why?'

'I don't know.'

'Did you meet anyone?'

'No! I avoided the main road and came in through the grounds . . . Just as I reached the front steps, the shot rang out . . . I'd like to see Else.'

'Do you know that someone has tried to poison her?'

Maigret was completely unprepared for Andersen's reaction to his words. The wounded man sat up all by himself, stared eagerly at the inspector and stammered, 'Really?'

He seemed overjoyed, released from a nightmare.

'Oh! I want to see her!'

Maigret went out into the hall to fetch Else, who was in her room, lying on the divan with empty eyes. Lucas was watching her sullenly.

'Would you come with me?'

'What did he say?'

She was still frightened, uncertain. After taking a few hesitant steps into the wounded man's room, she rushed over and hugged him, talking to him in Danish.

A gloomy Lucas was watching Maigret out of the corner of his eye.

'Can you figure any of this out?'

Instead of replying, the inspector shrugged and began issuing orders.

'Make sure that the garage owner has not left Paris . . . Telephone the Préfecture, have them send out a surgeon first thing in the morning . . . Even tonight, if possible.'

'Where are you going?'

'No idea . . . As for the surveillance around the grounds: keep it up, but don't expect anything.'

Maigret went downstairs, down the front steps, out to the main road, alone. The garage was closed, but the milky-white globes of the pumps were shining.

The light was on upstairs at the Michonnet villa. Behind the shade, the insurance agent's silhouette was still in the same place.

The night was cool. A thin mist was drifting

244

up from the fields, forming into waves about a metre above the ground. From over towards Arpajon came the increasingly loud sounds of an engine and clanking metal; five minutes later, a lorry pulled up at the garage, honking its horn.

A small door opened in the iron security shutter, revealing an electric light bulb burning inside the garage.

'Twenty litres!'

The sleepy mechanic worked the pump; the driver stayed high up in his cab. The chief inspector walked over, his hands in his pockets, his pipe between his teeth.

'Monsieur Oscar not back yet?'

'What? You here? . . . Well, no! When he goes to Paris, he only comes back the next morning.'

A moment's hesitation, then: 'Say, Arthur, you'd best pick up your spare: it's ready . . . '

And the mechanic fetched a wheel with its tyre from the garage, rolling it out and laboriously attaching it to the back of the lorry.

The vehicle drove off. Its red tail light dwindled into the distance. The mechanic yawned and sighed.

'Still looking for the murderer? At this hour? . . . Well, me, if I could just snooze my fill, I swear I wouldn't care one way or the other!'

A bell tower struck two o'clock. A train trailed sparks along the horizon.

'You coming in? . . . Or not?'

And the man stretched, impatient to get back to sleep.

Maigret went inside, looked at the white-washed walls, where red inner tubes and tyres of

245

every brand, most of them in bad shape, were hanging from nails.

'Tell me! What's he going to do with the wheel you gave him?'

'Huh? . . . Why, put it on his lorry, of course!'

'You think so? . . . It'll drive lopsided, his lorry, because that wheel hasn't the same diameter as the others . . . '

The mechanic began to look worried.

'Just a minute now . . . Maybe I mistook the wheel . . . Did I go and give him the one from old man Mathieu's van?'

There was a loud explosion: Maigret had just shot at one of the inner tubes hanging on the wall. And along with the escaping air, small white paper packets came pouring out of the collapsing tube.

'Don't move, you little rat!'

For the mechanic, bent over, was about to run at him head first.

'Watch it, or I'll shoot.'

'What do you want from me?'

'Hands up! . . . Now!'

He stepped smartly over to Jojo, patted his pockets and confiscated a fully loaded revolver.

'Go and lie down on your cot.'

Maigret pushed the door shut with his foot. One look at the mechanic's freckled face was enough to tell him that the fellow would not give up easily.

'Lie down.'

Glancing around, he saw no rope but spotted a coil of electric wire.

'Your hands!'

Realizing that Maigret would have to put down his revolver, the mechanic tensed for action, but got punched right in the face. His nose bled. His lip swelled up. The man growled in rage. Then his hands were tied and soon his feet as well.

'How old are you?'

'Twenty-one.'

'Released from where?'

Silence.

All Maigret had to do was make a fist.

'The reformatory at Montpellier.'

'That's better! And do you know what's in those little packets?'

The reply was a snarl: 'Drugs!'

The mechanic was flexing his muscles, trying to snap the wire bonds.

'What was in the spare tyre?'

'Don't know.'

'Then why did you give it to that driver rather than another?'

'I'm not talking any more!'

'Too bad for you!'

Five inner tubes were punctured one after another, but they did not all contain cocaine. Under a patch that had covered a long slit in one tube, Maigret found silverware stamped with the coronet of a marquis. Another tube held lace and some antique jewellery.

There were ten cars in the garage. Maigret tried to start each engine, but only one would work. So, armed with a monkey wrench backed up by a hammer, he got busy taking apart engines and cutting open petrol tanks.

The mechanic watched him with a mocking smile.

'Can't say we're short on the goods!' he sneered.

The tank in a four-horse-power car was crammed full of bearer bonds worth at least 300,000 francs.

'Is this the haul from the break-in at that big savings and loan company?'

'Could be!'

'And these old coins?'

'Dunno.'

There was more variety than in the back room of a second-hand shop. Everything imaginable: pearls, bank-notes, American currency, official stamps and seals that must have been used to forge passports.

Maigret was unable to search everywhere, but when he tore open the worn-out cushions of a sedan, he found still more: silver florins, which convinced him that everything in that garage was more than met the eye.

A lorry swept past on the main road. Fifteen minutes later, another went by without stopping, and the inspector frowned.

He was beginning to see how the business was run. The garage was a no-account place along the main road, fifty kilometres from Paris, not far from some big provincial cities such as Chartres, Orléans, Le Mans, Châteaudun.

No neighbours, aside from those living in the Three Widows house and the Michonnet villa.

What could they see? A thousand cars going by every day. At least a hundred of them stopped at the petrol pumps. A few would go in for repairs. The garage sold or changed tyres and wheels. Cans of oil and drums of diesel oil came and went.

One detail was especially interesting. Big lorries headed for Paris drove by every evening, delivering vegetables to Les Halles. Later that night or in the morning, they came back empty.

Empty? Weren't they the ones ferrying stolen merchandise in the baskets and crates of produce?

The enterprise could well be a regular, even daily event. A single tyre, the one concealing cocaine, was enough to show the extent of the trafficking, because that drug shipment was worth over 200,000 francs.

What's more, didn't the garage repaint and disguise stolen cars? No witnesses! Monsieur Oscar in the doorway, hands in his pockets. Mechanics working with monkey wrenches or blowtorches. The five red-and-white petrol pumps providing an innocent front . . .

The butcher, the baker, the tourists: didn't they stop by here like everyone else?

A bell rang in the distance. Maigret checked his watch. It was half past three.

'Who's your boss?' he asked, without looking at his prisoner.

The man just smiled.

'You know you'll wind up talking . . . Is it Monsieur Oscar? What's his real name?'

'Oscar!'

The mechanic was practically giggling.

'Did Monsieur Goldberg come here?'

249

'Who's that?'

'You'd know better than I! The Belgian who was murdered . . . '

'No kidding!'

'Whose job was it to knock off the Danish fellow on the Compiègne road?'

'Somebody got knocked off?'

No doubt about it: Maigret's first impression was panning out. He was up against a well-organized professional gang. And he soon had more proof. He heard a car coming, then a screech of brakes as it stopped outside the iron shutter. The horn sounded urgently.

Maigret rushed to the door, but before he could open it, the car sped away so fast he could not even guess its model.

Clenching his fists, he went back to the mechanic.

'How did you warn him off?'

'Me?'

And the fellow chuckled, holding up his wrists in their wire bonds.

'Talk!'

'Must be that it smells fishy here and that driver's got a good nose . . . '

Now Maigret was worried. He overturned the cot roughly, sending Jojo sprawling, and looked for a possible switch for a warning signal outside.

He found nothing under the bed, however. He left the man lying on the floor, went outside and saw the five pumps lit up as usual.

He was beginning to get really angry.

'There's no phone in the garage?'

'Go and take a look!'

250

'You do know you'll talk in the end . . . '

'I can't hear you!'

There was nothing more to be got from Jojo, a perfect example of a confident, experienced criminal. For a quarter of an hour, Maigret walked up and down fifty metres of the main road, searching without success for some possible signal.

The upstairs light at the Michonnet villa had been turned off. Only the Three Widows house was still lit, and the presence of the policemen surrounding the property was discreetly felt.

A limousine barrelled past.

'What kind of car does your boss have?'

To the east, dawn announced itself with a whitish haze that barely cleared the horizon.

Maigret studied the mechanic's hands. They were not touching anything that might have sent a signal.

A current of cool air came in through the little door standing open in the corrugated iron shutter over the garage.

Hearing the sound of an engine, Maigret started to go out to the road, but just as he noticed the approach of an open four-seater touring car, which wasn't doing more than thirty kilometres an hour and seemed about to pull in, the car exploded with gunfire.

Several men were shooting and bullets were rattling against the iron shutter.

Nothing could be seen except the glare of the headlights and the immobile shadows — heads, rather — just showing above the body of the car. Then came the roar of the accelerator . . .

251

Some broken windows . . . on the upper floor of the Three Widows house. The men in the car had kept shooting as they'd gone past.

Maigret had thrown himself flat on the ground and now stood up, his mouth dry, his pipe gone out.

He was certain: Monsieur Oscar had been driving the car that had just plunged back into the darkness.

8

Missing Persons

Before the chief inspector even had time to get out on to the road, a taxi raced up and slammed on its brakes in front of the petrol pumps. A man jumped out — and collided with Maigret.

'Grandjean!' exclaimed the chief inspector.

'Petrol, quick!'

The taxi driver was a nervous wreck, because he'd been speeding at over a hundred kilometres an hour in a car meant to do eighty at most.

Grandjean belonged to the highway patrol; there were two other inspectors in the taxi with him, and each man gripped a revolver in both fists.

The petrol tank was filled with feverish haste.

'How far ahead are they?'

'About five kilometres . . . '

The driver was waiting to take off again.

'You stay here!' Maigret ordered Grandjean. 'The other two will continue on without you.

'Don't take any risks!' he advised them. 'No matter what happens, we've got them. Tail them, that's all . . . '

The taxi set out. A sagging mudguard made a racket all down the road.

'Let's hear it, Grandjean . . . '

And Maigret heard him out, all the while keeping an eye on Jojo and the three houses and listening intently to the noises of the night.

'It was Lucas who telephoned me, told me to watch the owner of this place, Monsieur Oscar . . . I began following him at Porte d'Orléans. They had a big dinner at L'Escargot, where they spoke to no one, then went on to L'Ambigu . . . Until then, nothing to report. At midnight, they come out of the theatre and I see them head for the Chope Saint-Martin . . . You know the place; in the little dining room upstairs, there are always a few tough guys . . . So Monsieur Oscar walks in like he owns the joint. The waiters welcome him, the proprietor shakes his hand, asks him how business is going . . .

'As for the wife, her, she's right at home there too.

'They sit down at a table where there were already three guys and a tart. I recognized one of the guys, he owns a bar somewhere around République. The second had a junkshop, Rue du Temple. As for the third guy, I don't know, but the tart with him has got to be on record with Vice . . .

'They start drinking champagne, having a gay old time. Then they order crayfish, onion soup, what have you, a real blowout, like those people get up to: yelling, slapping their thighs, belting out a little song now and then . . .

'There was one jealous scene, because Monsieur Oscar was cuddling too close to the tart and his wife didn't care for her. That worked out in the end, thanks to a fresh bottle of champagne.

'Time to time, the *patron* came over to have a drink with his customers and he even stood them a round. Then, towards three o'clock, I think, the

254

waiter arrived to say Monsieur Oscar's wanted on the phone.

'When he came back from the booth, he wasn't laughing any more. He gave me a dirty look, because I was the only one there they didn't know. He spoke in a low voice to the others . . . They were in some kind of mess! They pulled the longest faces . . . The girl — I mean Monsieur Oscar's wife — had circles under her eyes and halfway down her cheeks and was drinking like mad to give herself some Dutch courage . . .

'There was only one guy who left with the couple, the fellow I didn't know, some kind of Italian or Spaniard . . .

'While they were saying goodnight and all that I got out ahead of them to the boulevard. I picked a taxi that didn't look too dilapidated and called two inspectors on duty over at Porte Saint-Denis.

'You saw their car . . . Well! They started going like blazes at Boulevard Saint-Michel. They were whistled down at least ten times, never even looked back. We had real trouble following them. The taxi driver — a Russian — claimed I was making him burn out his engine . . . '

'They're the ones who were shooting?'

'Yes!'

After hearing all the gunfire, Lucas had left the Three Widows house and now joined the inspector.

'What's going on?' he asked.

'How's the patient?'

'Weaker. I think he'll make it till morning, though. The surgeon should arrive soon. But what happened here?'

255

Lucas took in the garage's iron shutter, scarred by bullets, and the cot where the mechanic was still tied up with electric wire.

'An organized gang, then, chief?'

'And how!'

Maigret was unusually worried; it was the slight hunching of his shoulders that gave it away. His lips were clamped hard around the stem of his pipe.

'Lucas, you organize the dragnet. Phone Arpajon, Étampes, Chartres, Orléans, Le Mans, Rambouillet . . . You'd best take a look at the map . . . I want every police station on alert! Get the roadblock chains up outside the towns . . . We've got them, this bunch . . . What's Else Andersen doing?'

'I don't know. I left her in her room. She's very depressed.'

'You don't say!' barked Maigret with surprising sarcasm.

They were still standing out in the road.

'Where should I call from?'

'There's a phone in the hall of the garage owner's house. Start with Orléans, because they've probably gone through Étampes by now.'

A light came on in an isolated farmhouse surrounded by fields. The family was getting up. A lantern disappeared around the end of a wall, and then the windows of a stable lit up.

'Five o'clock . . . They're beginning to milk the cows.'

Lucas went off to force open the door of Monsieur Oscar's house with a crowbar from the garage.

As for Grandjean, he followed Maigret around without really understanding what was happening.

'The latest incidents are as clear as day,' grumbled the inspector. 'All we need to find out is what started it all . . .

'Look! Up there is a citizen who sent for me specifically to show me that he couldn't walk. He's been sitting in the same place for hours, without moving a muscle, not one muscle . . .

'Aha! Michonnet's windows are lit up, aren't they! And there I was, just now, looking for the signal! You can't understand the problem now . . . The traffic was going on by without stopping! But all that time, the bedroom window *was completely dark . . .* '

Maigret laughed like someone tickled pink.

And suddenly his colleague saw him pull a revolver from his pocket and aim it at an unbroken upstairs window, at the shadow of a head leaning back in an armchair.

The report was as sharp as a whip-crack. Then came the shattering of the window and a shower of glass shards into the garden.

Yet nothing moved in the bedroom. The shadow was intact behind the linen shade.

'What have you done?'

'Break down the door! . . . No — ring the bell instead! I'd be surprised if someone didn't open up.'

But no one did. The house was completely silent.

'Break it down!'

Grandjean was a big, burly man. He reared

back and threw himself three times at the door, which finally gave way, ripped off its hinges.

'Careful . . . Easy does it . . . '

They each had a weapon out. The first light they turned on was in the dining room. On the table, still sitting on the red check cloth, were dirty dinner dishes and a carafe with some white wine left in it. Maigret finished it off, right from the carafe.

There was nothing in the drawing room. Dust covers on furniture. The musty atmosphere of a room no one ever uses.

A cat was the only creature to run out of the white-tiled kitchen.

Grandjean kept looking uneasily at Maigret. They soon went upstairs to the landing and its three closed doors.

The inspector opened the one to the front bedroom.

The shade was stirring in a draught from the broken window. They saw a ridiculous object leaning against the armchair: a broom with a round turban of rags around the top, which stuck up over the back of the chair so it would look like a head in the shadow seen from outside.

But this sight did not amuse Maigret, who opened a connecting door and turned on the light in the neighbouring bedroom, which was empty.

The third door led to the attic. Apples lay on the floor, about two fingers' width apart from one another, and strings of green beans hung from a beam. There was a bedroom intended for a maid but unused, for it contained nothing but an old night table.

They went back downstairs. Maigret walked through the kitchen and out to the courtyard, which faced east, where the smudged halo of dawn was growing larger.

A small shed . . . A door that moved . . .

'Who's there?' he bellowed, brandishing his revolver.

There was a yelp of fright. No longer held from the inside, the door swung open, revealing a woman who fell to her knees.

'I haven't done anything! . . . I'm sorry! I . . . I . . . '

It was Madame Michonnet, her hair all mussed, her clothing flecked with plaster from the shed.

'Your husband?'

'I don't know! I swear I don't know anything! I'm so miserable, it's not fair . . . '

She was weeping. Her whole plump body seemed to soften and collapse. Her face had aged ten years, puffy from tears, sagging with fear.

'It wasn't me! I didn't do a thing! It's that man, across the way . . . '

'What man?'

'The foreigner . . . I know nothing about it, but he's the one, you can be sure of that! My husband isn't a murderer, or a thief . . . He's been honest all his life . . . It's him — with his bad eye! An evil eye! Ever since he came to the crossroads, everything's been going wrong . . . I . . . '

The chicken run was full of white hens pecking at some fat yellow grains of corn strewn on the ground. The cat was perched on a windowsill, its eyes gleaming in the semi-darkness.

'Stand up.'

'What are you going to do to me? Who fired a gun?'

It was pathetic. She was fifty years old and crying like a child. She was so utterly at a loss that when she got to her feet and Maigret automatically gave her shoulder a little pat, she almost threw herself into his arms, resting her head against his chest, in any case, and clinging to his jacket lapels.

'I'm only a poor woman,' she moaned. 'I've worked all my life! When I got married, I was the cashier in the biggest hotel in Montpellier . . . '

Maigret eased her away from him but couldn't stem her lamentation.

'I should have stayed where I was . . . Because I was a valued employee . . . When I left, I remember that the hotel manager — who thought quite highly of me — told me that one day I would be sorry . . .

'And it's true! I've worked harder than I ever had before . . . '

She broke down again. The sight of her cat brought fresh distress.

'Poor Kitty! You're not to blame for any of this, either! And my hens, my furniture, my little house! . . . Inspector, you know I think I could kill that man if he were right here! I felt it the first day I saw him — just the sight of that black eye of his . . . '

'Where is your husband?'

'How would I know?'

'He went out early yesterday evening, didn't he? As soon as I left here. He wasn't any more laid up than I am . . . '

Stumped for a reply, she looked frantically around as if for help.

'He actually does suffer from gout . . . '

'Has Mademoiselle Else ever been here?'

'Never!' she exclaimed indignantly. 'I won't have such creatures in my home.'

'How about Monsieur Oscar?'

'Have you arrested him?'

'Almost!'

'It would serve him right, too . . . My husband should never have mixed with people who aren't our sort, who have no education. Oh, if only men listened to women! What do you think will happen? Tell me! I keep hearing gunshots . . . If something happens to Michonnet, I believe I'll die of shame! And besides, I'm too old to return to work . . . '

'Get back into the house.'

'What should I do?'

'Have a hot drink and wait. Get some sleep, if you can.'

'Sleep?'

And the word released another flood of frantic tears, which she had to deal with by herself, however, for both men had left.

Maigret went back to the house, though, and unhooked the phone receiver.

'Hello, Arpajon? . . . Police! . . . Would you tell me what numbers were requested during the night by this line?'

He had to wait for a few minutes. At last, the answer came: 'Archives 27-45 . . . It's a big café near Porte Saint-Martin . . . '

261

'I know,' said Maigret. 'Did you have other calls from the Three Widows Crossroads?'

'Just a moment ago, from the garage, requesting various police stations . . . '

'Thanks!'

When Maigret rejoined Inspector Grandjean out on the road, a rain as fine as mist was beginning to fall, yet the sky was brightening to a milky white.

'Can you figure any of this out, chief?'

'I'm getting there . . . '

'That woman is faking it, isn't she?'

'She is perfectly sincere.'

'But . . . her husband . . . '

'Now, him, he's a different story. An honest man gone bad. Or, if you prefer, a crook who was born to be an honest man. There's nothing more complicated than that kind! They stew for hours trying to find a way out of trouble, coming up with incredible plots, playing their parts to perfection . . . Listen, what's still a mystery is what, for instance, made him decide at some point to turn crooked, so to speak. And we still need to find out what in heaven's name he was up to last night.'

And filling his pipe, the inspector went over to the front gate of the Three Widows house. An officer was standing guard.

'Any news?'

'I don't think we've found anything. We've surrounded the grounds. No one's been spotted, though.'

Maigret and Grandjean walked around the house, which was recovering its yellow colour in

262

the half-light, its architectural details just beginning to emerge from the gloom.

The drawing room had not changed at all from Maigret's first visit: the easel still held the sketch of a fabric design with large crimson flowers. Two symmetrical reflections in the shape of an hourglass gleamed on a record on the phonograph. The dawning day was filtering into the room like wisps of fog.

The same step creaked on the staircase. In his room, Carl Andersen had been groaning before the inspector appeared but fell silent when he saw him. Mastering his pain, if not his anxiety, he stammered, 'Where is Else?'

'In her room.'

'Ah!'

Seemingly reassured, he sighed and felt his shoulder, frowning thoughtfully.

'I don't think I'm going to die from this . . . '

It was his glass eye that was most painful to see, because it played no part in the life of his face, remaining separate, clear and wide open while all the facial muscles were moving.

'I'd rather she did not see me like this. Do you think my shoulder will recover? Will a good surgeon be coming?'

Like Madame Michonnet, he was reduced to a child in his anguish. His eyes were pleading. He was asking to be reassured. What seemed to concern him the most, however, was the damage that his injuries might do to his appearance.

On the other hand he was displaying extraordinary will-power, a remarkable capacity for rising above his suffering. Maigret, who had seen his two wounds, knew what he was going through.

'Tell Else . . . '

'You don't want to see her?'

'No. I had better not. But tell her that I am here, that I will recover, that . . . I am perfectly lucid, that she should have confidence, have faith. Repeat that word to her: faith! Tell her to read a few verses in the Bible: the story of Job, for example . . . That makes you smile, because the French don't know the Bible well. Faith! . . . *And I shall always know my own* . . . God is speaking . . . God who knows his own . . . Tell her that! Also: *There will be more joy in heaven over one sinner* . . . She'll understand. And *The just man is tested nine times in a day* . . . '

It was astonishing. Wounded, in pain, bed-ridden under police guard, he was serenely quoting Holy Scripture.

'Faith! You will tell her, won't you? Because the only true example is innocence.'

He scowled. He had caught a fleeting smile on Grandjean's face. And between his teeth, he muttered to himself, '*Franzose!*'

Frenchman . . . In other words, unbeliever! Sceptic, free-thinker, recreant, apostate!

Discouraged, he turned his face to the wall and stared at it with his one good eye.

★ ★ ★

'Tell her . . . '

Except that when Maigret and his colleague pushed open the door of Else's room, no one was there.

A hothouse atmosphere. An opaque cloud of aromatic tobacco smoke. And a feminine presence overwhelming enough to infatuate a schoolboy or even a grown man . . .

But not a living soul! The window was closed: Else had not left that way.

The painting hiding the niche in the wall, the tube of veronal, the key and the revolver was in its place . . .

Maigret slid it to one side. The revolver was missing.

'Stop looking at me like that, dammit!' exclaimed Maigret, glaring angrily at Grandjean, who was standing at his heels, gazing at him in beatific admiration.

Then the inspector bit down on his pipe so hard that he snapped the stem and sent the bowl rolling along the rug.

'She's run off?'

'Shut up!'

He was furious, out of line. Shocked, Grandjean did his best to stand perfectly still.

Day had not yet broken; that grey mist still drifted along the ground but brought no light. The baker's car drove by on the road, an old Ford with front wheels that wobbled along the asphalt.

Suddenly Maigret dashed to the hallway and down the stairs. And at the very moment when he reached the drawing room, where the French windows were standing open to the grounds, there was a ghastly cry, a death cry, the wavering howl of a beast in agony.

It was a woman crying out, her voice half

265

stifled in some mysterious way.

It was far away or quite close by. It could have come from the eaves. It could have come from beneath the ground.

And it spread such anguish that the man on guard at the gate came running up, his face haggard.

'Chief inspector! Did you hear that?'

'Silence, damn it all!' shouted Maigret, at the absolute end of his tether.

Before he'd even finished speaking a shot was fired, but the report was so muffled that no one could tell whether it had come from the left, the right, the grounds, the house, the woods or the road.

Then they heard footsteps on the stairs. Carl Andersen was coming down them, stiffly, a hand clamped to his chest, and he was yelling like a madman, 'It's her!'

He was panting . . . His glass eye never moved. No one could tell at whom he was staring so wildly with the other one.

9

The Lineup

For a few seconds, about as long as it took the last echoes of the shot to die away, nothing happened. They were all waiting for another. Carl Andersen walked outside and over to a gravel path.

It was one of the policemen stationed in the grounds who dashed towards the kitchen garden, in the middle of which stood a raised well topped by a pulley. He leaned over it, but quickly jerked back and blew his whistle.

'Take him away, by force if you have to!' Maigret shouted to Lucas, pointing to the tottering Andersen.

In the thin light of dawn, now everything happened at once.

Lucas signalled to one of his men. The two of them approached the wounded man, spoke with him briefly and, as he would not cooperate, tipped him over and carried him away, struggling and protesting hoarsely.

Meanwhile, Maigret was approaching the well but stopped in his tracks when the policeman yelled, 'Watch out!'

And another bullet whistled through the air as the underground report reverberated in long echoing waves.

'Who's down there?'

'The girl . . . and a man. They're fighting hand to hand . . . '

The inspector went over cautiously, but could see almost nothing down the well.

'Your flashlight . . . '

He had time to get only the briefest impression of what was happening before a bullet almost hit the flashlight.

The man was Michonnet. The well was not deep. It was wide, however, and completely dry.

There were two of them down there, locked in a struggle. As far as Maigret could tell, the insurance agent had a hand around Else's throat as if to strangle her. She had a revolver in one fist, but Michonnet's other hand was around hers, controlling where the gun was aimed.

'What are we going to do?' asked the appalled policeman.

They could hear occasional groans; it was Else, suffocating, battling ferociously.

'Michonnet, give yourself up!' Maigret called out clearly, as a matter of form.

Without a word the other man fired the revolver into the air, and the inspector did not hesitate any longer. The well was three metres deep. Maigret suddenly jumped in, landing literally on Michonnet's back and pinning down one of Else's legs as well.

It was total chaos. One more shot went off, grazing the wall of the well before vanishing into the blue, while Maigret punched Michonnet's skull with both fists, just to be on the safe side. At the fourth blow, the man looked at him like a wounded animal, staggered and fell backwards with a black eye and dislocated jaw.

Else, who was holding her throat with both hands, was gasping for breath.

It was both tragic and absurd, this battle in the murky light at the bottom of a well smelling of saltpetre and slime.

The epilogue was even more absurd: Michonnet was hauled up by the pulley rope, limp and groaning; Else, whom Maigret held up to the policeman, was filthy, her black velvet dress blotched with big smears of greenish moss.

Neither she nor her adversary had completely lost consciousness. They were exhausted and sore, however, like clowns after a fake boxing match who lie collapsed in a disheartened heap together, still swinging feebly at nothing.

Maigret had picked up the revolver. It was Else's, the one taken from the niche in her bedroom. There was one bullet left.

Arriving from the house, Lucas looked worried and sighed as he took in the scene.

'I had to tie him to his bed.'

The policeman had moistened a handkerchief with water and was dabbing the girl's forehead.

'And where'd these two come from?' the sergeant continued.

Suddenly Michonnet, despite not having even enough strength left to stand up, threw himself at Else, his face convulsed with fury. He never reached her, for Maigret gave him a kick that sent him tumbling a good two metres away.

'That's enough of this farce!' he bellowed.

Then he laughed almost to tears, the look on

Michonnet's face was so funny. He was like one of those infuriated kids you carry off under your arm, spanking them as you go, yet they keep wriggling, howling, crying, lashing out and trying to bite, refusing to accept that they're helpless.

For Michonnet was crying! Crying and grimacing miserably! He was even shaking his fist!

Else was finally back on her feet, rubbing her hand over her forehead.

'I really thought I was done for,' she sighed, smiling weakly. 'He was squeezing so hard . . . '

One cheek was black with dirt and there was mud in her tangled hair. Maigret wasn't much more presentable.

'What were you doing in the well?' he asked.

She looked at him sharply. Her smile vanished. In a single moment, she seemed to have recovered all her sangfroid.

'Answer me.'

'I . . . I was taken there by force . . . '

'By Michonnet?'

'That's not true!' screamed the man.

'It is true. He tried to strangle me . . . I think he's insane.'

'She's lying! She's the one who's insane! Or rather, she's . . . '

'She's what?'

'I don't know! She's . . . She's a viper whose head should be crushed on a stone!'

Meanwhile, dawn had broken. Birds were twittering in all the trees.

'Why did you take your revolver?' Maigret asked Else.

270

'Because I was afraid of a trap . . . '

'What trap? Hold on a minute! One thing at a time. You just said that you were attacked and put into the well.'

'She's lying!' repeated Michonnet, gulping convulsively.

'Then show me,' Maigret went on, 'where this attack took place.'

Looking around her, Else pointed over to the front steps.

'It was there? And you didn't scream?'

'I couldn't . . . '

'And this scrawny little fellow managed to carry you all the way over to the well, lugging fifty-five kilos?'

'Yes, it's true.'

'She's lying!'

'Make him be quiet!' she said wearily. 'Don't you see he's crazy? And has been for a while, too.'

They had to restrain Michonnet, who was about to go after her again.

They formed a small group in the kitchen garden: Maigret, Lucas, two inspectors, all looking at the insurance agent with the swollen face and Else, who even while talking had been trying to clean herself up.

For some strange reason, this entire episode had not risen to the level of tragedy, or even drama. It was more like buffoonery.

The feeble morning light might well have had something to do with it. And perhaps everyone's fatigue, even their hunger.

Things got worse when they saw a simple soul walking hesitantly down the road, a woman who

271

peered through the bars of the front gate, finally opened it and caught sight of Michonnet.

'Émile!' she exclaimed.

It was Madame Michonnet, more bewildered than distressed, who now pulled a hankie from her pocket and burst out crying.

'It's that woman again!'

She looked like someone's good old mother, battered by events and falling back on the soothing bitterness of tears.

Maigret noticed with amusement how Else's face seemed to come into tight focus as she looked at everyone around her in turn. A pretty face, delicate, gone suddenly sharp-featured and tense.

'What were you planning on doing in the well?' he asked cheerfully, as if he were saying, 'Enough of this! Admit it, there's no point in pretending any more.'

She understood. Gave him an ironic smile.

'I think we're done for,' she conceded. 'Only, I'm hungry, I'm thirsty, I'm cold and I'd really like to clean myself up a bit. And then we'll see . . . '

She wasn't playing a part. On the contrary, she was admirably to the point.

All alone in the middle of the group, she was relaxed, watching the pitiful Michonnet and his weeping wife with an amused air, and when she turned to Maigret her eyes said, 'Poor things! Us, we're two of a kind, aren't we! We'll talk later. You've won . . . but admit it: I put on quite a show!'

No fear, no embarrassment, either. No theatrics at all.

It was the real Else at last — and she was enjoying this moment of truth.

'Come along with me,' said Maigret. 'Lucas, you take care of the other one . . . As for his wife, she can go home or stay here, either way.'

★ ★ ★

'Come in! You're not disturbing me . . . '

It was the same room, up there, with the black divan, the insistent perfume, the hiding place behind the water-colour. It was the same woman.

'Carl is well guarded, at least?' she asked, jerking her chin towards his room. 'Because he'd be even harder to control than Michonnet! . . . You may smoke your pipe.'

She poured some water into the basin, calmly pulled off her dress as if that were the most natural thing in the world, and stood there in her slip, without any fuss or provocation.

Maigret recalled his first visit to the Three Widows house, when Else had been as enigmatic and distant as a cinema vamp, and he remembered the disturbing, enervating atmosphere with which she could surround herself.

Had she played her part well, the alluring, wilful young thing who talked about her parents' castle, the nannies and governesses, her father's strict principles?

Well, that was yesterday! One gesture was more eloquent than any words: the way she'd stripped off her dress and was now looking at herself in the mirror before washing her face.

The classic tart, earthy, vulgar and sly.

'Admit that you fell for it!'

'Not for long!'

She wiped her face with a corner of the Turkish towel.

'Sure! . . . Just yesterday, when you were here and I flashed you a peek at one breast, your mouth was dry and your forehead sweaty, like the nice fat old fellow you are. That won't work with you now, of course. Even though I haven't lost any of my looks . . . '

She threw out her chest and happily admired her lithe and barely clad figure.

'Between us, what tipped you off? I made a mistake?'

'Several.'

'Such as?'

'Talking a mite too much about the castle and the grounds . . . When you really live in a castle, you usually call it the house, for example.'

She had pulled aside the curtain of a wardrobe and was studying her dresses.

'You'll be taking me to Paris, naturally! And there will be photographers there . . . What do you think of this green dress?'

She held it up to herself to judge the effect.

'No: black is still my best colour . . . Will you give me a light?'

She laughed, for, in spite of everything, Maigret was slightly affected by the subtle eroticism she managed to instil in the atmosphere, especially when she went over for him to light her cigarette.

'Well! Time to get dressed . . . The whole thing's a scream, don't you think?'

274

Her accent made even common slang sound strangely appealing . . .

'How long have you been Carl Andersen's mistress?'

'I am not his mistress. I am his wife.'

She ran a mascara wand along her eyelashes, freshened the pink in her cheeks.

'Were you married in Denmark?'

'You see, you still don't know a thing! And don't count on me to talk, I'm no snitch . . . Anyway, you won't hold me for long. How soon after I'm arrested do I get booked?'

'Right away.'

'Too bad for you! Because they'll find out that my real name is Bertha Krull and that for just over three years now the Copenhagen police have had a warrant out for my arrest. The Danish government will ask for extradition . . . There! I'm ready. Now, if you'll allow me, I'd like a bite to eat . . . Don't you think it smells musty in here?'

She went over to open the window, then came back to the door. Maigret left the bedroom first. She then slammed the door shut, slid the bolt, and he could hear her running to the window.

Had Maigret been ten kilos lighter, she would probably have got away. The bolt had only just gone home when, without losing a second, he hurled himself full tilt against the door.

And it gave way at once, falling flat with its lock and hinges ripped off.

Else was sitting astride the window-sill. She hesitated . . .

'Too late!' he said.

She turned around, breathing a touch heavily, her forehead slightly damp.

'I don't know why I bothered to dress myself up!' she remarked sarcastically, pointing out a tear in her dress.

'Will you promise me you won't try again to escape?'

'No!'

'In that case, I warn you that I will shoot at the slightest false move.'

And he kept his revolver in his hand from then on.

'Do you think he'll make it?' she asked as they passed Carl's door. 'He's got two bullets in him, hasn't he?'

He looked at her and although at that moment he would have been hard put to read her mind, he thought he detected in her face and voice a mixture of pity and resentment.

'It's his fault too!' she decided, as if to set her conscience at rest. 'I only hope there's still something to eat in the house . . . '

Maigret followed her into the kitchen, where she searched the cupboards and finally unearthed a tin of rock lobster.

'Won't you open it for me? . . . Don't worry, I promise I won't take advantage and make a run for it.'

There was a strangely companionable feeling between the two of them that Maigret rather enjoyed. There was even something intimate in their relationship, and the faintest undercurrent of possibilities.

She was having fun with this big, placid man

who had bested her but whom she knew she was impressing with her dash and daring. As for him, he was savouring this most unusual familiarity perhaps a little too much.

'Here you are . . . Eat quickly.'

'We're leaving already?'

'I've no idea.'

'Just between us . . . Exactly what have you found out?'

'Doesn't matter.'

'Are you carting off Michonnet as well, that idiot? Still, he's the one who scared me the most . . . Back in the well I really thought I'd had it. His eyes were bulging out of his head . . . He was squeezing my throat with everything he had.'

'Were you his mistress?'

She shrugged, the kind of girl for whom such details have almost no importance.

'And Monsieur Oscar?' he added.

'What about him?'

'Another lover?'

'You'll have to find all that out by yourself. Me, I know exactly what's waiting for me. I've got five years to do in Denmark: accessory to armed robbery and resisting arrest. That's when I caught this bullet.'

And she pointed to her right breast.

'As for the rest, this lot here will cope on their own!'

'Where did you meet Isaac Goldberg?'

'I've got nothing to say.'

'You'll have to talk at some point . . . '

'And just how do you think you can make me?'

She was answering while eating some rock lobster without any bread, because there was none left in the kitchen. They could hear a policeman walking up and down in the drawing room while he kept an eye on Michonnet, slumped in an armchair.

Two cars pulled up at the same time outside the front gate, which was opened to allow them to come up the drive and around to the front steps.

In the first car sat an inspector, two gendarmes, Monsieur Oscar and his wife.

The other car was the taxi from Paris, in which an inspector was guarding a third person.

The three prisoners were wearing handcuffs, but they kept up a good front, except for the garage owner's wife, whose eyes were red.

Maigret took Else into the drawing room, where Michonnet tried yet again to rush towards her.

The prisoners were brought inside. Monsieur Oscar behaved almost as casually as an ordinary visitor, but he did wince when he saw Else and Michonnet. The other man, who might have been an Italian, decided to brazen it out.

'Great! A family reunion! Are we having a wedding, or reading a will?'

'Luckily, we brought them in without any trouble,' the officer explained to Maigret. 'On the way through Étampes, we picked up two gendarmes who had been informed of the situation and seen the car go past without being able to stop it. Fifty kilometres from Orléans the fugitives had a flat tyre, halted in the middle of the road and trained

278

their revolvers on us . . . The garage owner was the first one to think better of it — otherwise we'd have had quite a gun battle.

'We started towards them; the Italian did fire at us twice with his Browning, but missed.'

'Well, now,' observed Monsieur Oscar. 'In my house, I served you a drink, so allow me to point out that it's rather parched around here . . . '

Maigret had had the mechanic fetched from the garage and seemed to be counting heads.

'All of you go and line up against the wall!' he ordered. 'At the other end, Michonnet . . . No use trying to get near Else.'

The little man glared at him and went to stand at the end of the line, with his drooping moustache and his eye still swelling from all those punches.

Next came the mechanic, whose wrists were still bound by the electric wire. Then the garage owner's wife, thin and woebegone, and the garage owner himself, who was much annoyed at being unable to put his hands into the pockets of his baggy trousers. Finally, Else and the Italian, who must have been the ladies' man of the gang and had a naked woman tattooed on the back of one hand.

Maigret looked them over slowly, one by one, with a satisfied little smile, then filled his spare pipe, strode over to the front steps to open the French windows and called out, 'Take their surnames, given names, occupations and addresses, Lucas . . . Let me know when you're done.'

The six of them stood all lined up. Pointing to Else, Lucas asked, 'Should I cuff her as well?'

'Why not?'

At which Else responded hotly, 'That's really rotten of you, inspector!'

The grounds were brimming with sunshine. Thousands of birds were singing. On the horizon, the weathercock of a little village church steeple was glistening as if it were solid gold.

10

Looking for a Head

When Maigret returned to the drawing room, where the wide-open French windows were welcoming the spring air, Lucas was wrapping up his interrogation in an atmosphere not unlike that of a barrack room.

The prisoners were still lined up against a wall, albeit in a less orderly fashion. And at least three of them were acting distinctly unimpressed by their police captors: the garage owner, his mechanic Jojo and the Italian Guido Ferrari.

Monsieur Oscar was dictating to Lucas.

'Occupation: garage proprietor and mechanic. Add on former professional boxer, licensed in 1920. Middleweight champion of Paris in 1922 . . . '

Some officers brought in two new recruits: garage employees who'd just shown up as usual for work. They were placed in the lineup with the others. One of them, who had the mug of a gorilla, simply drawled, 'That's it? We're busted?'

They were all talking at once, like children when their teacher is out of the room. They nudged one another with their elbows and cracked jokes.

Only Michonnet still presented a sorry sight, hunched over and glowering at the floor.

As for Else, she watched Maigret almost as if

281

he were her accomplice. Hadn't they understood each other remarkably well? Whenever Monsieur Oscar made a bad pun, she smiled discreetly at the inspector.

As far as she was concerned, she was a cut above all this.

'Let's have some silence, now!' thundered Maigret.

But at that same moment, a small sedan drew up at the front steps. The driver was well dressed and carried a leather instrument case under his arm with an air of importance. He came briskly up the steps only to stare in astonishment at the row of suspects that suddenly confronted him.

'The patient?'

'Would you take care of this, Lucas?'

It was an eminent surgeon from Paris, called in to attend to Carl Andersen. He went off with a worried look while the sergeant led the way.

'D'ja catch the look on that doc's kisser?'

Only Else had frowned, and her eyes had gone a little less blue . . .

'I called for silence!' said Maigret clearly. 'Save the wisecracks for later. What you seem to be forgetting is that at least one of you looks likely to pay for this with his head.'

And he looked slowly up and down the line. His speech had produced the desired effect.

The sun was the same; there was spring in the air. The birds kept on chirping in the trees and the shade from the foliage still trembled on the gravel path.

In the drawing room, though, one felt that mouths had gone drier, that cheekiness was draining away . . .

Still, Michonnet was the only one who moaned, and so unwittingly that he was himself the most surprised of all and turned his head aside, embarrassed.

'I can see you've understood!' continued Maigret, beginning to pace the room with his hands behind his back. 'We'll try to save time. If we're unsuccessful here, we'll keep going at Quai des Orfèvres . . . You must know the place, right? Good! . . . First crime: Isaac Goldberg is shot at point-blank range. Who brought Goldberg to the Three Widows Crossroads?'

They were silent, all looking at one another with no love lost, while over their heads the surgeon could be heard moving around.

'I'm waiting! I repeat: we'll continue this at police headquarters — and there, you'll be grilled one by one . . . Goldberg was in Antwerp. There was about two million in diamonds to unload . . . Who got the ball rolling?'

'I did!' said Else. 'I'd met Goldberg in Copenhagen. I knew stolen jewels were his specialty. When I read about the burglary in London and the papers said the diamonds had to be in Antwerp, I assumed Goldberg was in on it. I talked to Oscar about it . . . '

'Thanks a lot!' muttered the garage owner.

'Who wrote the letter to Goldberg?'

'She did.'

'Let's keep going . . . He arrives during the night. Who's at the garage at that point? . . . And most importantly, whose job is it to kill him?'

Silence. The sound of Lucas coming downstairs to speak to an officer.

283

'Hop it to Arpajon,' he told the officer, 'and bring back the first doctor you can find to help the professor, along with some camphorated oil. Got that?'

Lucas headed back upstairs while Maigret, his brow furrowed, studied his flock.

'We'll jump back a little in time . . . I think that will be simpler. You: when did you become a fence?'

He was looking hard at the garage owner, who seemed to find this question less prickly than the previous ones.

'That's it! Now you're talking! You admit yourself that I'm nothing but a fence. And maybe not even that . . . '

He was an incredible ham. He looked from one to another of the others, trying to make them smile.

'My wife and I, we're practically honest folks. Right, honey? . . . It's quite simple: I was a boxer. I lost my title in 1925 — and all I got offered was a job at the Foire du Throne fairgrounds in Paris! Not nearly enough for me. We had some friends who were legit and some who weren't. One guy — he was arrested two years later — was raking it in at the time, selling stuff he'd got on credit.

'I thought I'd try that, but since I'd been a mechanic when I was younger, I decided to start with garages, thinking I'd get my hands on cars, tyres, spare parts, sell it all on the quiet and clear off. I was counting on making 400,000 or so!

'Trouble was, I was late out of the gate. The big places were thinking twice before letting the goods leave home on credit.

'I got brought a stolen car to freshen up . . . A guy I'd met in a bar near the Bastille. You can't imagine how easy it is!

'Word got around in Paris. I was in a cushy spot, seeing as I'd hardly any neighbours. I turned ten or twenty cars around . . . Then one turned up, I can still see it today: full of silverware stolen from a villa around Bougival. We squirrelled that lot away, got in touch with second-hand dealers in Étampes, Orléans and even farther away.

'We got used to this routine . . . A sweet racket . . .

'Has he found out about the tyres yet?' he asked, turning towards Jojo, who sighed.

'He sure has . . . '

'You know how wacky you look with your electric wire? Add a plug and you'd be a blinking lamp!'

Maigret cut him off.

'Isaac Goldberg arrived in his own car, a Minerva. There was a welcoming party, because the idea wasn't to buy his diamonds, even on the cheap, but to steal them. And to do that you had to bump him off. So there was a bunch of you in the garage, that's to say in the house behind it . . . '

Absolute silence. This was the sore spot. Once again Maigret looked them all in the face one by one . . . and saw a few drops of sweat on the Italian's forehead.

'You're the killer, right?'

'No! It's . . . It's . . . '

'Who?'

'It's them, it's . . . '

'He's lying!' yelled Monsieur Oscar.

'Who got the nod?'

Shrugging cockily, the garage owner said, 'The guy upstairs, so there!'

'Say that again!'

'The guy upstairs!'

But he didn't sound as sure of himself this time around.

'Else, come over here!'

Maigret pointed to Else, with the confidence of a conductor with the most diverse instruments at his command who knows his motley orchestra will still perform in perfect harmony.

'You were born in Copenhagen?'

'If you keep using my name, chief inspector, everyone will think we slept together . . . '

'Answer me.'

'Hamburg!'

'What was your father's occupation?'

'Docker.'

'He's still alive?'

Her whole body shuddered. She looked at her companions with a sort of uneasy pride.

'They cut his head off, in Düsseldorf.'

'Your mother?'

'A drunk.'

'What were you doing in Copenhagen?'

'I was a sailor's girl. Hans! A handsome fellow I'd met in Hamburg. He took me along with him. He belonged to a gang. One day we decided to knock over a bank, had it all set up. We were supposed to get millions in a single night. I was the lookout . . . But someone snitched on us, because just when the men started in on the

286

safes, the cops surrounded us.

'It was at night, you couldn't see a thing . . . We were scattered . . . There were shots; people yelling, chasing us. I got hit in the chest and began to run. Two policemen grabbed me. I bit one of them, kicked the other in the stomach and he let me go . . .

'But I was still being chased. And then I saw a wall: I hauled myself up . . . I literally fell off the other side and when I came to there was a tall young man, very chic, upper-class, looking at me with bewilderment and pity . . . '

'Andersen?'

'That isn't his real name. He'll tell you *that* only if it suits him to. It's a well-known name . . . They're people with entrée to the royal court, who spend half the year in one of the most lovely castles in Denmark and the other half in a great mansion with grounds as large as an entire city neighbourhood.'

An officer arrived accompanied by a short, flushed, pop-eyed man. It was the doctor requested by the surgeon. He stopped short before the strange gathering, especially at the sight of handcuffs on almost everyone's hands, but he was hustled on up to the first floor.

'After that . . . '

Monsieur Oscar snickered. Else gave him a fierce, almost venomous look.

'They can't understand,' she murmured. 'Carl hid me in his parents' mansion and took care of me himself, with a friend who was studying medicine. He had already lost an eye in that plane crash. He wore a black monocle . . . I think

287

he considered himself permanently disfigured. He was convinced that no woman could love him, that whenever he had to remove his black eyeglass, revealing his sewn-up eyelid and fake eye, he would become repulsive . . . '

'Did he love you?'

'It wasn't exactly that. I didn't understand at first . . . and they,' she added, pointing to her accomplices, 'will never understand. It was a Protestant family. Carl's first impulse was to save a soul, as he put it . . . He made long speeches, read me chapters from the Bible. Yet at the same time, Carl was afraid of his parents. Then one day, when I was almost well again, he suddenly kissed me on the mouth — and ran away. I didn't see him for almost a week. Well, I was able to watch him from the dormer window of a servant's room where I was kept hidden . . . He walked for hours in the garden with his head hanging, visibly unhappy.'

Monsieur Oscar was actually slapping his thighs in delight.

'It's just like a novel!' he exclaimed. 'Keep going, honey-bunch!'

'That's all there is . . . When he came to see me again he said he wanted to marry me, that he couldn't do that in his country, that we were going abroad . . . He claimed that he had understood at last what life was all about, that he had found his reason for living and would no longer be a useless human being . . . And stuff like that . . . '

Her voice was becoming more common again.

'We got married in Holland under the name of

Andersen. I was enjoying myself. I think I even fell for his fairy tale, too. He would tell me the most amazing things . . . He made me dress like this, like that, learn table manners, ditch my accent . . . He had me read books. We used to visit museums.'

'How about that, my angel!' Monsieur Oscar exclaimed to his wife. 'When we're sprung from the big house, we'll go and visit museums too, won't we? And hold hands, making sheep's eyes at the Mona Lisa . . . '

'We came to live out here,' Else went on quickly, 'because Carl was always afraid of running into one of my old accomplices. He had to work because he'd renounced his parents' fortune. As a precaution, he passed me off as his sister, but he still worried . . . Whenever anyone rang at the front gate it made him jump, because Hans managed to escape from prison and no one knows what happened to him . . . Carl loves me, that's for sure.'

'And yet . . . ' said Maigret thoughtfully.

'I'd like to see what you'd have done here!' snapped Else. 'Alone, always alone! With nothing but talk about goodness, beauty, the salvation of the soul, human destiny and being worthy of the Lord . . . And those lessons in deportment! And when he went anywhere he locked me in, supposedly to save me from temptation. The truth is he was ferociously possessive . . . and passionate, too!'

'Now no one can say I don't know a good thing when I see it!' crowed Monsieur Oscar.

'And what did you do?' Maigret asked him.

'I spotted her, for God's sake! It was easy: I could tell she was putting on all those fancy manners. For a while I even wondered if the Danish fellow wasn't a fake as well. But I didn't trust him. I preferred to sniff around the tart . . . Oh, now honey, don't get upset, you know I've always come back to you in the end! The other stuff is just business. Anyway, I used to prowl around that dump when ol' One-Eye wasn't there. We started talking one day, her at the window, being as the bird was in a cage. She saw right away how matters stood. I tossed her a ball of wax to take an impression of her lock . . . The next month we met at the far end of the grounds to talk shop. No magic needed! She was sick of that blue-blood of hers . . . She had a hankering for her old life is all!'

'And since then,' said Maigret slowly to Else, 'you've been regularly slipping veronal into Carl Andersen's food at night?'

'Yes . . . '

'And you would go to meet Oscar?'

The garage owner's wife had red eyes but was holding back her tears.

'They deceived me, chief inspector! At first my husband told me she was just a pal, that rescuing her from that hole was really a good deed! Then he used to take us both for evenings out in Paris, we'd have wild times with our friends . . . I never suspected a thing until the day I . . . found them . . . '

'And so what? All men aren't monks . . . She was wasting away, poor dear.'

Else was quiet. There was a sad look in her

290

eyes, and she seemed uneasy.

Suddenly Lucas came back downstairs.

'Are there any methylated spirits in the house?'

'What for?'

'To disinfect the instruments.'

It was Else who rushed to the kitchen and looked through all the bottles.

'I found it! . . . Are they going to save him? Is he in any pain?'

'Filthy bitch!' growled Michonnet, who had been dead to the world since the beginning of this interrogation.

Looking Michonnet straight in the eye, Maigret asked the garage owner, 'And this one?'

'You haven't figured that out yet?'

'Just about . . . There are three houses at the crossroads. Every night was suspiciously full of comings and goings: the vegetable lorries, coming back unloaded from Paris, were bringing in the stolen goods. The Three Widows house posed no threat, but the villa . . . '

'Not to mention that we needed someone respectable to sell certain items out in the countryside.'

'So Else was assigned to rope in Michonnet?'

'Why waste a pretty girl? He was swept off his feet! She brought him along one night and we reeled him in with champagne. Another time we took him to Paris for one of our best blow-outs, while his wife thought he was off on a tour of inspection. He was done for! Take it or leave it, we told him. The best part was that he thought she'd fallen for him and he turned as jealous as a schoolboy. Isn't that the limit? And him with the mug of a department store cashier!'

There was some kind of noise upstairs and Maigret saw Else go dead white. From then on she ignored the interrogation and listened intently to the proceedings overhead.

They heard the surgeon's voice.

'Hold him . . . '

Outside, two sparrows were hopping around on the white gravel path.

Filling a pipe, Maigret reviewed the prisoners once again.

'Now all we need to know is, who the killer was . . . Quiet!'

'In my case, for fencing, I shouldn't get more than — '

The inspector silenced Monsieur Oscar with an impatient glare.

'Else learns from the papers that the jewellery stolen in London and valued at two million must be in the possession of Isaac Goldberg, whom she met when she belonged to the gang in Copenhagen. She writes to him to set up a meeting at the garage, with a promise to purchase the diamonds at a good price . . . Goldberg, who remembers her from before, does not suspect trouble and arrives in his car.

'Champagne is served, in the house . . . Reinforcements have been called in — in other words, you are all there. The problem is getting rid of the corpse, once the murder has been committed . . .

'Michonnet must be nervous, because, for the first time, he'll be involved in a real crime . . . But he is probably given more champagne than the others.

'Oscar's probably for dumping the body in a ditch someplace far away.

'It's Else who comes up with an idea . . . Quiet! . . . She's had enough of living locked in during the day and having to hide at night. She's had enough of the speeches about virtue, goodness and beauty! She's also had enough of her boring life, and of counting each sou . . .

'She's come to hate Carl Andersen. But she knows he loves her enough to kill her rather than lose her.

'She's drinking! She's flying high! She has a bold, exciting idea: to pin the crime on Carl! On Carl, who is so blinded by love that he will never even suspect her.

'Isn't that so, Else?'

For the first time, she turned her head away.

'The Minerva, disguised by Oscar's crew, will be sent far away to be sold or abandoned. The real culprits must be placed beyond suspicion. And Michonnet is the most afraid! His car will therefore be 'stolen', which is the best way to camouflage him. He'll be the one to complain first to the police, fretting about the disappearance of his six-cylinder car. But the police must also go looking for the corpse over at Carl's place. And that's when someone has the bright idea of switching the cars.

'The corpse is installed at the wheel of Michonnet's car. Andersen, as usual, has been drugged and is fast asleep. The car is driven into his garage. The little jalopy is placed inside Michonnet's.

'The police will be flummoxed! And even

better, this aloof Danish fellow passes among the locals for half mad . . . The country folk are spooked by his black monocle.

'Suspicion will fall on him! And everything about this case is so bizarre that it will fit his appearance and reputation like a glove. Besides, after his arrest, won't he kill himself to avoid the scandal that might reflect upon his family if his true identity were ever discovered?'

The little doctor from Arpajon poked his head around the half-open door.

'Another man, to hold him . . . We're having trouble putting him to sleep . . . '

The doctor was flushed, impatient. There was an officer out in the garden.

'You go!' Maigret shouted to him.

And at that same moment received an unexpected blow to the chest.

11

Else

It was Else, who had flung herself on him, sobbing convulsively, pleading with him.

'I don't want him to die!' she stammered. 'Please! . . . I . . . This is awful . . . '

The moment was so gripping and she seemed so truly sincere that the others, those sinister men lined up against the wall, neither sneered nor even smiled.

'Let me go upstairs! I'm begging you! You can't understand . . . '

But Maigret pushed her aside! She went to collapse on the dark divan where he'd seen her that first time, an enigmatic figure in her high-necked black velvet dress.

'I'm nearly done! . . . Michonnet played his part perfectly. And all the more believably in that he had to act like a ridiculous little fellow caught up in a bloody crime who thinks only of his car. The police investigation begins; Carl Andersen is arrested. And it just so happens that he does not commit suicide and is even released.

'Not for a moment has he suspected his wife. He will never suspect her. He would defend her even against all evidence.

'But now we learn that Madame Goldberg, who might know and reveal who drew her husband into this trap, is coming here.

'The same man who shot the diamond merchant lies in wait for her . . . '

The chief inspector looked at his audience one by one, then pressed on as if in a hurry to be done with it.

'The murderer has put on Carl's shoes, which will be found here covered in mud from the field . . . That's overdoing things! But Carl must be found guilty or else the real murderers will soon be unmasked. Now panic sets in.

'Andersen has to go to Paris because he needs money. The same man who committed the first two crimes waits for him along his route and, posing as a policeman, gets into his car beside him.

'It isn't Else who came up with that . . . I have the feeling it's Oscar.

'Does he talk to Andersen about escorting him to the border, or confronting him with some witness in a town up north?

'Andersen is made to drive across Paris. The Compiègne road goes through dense woods. The murderer shoots, again at point-blank range. No doubt he hears another car behind them . . . and in a rush he pushes the body out into the roadside ditch. On the way back he'll conceal the body more carefully.

'The immediate concern is to divert all suspicion. That's been done. Andersen's car is abandoned a few hundred metres from the Belgian border.

'The police naturally conclude that — he fled the country! So he is guilty . . .

'The murderer returns with another car. The victim is no longer in the ditch and there are tracks suggesting that he isn't dead.

'The man assigned to this murder telephones Monsieur Oscar from Paris: he refuses to come anywhere near this area again, it's too full of cops.

'Carl's devotion to his wife is now common knowledge. If he's alive, he'll come back. If he comes back, he might talk . . .

'They have to finish the job. No one feels up to it. Monsieur Oscar doesn't like to get his hands dirty . . .

'Isn't this the moment to use up Michonnet? The man who has sacrificed everything to his love for Else and can be set up to take the last fall?

'The plan is carefully crafted. Monsieur Oscar and his wife go off to Paris, very publicly, describing their intentions in detail.

'Monsieur Michonnet sends for me and shows that he is immobilized in his armchair by gout.

'He has probably read some crime novels. He uses tricks now, just as he does in his insurance dealings. I've hardly left the house when a broomstick and ball of rags have replaced him in the chair — and this stage setting works. From outside, the illusion is flawless . . . And Madame Michonnet, terrorized, agrees to play along by pretending, behind the shade, to take care of the invalid.

'She knows there is a woman involved, and she is jealous, too. But she wants to save her husband in spite of everything because she still hopes he'll come back to her.

'She's not mistaken: Michonnet has sensed

that he's been played for a fool. He no longer knows if he loves or hates Else, but he does know that he wants her dead.

'He knows the house, the grounds, all the ways in or out . . . Perhaps he knows that Else usually drinks some beer in the evening.

'He leaves a poisoned bottle open in the kitchen. He lies in wait outdoors for Carl's return.

'He fires at him . . . He is near collapse. There are policemen everywhere. He winds up hiding in the well, which dried up long ago.

'All that was only a few hours ago. And meanwhile, Madame Michonnet has had to play her part, follow certain instructions . . . If something fishy happens around the garage, she must telephone the Chope Saint-Martin in Paris.

'Well, I turn up. She sees me go inside the garage. I fire off some shots . . . and she turns off the light, warning the drivers in the gang not to stop.

'The telephone call works. Monsieur Oscar, his wife and Guido, who goes along with them, jump into a car with their revolvers and drive by here at top speed, trying to shoot me dead since I might well be the only person who knows something.

'They take the road to Étampes and Orléans. Why? When they could flee via another route, in a different direction?

'Because along that road travels a lorry carrying a spare tyre collected from the mechanic . . . *and that tyre contains the diamonds!*

'They must catch up with the lorry and only then, their pockets full, make for the border . . .

298

'So far so good? . . . Be quiet: I'm not asking *you* anything! . . . Michonnet is down his well. Else, who knows the grounds, suspects that he's hiding there. She knows he's the one who tried to poison her. She harbours no illusions about the fellow. Arrested, he will spill everything. So she decides to get rid of him.

'Did she accidentally fall in? In any case, she ends up in the well with him, holding a revolver. But he grabs her throat with one hand . . . and gets the other around the wrist of her gun hand. They struggle in the darkness. A shot is fired . . . Else cries out in spite of herself, because she's afraid of dying.'

He struck a safety match to relight his pipe.

'What do you say to that, Monsieur Oscar?'

'I'll defend myself,' he said glumly. 'I'm not saying anything . . . except that I'm just a fence.'

'He's lying!' yelped his neighbour, Guido Ferrari.

'Ah! . . . You, I was waiting for you, pal. Because you're the shooter! All three times! First you shot Goldberg, then his wife, and finally, in the car, Carl Andersen. Oh, yes! You're a hired gun if ever I saw one.'

'Not true!'

'Calm down . . . '

'It's not true! Not true! . . . I don't want . . . '

'You're fighting for your life, but Carl Andersen will soon identify you . . . and the others will abandon you. They're not looking at anything but jail time.'

Then Guido drew himself up, pointed at the garage owner and exclaimed viciously, 'He's the one who gave the orders!'

'Goddamn you!'

And before Maigret could step in, Monsieur Oscar had slammed his handcuffed fists down on the Italian's skull, yelling, 'You scum! You'll pay for that . . . '

They must have lost their balance because they wound up on the floor, still thrashing around grimly, but the handcuffs made them clumsy.

That was the moment the surgeon chose to come downstairs.

He was wearing a light-grey hat and gloves to match.

'I beg your pardon . . . I was told that the chief inspector was here.'

'That's me.'

'It's about the wounded man . . . I believe he'll pull through. But he must have absolute quiet. I suggested my clinic, but it would seem that it's not possible. In half an hour at the most he will be coming to, and I would recommend — '

A shriek. The Italian was biting the nose of the garage owner, whose wife rushed to Maigret.

'Quick! See what . . . '

The two men were kicked apart while the surgeon, aloof, lips pursed in disgust, walked out to his car and started the engine.

Michonnet was crying quietly in his corner, refusing to look around him.

Grandjean arrived.

'The police van's here.'

The culprits were bundled outside, one after the other. Gone were the sneers and any effort at bravado. At the back of the van there was almost a fresh scuffle between the Italian and the man next to him, a mechanic from the garage.

'Thieves! Thugs!' shouted the Italian, crazed with fear. 'I never even got the money you promised me!'

Else was the last to go. At the moment when, reluctantly, she was about to step through the French windows on to the sunlit steps, Maigret stopped her with a single word.

'Well?'

She turned towards him, then looked up at the ceiling. Towards the room where Carl was lying.

It was impossible to say whether she would start crying again or muttering curses.

A rather long silence. Maigret was looking her in the eye.

'In the end ... No! I don't want to say anything bad about him.'

'Say it!'

'You know ... It's his own fault! He's half mad. He was intrigued when he learned that my father was a thief, that I was part of a gang. That's the only reason he loved me ... And if I'd become the well-behaved young woman he tried to make of me, he would quickly have lost interest and ditched me ... '

She turned her face away to add in a soft voice, almost bashfully, 'Still, I wouldn't like anything bad to happen to him ... He's ... How can I put it ... He's a nice guy ... And slightly cracked!'

And she smiled.

'I suppose I'll be seeing you ... '

'It was Guido who did the killing, right?'

He'd gone too far. Her expression hardened again.

'I'm no squealer.'

Maigret followed her with his eyes until she climbed into the police van. He saw her look back at the Three Widows house, shrug and toss a joke at the gendarme hustling her along.

'We could call this the case of the three mistakes!' he told Lucas, who was standing at his side.

'Whose mistakes?'

'Else's, first of all, when she straightened the snowy landscape, smoked downstairs, brought the phonograph up to her bedroom, *where she was supposedly locked in* — and when she felt she was in danger, she accused Carl while pretending to defend him.

'The insurance agent's mistake, when he sent for me to show that he would be spending the night at his window.

'Jojo the mechanic's mistake, when he saw me suddenly turn up and, fearing I might discover everything, sent a driver away with a spare wheel full of diamonds that was *too small for the lorry*.

'Otherwise . . . '

'Otherwise? . . . '

'Well, when a woman like Else lies with such perfection that she winds up believing her own story . . . '

'I told you so!'

'Yes . . . She could have become something extraordinary. If that fire inside her hadn't flared back up at times, as though that criminal underworld were calling to her . . . '

*   *   *

Carl Andersen hung for almost a month between life and death. Learning of his condition, his family seized their chance to bring him back to Denmark, where they placed him in a convalescent home that bore a strong resemblance to a lunatic asylum. He did not, therefore, appear in Paris as a witness at the trial.

To everyone's surprise, the request for Else's extradition was refused; she had first to spend three years in the women's prison of Saint-Lazare in Paris.

It was in the visiting room there that Maigret found Andersen arguing with the prison warden three months later, presenting his marriage licence and demanding permission to see the prisoner.

He had hardly changed at all. He still wore his black monocle, but his right shoulder was now a little stiffer.

Catching sight of the inspector, he became flustered and turned his face away.

'Your parents let you leave again?'

'My mother died. I received an inheritance.'

It was his, that limousine parked fifty metres from the prison, with a chauffeur in a fancy uniform behind the wheel.

'And you're still trying, in spite of everything?'

'I'm moving to Paris.'

'To come and visit her?'

'She is my wife . . . '

And his single eye searched Maigret's face in dread of finding irony or pity there . . .

The inspector simply shook his hand.

At the prison in Melun, two women would arrive together for their visits like inseparable friends.

'He's not a bad fellow,' Oscar's wife would say. 'He's even too kind, too generous. He gives twenty-franc tips to café waiters! That's what did him in. That and women!'

'Before he met that woman, Monsieur Michonnet would never have filched a single sou from a client. But he swore to me last week that he never even thinks of her now . . .'

On Death Row, Guido Ferrari spent his time waiting for his lawyer to arrive, bearing his pardon. But one morning, five men appeared instead to carry him away, struggling and screaming.

He refused the cigarette and the glass of rum, then spat at the chaplain.

We do hope that you have enjoyed reading this large print book.

Did you know that all of our titles are available for purchase?

We publish a wide range of high quality large print books including:
**Romances, Mysteries, Classics
General Fiction
Non Fiction and Westerns**

Special interest titles available in large print are:
**The Little Oxford Dictionary
Music Book
Song Book
Hymn Book
Service Book**

Also available from us courtesy of Oxford University Press:
**Young Readers' Dictionary
(large print edition)
Young Readers' Thesaurus
(large print edition)**

For further information or a free brochure, please contact us at:
**Ulverscroft Large Print Books Ltd.,
The Green, Bradgate Road, Anstey,
Leicester, LE7 7FU, England.
Tel:** (00 44) 0116 236 4325
Fax: (00 44) 0116 234 0205

Other titles published by Ulverscroft:

MAN'S HEAD &
THE DANCER AT THE GAI-MOULI

Georges Simenon

A rich American widow and her maid have been stabbed to death in a brutal attack. All the evidence points to Joseph, a young drifter, and he is soon arrested. But what is his motive? Or is he just a pawn in a wider conspiracy? Inspector Maigret arranges his escape from prison in order to prove his innocence . . . In Liege, two teenage boys prepare to raid money from a nightclub till after closing — and find not francs, but a dead customer. Maigret is called in to discover who would want to kill the wealthy playboy son of an Athens banker.

THE TWO-PENNY BAR &
THE SHADOW PUPPET

Georges Simenon

While visiting a criminal in his cell, Inspector Maigret is told of a man who'd been spotted dumping a body in a Parisian canal some years ago. Later, at a popular inn, Maigret finds himself in the very place the suspected killer was last seen, and is pulled deep into a web of blackmail and deceit . . . A scientist is shot dead in his laboratory, his body within easy view of the surrounding apartments. Did anyone see anything? Why was he killed? Summoned to investigate, Maigret uncovers a tragic story of desperate lives, unhappy families, addiction, and a terrible, fatal greed.

CRIME IN HOLLAND & THE GRAND BANKS CAFÉ,

Georges Simenon

When a French professor visiting the Dutch town of Delfzijl is accused of murder, Detective Chief Inspector Maigret is sent to investigate. The community seem happy to blame an unknown outsider, but there are culprits closer to home, including the dissatisfied daughter of a local farmer, the sister-in-law of the deceased, and a notorious crook. And in *The Grand Banks Café*, Maigret investigates the murder of a captain soon after his ship returns from three months of fishing off the Newfoundland coast. The ship's wireless operator has been arrested for the murder — but the sailors all blame the Evil Eye . . .